BEFORE IT'S TOO LATE

BEFORE IT'S TOO LATE

JOHN J. SCALERCIO

Copyright © 2013 by John J. Scalercio.

Library of Congress Control Number: 2013906776
ISBN: Hardcover 978-1-4836-2574-4
Softcover 978-1-4836-2573-7
Ebook 978-1-4836-2575-1

All rights reserved. No part of this book may be reproduced or transmitted in any form or by any means, electronic or mechanical, including photocopying, recording, or by any information storage and retrieval system, without permission in writing from the copyright owner.

This is a work of fiction. Names, characters, places and incidents either are the product of the author's imagination or are used fictitiously, and any resemblance to any actual persons, living or dead, events, or locales is entirely coincidental.

This book was printed in the United States of America.

Rev. date: 05/20/2013

To order additional copies of this book, contact:
Xlibris Corporation
1-888-795-4274
www.Xlibris.com
Orders@Xlibris.com
126758

To my father, who always encouraged me to better myself and never give up on my dreams; my mother who has always been there for me, even though I have not always been there for her; my wife, without whose encouragement and support this book would have not been completed; my children, who have never let me down and are, to this day, my greatest joy; and to my two sisters, the youngest of whom was born with and died from the blood disorder discussed in this book, prior to reaching her ninth birthday.

I want to thank both Janice Hetfeld, for writing the novel cover synopsis and the narrative that was used for external marketing, and Attorney Ben Hetfeld, for giving Janice the time away from his law firm to assist me in making this novel a reality.

CHAPTER 1

A silver-colored Lexus came to a screeching stop outside Derry Memorial Hospital. A man wearing a navy blue tee shirt and soiled blue denim jeans ran through the opened front door.

"What do we have?" asked Dr. Rossi.

The nurse, finding it difficult to keep pace with Dr. Rossi, said, "A man in his early twenties with a knife wound in the abdomen."

"What's his vitals?"

"Ninety-five over seventy and dropping."

"Is he in the OR?"

"They're prepping him now."

Rossi ripped off his tee shirt as he approached the doctors' lounge. He turned toward the nurse and said, "Tell Dr. Kaunert to begin anesthesia."

"Dr. Kaunert isn't here . . . Dr. Casey is on call today."

Rossi snapped back. "Then tell Dr. Casey to begin anesthesia."

"Right away, Doctor."

Rossi entered the doctors' lounge and changed into his surgical gown. He then washed his hands and arms before slipping on his latex gloves. Moments later, Rossi stepped into the triage area and barked out orders like a field general.

"Talk to me!" screamed Rossi.

Dr. Casey glanced at the monitor to his right. "Ninety over sixty-three."

A concerned look flashed across Rossi's face. "We don't have much time . . . Is he ready to go?"

"He's ready," said Casey.

Rossi extended his right hand, and the nurse instinctively handed him the scalpel. He carved a twelve-inch incision near the wound site rather than the preferred conservative eight-inch cut. Finding the cause of the rapid drop in blood pressure and averting a possible cardiac arrest were of greater importance than creating a smaller, more cosmetic incision.

Rossi realized little time remained until the patient's blood pressure dropped to a critically low level that resuscitation would be impossible. He prayed he would not find a severed artery as he reflected the fascia and the muscles adjacent to the wound.

"Eighty over sixty," called out Casey.

"Suction!" shouted Rossi, instructing the nurse to clear the blood from the surgical site.

Rossi continued to reflect the tissue, searching for the cause of the drop in blood pressure.

"I'm almost there," said Rossi. "I think—"

Dr. Casey interrupted Rossi in mid-sentence. "Systolic is now sixty-five. I can't get a diastolic."

"The knife punctured the liver," said Rossi, "but the arteries appear intact."

Rossi extended his right hand toward the surgical nurse. The nurse, from years of working alongside Dr. Rossi in the operating room, instinctively slapped the hemostat into the palm of his hand.

Rossi took the hemostat and clamped the vein that supplied blood to the liver.

"We're losing him, Bill," said Casey.

Rossi sutured the laceration in the liver and repositioned the muscles in their appropriate place.

Casey kept his eyes fixated upon the monitor. Moments later, he let out a sigh of relief as he informed the surgical team that the blood pressure was beginning to stabilize.

After placing the final suture, Rossi and the other members of the surgical team focused their attention to the EKG monitor. They noticed that the patient's blood pressure had begun to improve, and within minutes, the blood pressure had risen to an acceptable value of one hundred eighteen over seventy-eight.

"Turn off the juice," said Rossi as he jokingly asked Dr. Casey to reverse the anesthesia process.

Casey reversed anesthesia while the surgical team restored the operating room back to its presurgical state. Everyone had begun to redirect their focus away from the patient and onto their own responsibilities. Consequently, no one noticed that Dr. Rossi had picked up a scalpel from the table. With one swift motion, Rossi turned and thrust the scalpel into the patient's heart.

"What are you doing?" yelled Casey.

Rossi laughed as he walked away from the body.

Just then, the alarm clock sounded and awakened Rossi from his sleep.

Rossi felt exhausted, even though he had slept for seven hours. He sat on the edge of the bed and gathered his thoughts before jumping into the shower. *If he had only died on the operating table, then none of this would have happened.*

Rossi swung open the shower door and reached for the water faucet. Tilting his head backward, he stood beneath the oversized shower head and allowed the water to cascade off his forehead. *If the traffic light was red instead of green, I would have arrived at the hospital too late to save the bastard.*

Rossi stepped out of the shower and thought about the man who stole his daughter's life. He wanted him dead. He wanted him to suffer as she suffered.

As Rossi brushed his teeth, he glanced upward and wiped the steam that blanketed the mirror. The reflection he saw in the mirror was that of a man who was once a caring health professional, a pillar in the community. Rossi knew he was no longer that same person; he had become a vindictive and calculating individual. He no longer respected the man he saw in the mirror.

CHAPTER 2

Twenty Years Earlier

Bill Rossi was the oldest of three children from an Italian household. His skin tone was different from most people of Mediterranean ancestry. His light complexion and sandy brown hair, which he parted to the left side of his head, gave him the look of a taller Robert Redford. His unassuming manner and exuberant personality more than compensated for his five-foot-nine-inch body height.

Rossi enrolled at Temple University in the fall of 1976. He studied into the wee hours of the night during the week, but on weekends, he often drove to the Jersey Shore. Rossi loved Ocean City, and he often fantasized about working at the shore for the summer.

Between his junior and senior years of college, Rossi decided it was time to turn in his shovel and hard hat and head to the Jersey Shore. He secured a bartending job at Tony Mart's, the largest nightclub on the East Coast. Although his expertise as a bartender was limited, he never believed his employment at the club was tenuous. He understood that the management regarded bartenders who were adept at stuffing cash registers a more valuable commodity than bartenders who were skilled in making "Slow Gin Fizzes."

Rossi enjoyed his summer at the shore more than he could have imagined. Unlike the summers back home in Philadelphia, where he endured five days of work so he could enjoy the weekend, the days and nights at the shore were filled with endless activities. It was as though weekends were seven days long.

At the end of summer, Rossi returned to Philadelphia for his final year of college and discovered that he had been assigned to Tower C dormitory, the only dormitory on campus designated as single occupancy. Although he was pleased with his dormitory assignment, he was disappointed to learn that his room was near the elevator. He believed that the chatter from the students waiting to enter or exit the elevator would distract him from his studies. However, what Rossi didn't realize at the time was that this room location would have an unexpected impact on his life.

CHAPTER 3

A rigorous academic schedule, including organic chemistry, genetics, and calculus, required Rossi to put his nose to the grind to attain the level of success necessary to gain admittance into medical school. However, the first several weeks of classes are generally less demanding, so Rossi would often prop his dormitory door wide open with the intent of meeting some new people. Each time the elevator doors separated, Rossi glanced away from his textbook to see who was coming onto his floor.

John McNamara, an engineering student he met the previous day, stepped out of the elevator with an entourage of girls. Several of the girls were knockouts; others were not as attractive. One of the girls who walked arm in arm with McNamara caught Rossi's eye. She was petite and shapely, with ash brown hair that extended well below her shoulders. Her large brown eyes and high cheekbones accentuated her ovoid tapered face. Rossi believed she was far too beautiful to be dating this geeky-looking guy.

Rossi wanted to meet her, but he never found her alone. She was always with McNamara or one of her female friends. However, the opportunity to meet this girl finally presented itself when Rossi least expected it—on Thanksgiving Day.

Examinations in chemistry and genetics were scheduled for the Monday following Thanksgiving. Rossi, realizing he would be tempted to watch football games rather than memorize the various reactions necessary to pass the upcoming chemistry examination, decided to return to campus following Thanksgiving dinner.

With chemistry notes in hand, Rossi heard the familiar chime of the elevator just before opening its doors. Instinctively, he turned his head toward the elevator. He wondered what other fool sacrificed his holiday for a weekend of studies. When the beige-colored doors separated, he was surprised to see that it was the girl whom he longed to meet—McNamara's girl. And she was alone!

The girl smiled at Rossi as she passed his doorway.

"What are you doing here?" he asked.

The girl was taken aback by his question. She remembered seeing this boy on several occasions, but they had never spoken.

"Pardon me!" she replied.

"Why are you here? Why aren't you at home, eating turkey with your family?"

The girl debated whether she should enter into a conversation with someone she didn't know. However, he seemed nonthreatening, and she found him attractive.

"I live too far away to drive home for the weekend . . . I'm from South Carolina."

"Couldn't you have flown home?"

"Not on my budget! I'm one of those out-of-state students who have the privilege of paying a higher tuition for my education."

Rossi realized there may never be a better time than now to meet this girl, so he decided to seize the opportunity.

"My name's Bill . . . Bill Rossi."

"I'm Terri Gullum."

Rossi stepped out of his room and into the hallway. "It's been so quiet here."

"It does seem a little eerie."

"Would you like to come in? I can offer you some turkey leftovers."

"I can't . . . My friend's expecting me."

"Who might that be?"

"John McNamara . . . the guy in 914."

Rossi felt a lump develop inside his throat. "I've seen the two of you around campus. Are you guys dating?"

"No . . . we're just friends."

The lump in Rossi's throat began to dissipate. "I thought you two were an item."

"No . . . just friends."

"Did you ever borrow one of his pencils?"

"Excuse me?"

"One of the pencils from his pocket protector."

Terri smiled. "That's not nice."

"I'm sorry . . . I just couldn't help myself. Please come in for a minute."

"I can't . . . I'm already late."

"I suppose you'll be going home for Christmas."

"I'm leaving after my last final on December 14. Can't wait."

"If I don't get a chance to talk to you before you leave, have a great time."

"You too."

As Terri walked down the hallway, Rossi fired off one departing comment. "Don't take any pencils home with you."

Terri turned back toward Rossi and smiled. "See you in January."

Terri arrived at the Philadelphia International Airport two hours before her scheduled flight to South Carolina. Upon arriving in Charleston, she made her way to Allegheny Airline's baggage area and scanned the terminal for her father. Even though Terri and her father had planned to meet at the curbside near Terminal B, she knew he would be somewhere near the baggage claim area to greet her.

Terri glanced both left and right for her father, but she didn't see him anywhere. She was now beginning to think that perhaps he was indeed waiting for her outside in his Ford pickup truck. Staring at the conveyer belt as it zigzagged its way like a caterpillar, Terri saw her oversized navy blue American Tourister suitcase and matching garment bag race toward her. As she leaned over to pick up her garment bag, Terri caught a whiff of Old Spice. It was a scent she recognized from the time she was a little girl.

"I'll get that for you, little lady," said John Gullum. "Southern men don't let their women pick up anything heavy. You might break a fingernail!"

"I knew you'd be here," said Terri.
"How did ya know that?"
"Because you're *always* there for me."
"And all this time, I didn't think you noticed."
Terri hugged her father and gave him a kiss on the cheek. "I've missed you, Daddy."
"I missed you too, honey." Gullum gathered the luggage and directed Terri to the short-term parking lot.
"How's Mom been?"
"Ornery as ever!"
"And I bet you love every minute of it."
"Wouldn't want it any other way."

Sue Gullum spent the past two days baking pecan pies and other food items that she knew Terri enjoyed. Terri had not been home in nearly four months, and Sue wanted this to be a memorable evening for her.
When Sue saw Terri climb out of the pickup truck, her eyes swelled with tears. She couldn't believe that her daughter looked so grown up. Like a moth that transformed itself into a butterfly, Terri had evolved into a beautiful young woman.
"Welcome home, honey," said Sue as she ran down the front steps of the porch. "How's the college girl?"
"Great! College is a blast."
"What have you been doing at school?"
"I'll tell you all about it during dinner," said Terri as she and her mother walked up the porch steps. Before reaching the top of the steps, Terri turned toward her mother and asked if they were having dinner at home or dining out.
Sue smiled at her daughter and said, "I threw together some leftovers."
Terri tried to conceal her disappointment with "must-go" food. "Sounds great . . . I'm so hungry!"
Sue read the disappointment in Terri's eyes as if her daughter's face were a billboard. "I was only kidding, honey. I prepared a stuffed turkey with mashed potatoes, gravy, and black-eyed peas."

"You shouldn't have gone to all that trouble, Mother. We could have grilled steaks."

"Terri, were you home for Thanksgiving?"

"No."

"Well, we're celebrating Thanksgiving today."

A tear ran down Terri's right cheek. "What's for dessert?"

Sue leaned over and whispered, "Pecan pie."

CHAPTER 4

Terri entered the dining room after treating herself to a hot bubble bath.

"Is there anything I can do?" asked Terri.

"No, honey . . . I think we're ready to sit down to dinner . . . Let me get your father."

Sue walked into the family room and noticed that her husband was slouched down in his favorite chair. He had fallen asleep while watching *Kojak*.

"John, we're ready for dinner."

Gullum yawned as he stretched his arms high above his head. "Would you mind very much if I ate my dinner here so that I could watch the end of the program?"

Sue stared at him with daggerlike eyes. "You got to be kidding."

"Gotch-ya!" He jumped out of his recliner and made his way into the dining room.

Terri controlled much of the dinner conversation. She wanted to hear who was dating whom, and she wanted to hear about the supposed marital affair between the female gym teacher and the algebra teacher.

Sue didn't want to discuss what was going on in Charleston; she wanted to know what her daughter had been doing while away at school. When the opportunity presented itself, Sue directed the dinner conversation toward her topic of interest.

"Enough about what's been happening here in Charleston. Tell me what you've been doing at school."

"I've been studying really hard."

"And your mother thought you'd been goofing off."

Terri glanced at her father and smiled. "And I've made a lot of friends."

"What would college life be without friends?" Gullum stated sarcastically.

"And I met a boy just before coming home for Christmas."

Sue and John locked eyes before turning their focus back onto Terri.

"A boy as in boy friend or boyfriend?" asked Sue.

"I'm not sure . . . I guess he's just a friend."

"I'd like to hear more about this boy," said Sue.

"So would I," blurted John.

Terri took a bite of her mother's mouthwatering pecan pie before answering the question. "I met a boy named John McNamara during orientation. When I visited him in his dormitory room—"

"Wait a minute, little girl . . . You were in his dormitory room?" asked Gullum with a concerned tone in his voice. "We didn't raise you to visit boys in their bedrooms. Southern girls don't act like that . . . Southern girls have dignity!"

"We're just friends, Dad . . . He's someone I goof around with. Besides, he's not the boy I was talking about."

Gullum let out a sigh of relief. "I'm sorry, honey."

"The boy I was talking about lives on the same floor as John McNamara. Sometimes I'd see him because his room faces the elevator."

"Would anyone like a scoop of ice cream on their pie?" asked Gullum.

"Keep quiet, John," scolded Sue. "Go on, Terri . . . Don't mind your father."

"Since my friend and I lived too far away to go home for Thanksgiving, we decided to have dinner together. I picked up a couple of chili dogs and a basket of fries from the Original Hot Dog Shop and brought the food to his room to eat. As I stepped out of the elevator, I noticed that one of the rooms had its door propped open. I peeked into the room as I walked by and saw this boy sitting at his desk. He smiled at me and motioned for me to come inside. I hesitated momentarily before entering his room, even though he appeared to be as harmless as a baby. He said his name was Bill Rossi and that he was a fourth-year student. I thought he also lived too far away since he was still on campus, but I was wrong. He lives nearby, in Philadelphia, but he decided to return to his room because he needed to prepare for some upcoming examinations. He's hoping to be accepted into medical school."

"I like him already," said Gullum jokingly.

Sue shot another dart at her husband from across the dinner table. "Go on, honey."

"That's about it. The next thing I knew it was time to come home for Christmas."

"Did he ask to see you when you return to school?" Sue asked inquisitively.

"We just said we'll see each other next semester."

Sue paused momentarily before continuing with her interrogation. "What does Bill look like? Is he short or tall? Does he have light or dark hair?"

"Does he have a tattoo?" asked Mr. Gullum.

"He's handsome," replied Terri. "He looks like an actor, but I can't remember his name. He starred in the movie *Butch Cassidy and the Sundance Kid*. He played the Sundance Kid."

"Do you mean Robert Redford?" asked Gullum.

"Yes, Daddy. He looks like Robert Redford, only taller. He's about five feet nine, and he has sandy blond hair. And he's athletic looking."

"He's welcome here anytime," said Sue in a sensual tone of voice.

"He might have a girlfriend," said Terri.

"Why do you say that?"

"I don't know . . . just a hunch."

Sue smiled at her daughter and said, "If it's meant to be, it will be."

Terri hoped it was meant to be.

CHAPTER 5

Terri's return flight to Philadelphia departed at 1:10 pm. Although she enjoyed the time spent with her parents, Terri was excited to return to school in hopes of beginning a relationship with this Robert Redford look-alike.

The professor posted the reading list for the semester's literature course on the blackboard. Terri scribbled the titles of the novels in her notebook before arranging her books at the top right-hand corner of her desk. As the minute hand of the clock inched closer to the witching hour, Terri fidgeted in her chair and waited for the teacher to dismiss class.

She exited Crawford Hall immediately following her English class and raced across campus to meet McNamara. Truth be known, she had no desire to visit McNamara; she wanted to see Bill Rossi. Since returning to school following Christmas break, Terri tried to cross paths with him several times. But each attempt to see Rossi was futile, and Terri returned to her room each night filled with disappointment. She even made plans to study with McNamara one evening with the hope of finding Rossi in his room; however, once again, Terri experienced disappointment in finding his door closed. She considered knocking on the door but decided against it. She didn't want to appear as though she were chasing him.

As Terri walked through the tower's lobby on her way to the mail room the following evening, she was surprised to see Rossi. He was standing alongside the student bulletin board, talking with an attractive red-haired girl. The girl didn't look like a college student;

she was too well dressed. She wore a black and white silk blouse with black wool slacks.

Terri's heart stopped momentarily when she saw the girl. She tried to assess whether they were friends or whether they were dating each other. The longer Terri watched from afar, the more she believed they were more than friends.

Terri now began to second-guess the conversation she had with Rossi on Thanksgiving night. She tried to recall what was said and *how* it was said. She remembered Rossi say he would see her in January. But did he mean he would see her around campus when school reconvened, or did he imply that he wanted to see her romantically? She hoped it was the latter. However, as Terri continued to mull over the words which were spoken that November night, she realized it was she, and not Rossi, who said they would see each other in January. And if she was the one who said they would see each other in January, then perhaps the attraction she believed they had for each other was one-sided. Not wishing to be seen, Terri fled the tower's lobby.

CHAPTER 6

Pi Kappa Alpha's Sweethearts Dance, a semiformal party held in February of each year, was regarded by the fraternity members as the premier party of the year. Rossi had not attended the Sweethearts Dance since his freshman year at Temple. Now in his final year of college, Rossi felt the need to partake in this year's event. However, one obstacle stood in his way; he was not dating anyone at the moment. He searched through his cerebral rolodex for the perfect date. Regardless how many times he scanned his memory bank, Terri Gullum's name kept popping up. But he hadn't seen her around campus since Christmas break, and he didn't have the foggiest idea how to find her.

Knowing that all freshmen dormitory residents ate their meals at either the tower's cafeteria or the Lothrop dining hall, Rossi flipped a coin to determine where he would situate himself. If the coin came up heads, then he was off to the tower's cafeteria; otherwise, he would position himself at Lothrop hall. As the quarter fell to the ground, the face of George Washington appeared.

Rossi stood near the tower's stairwell two consecutive evenings in hopes of seeing Terri, but she was nowhere to be found. He was now beginning to believe that she ate her meals at the Lothrop facility. However, as the dining hall was about to close on the third day, Rossi saw Terri enter the tower's lobby and descend the cafeteria stairs. She was with three other girls. Taking precautions so not to be seen, he followed her from a distance. Rossi considered stopping by Terri's dinner table and striking up a conversation with her, but he decided against it. He believed it was inappropriate to ask her out on a date while she was eating dinner.

Rossi inhaled his dinner and darted up the cafeteria stairwell without being seen. Thirty minutes later, surrounded by an entourage of friends, Terri emerged from the dining area. Rossi didn't want to approach her while she was with her friends. However, if he failed to seize the moment, then the opportunity to approach her may not occur again until after the dance. He needed to act immediately.

Rossi slithered through the crowd of students like a running buck maneuvering his way through a group of defenders. He successfully kept himself out of view until he emerged directly in front of Terri.

"Hey there," he said.

Terri's throat narrowed as if she were experiencing an anaphylactic reaction. "Hey yourself!"

"May I speak with you?"

Terri excused herself from her friends before following Rossi to a more private location near the northeast corner of the lobby.

"Thanks for staying behind," said Rossi.

"No problem . . . We were about to split up anyhow."

"Did you have a nice holiday?"

"Yes, I did . . . What about you?"

"Me too." Rossi paused momentarily. "My fraternity is having a party on Saturday night, and I'd like to take you, if you're not busy."

Terri couldn't believe what she was hearing. Just a few days ago, she had given up hope of ever speaking with Rossi again. Now he was asking her out on a date!

"I don't have any plans for Saturday night."

Rossi tried to conceal his excitement. "Great. Then it's a date. I'll pick you up around seven thirty."

"Seven thirty will be fine."

"Where do you live?"

"At 436 Amos Hall. You'll have to ask the security guard to call my room."

"I'll see you on Saturday."

"I'll be ready."

CHAPTER 7

Even though Rossi partied into the wee hours on Friday night with several of his fraternity brothers, he dragged himself out of bed by 8:00 am. He promised the fraternity social director that he would oversee the pledges as they decorated the house for the Sweethearts Dance. However, before making his way to the PiKa house, Rossi decided to eat breakfast; he needed to squelch the nauseous sensation he acquired from consuming too many boilermakers at Peter's Pub.

Before entering the cafeteria, Rossi walked across the tower's lobby to pick up an abandoned edition of this morning's *Philadelphia Inquirer* newspaper. He sat down on one of the benches facing the cafeteria and turned to the sports section. He wanted to read the article describing how Ron Stackhouse of the Pittsburgh Penguins single-handedly defeated the Flyers with two third period goals.

Glancing away from his newspaper, Rossi happened to see Terri make a bee's line to the cafeteria. He focused his attention on her as she descended the cafeteria stairs. She was wearing a gray sweat suit beneath a cheap-looking full-length white rabbit coat. And her hair looked as if it hadn't been stroked by a brush in weeks. She looked disgustingly unattractive.

Not wanting to be seen, Rossi hid behind a pillar. *What did I ever find attractive about her?* Once Terri entered the cafeteria, he emerged from behind the pillar. He no longer wanted to take her to the party tonight, but he was too much of a gentleman to cancel his date with her. He would never hurt anyone intentionally.

Rossi now turned his attention to the far end of the lobby where his friend and fraternity brother, Tom D'Orio, was playing pinball.

"How's it going, buddy?"

"Still hungover from last night."

"Are you going to the party tonight?"

"Probably."

"Are you bringing a date?"

"No. Claire went home for the weekend."

"She would rather visit her parents than party with us?"

"Na . . . her grandfather fell and fractured his hip. They operated on him yesterday afternoon."

"Is he all right?"

"Who knows? The guy's eighty-nine years old . . . They say old people don't heal very quickly."

Rossi became unusually quiet. D'Orio sensed there was something wrong. "What's the problem, big guy? You look uptight?"

Rossi hesitated momentarily before answering. "I asked this girl to the party tonight and . . ."

D'Orio patiently waited for Rossi to continue with his comment. When Rossi failed to complete his thought, D'Orio interjected. "You asked this girl to the party and . . . ?"

"I asked this girl to the party, but I don't want to take her any longer."

D'Orio inched closer to Rossi. "What did you say?"

"I don't want to take her to the party tonight!"

"Why not?"

"I saw her this morning."

"And?"

"Man, she looked real bad."

"You can't blow her off."

"I know . . . but maybe you can help me out."

"Don't drag me into this," said D'Orio.

"You got to help me out, bro."

"What do you want me to do?"

"Maybe you can dance with her a couple of times . . . and ask some of the guys to do the same."

"Don't even think about dumping her off on me," D'Orio stated emphatically.

"I really need your help, man. How about it?"

D'Orio shook his head back and forth. He now wished he had gone to Denny's for breakfast rather than the tower's cafeteria. "You'll owe me a big one for this," said D'Orio.

"I'll buy you a Big Mac."

"Ten Big Macs."

With a midterm physics examination scheduled for Monday afternoon, Rossi returned to his dormitory room to review the laws governing atomic fusion. However, he found it difficult to concentrate on his studies; he kept thinking about the homely looking girl clad in some type of animal outer garment.

Glancing at his wristwatch, Rossi turned the television channel to the 6:30 pm news with Walter Cronkite. Rossi despised Cronkite, but he preferred doing almost anything rather than preparing himself for tonight's date with Terri. Following the news broadcast, Rossi realized he couldn't procrastinate any longer; he had to get dressed for tonight's party. With the speed of a snail crossing an eight-lane highway, Rossi walked toward the shower stall. Afterward, he shaved off his two-day old stub and combed his hair before sprinkling some British Sterling on his neck and chest.

Rossi arrived at Amos Hall at 8:15 pm. He hoped Terri would be so enraged about his being forty-five minutes late that she would cancel their date. But no such luck. The security attendant informed Rossi that Ms. Gullum would be downstairs momentarily. Finding it difficult to conceal his disappointment, Rossi thanked the woman before sitting down on the sofa opposite the elevator.

Be pleasant, Rossi told himself. *Don't be rude.*

Moments later, Terri stepped out of the elevator and walked toward him.

"I'm really excited about tonight!"

Rossi couldn't believe this was the same girl who scampered down the cafeteria stairwell this morning, sporting an outfit which could have been purchased from any number of thrift stores. This girl wore a low-cut white silk blouse with a navy blue wool skirt.

"So am I," he said.

Rossi couldn't take his eyes off her. She looked better than he had remembered. And her hair was done differently; it was pinned back into a bun, showcasing her large brown eyes, high cheekbones, and flawless facial skin.

"You look absolutely great!"

"It's the clothes," she said.

"You'd look great wearing anything." Rossi knew that was a lie. It was only a few hours ago that he thought she resembled Don Quixote's Dulcinea.

"You look good yourself."

CHAPTER 8

Rossi handed Terri's coat to a pledge upon entering the fraternity house and then escorted her toward the bar. "Can I get you a glass of wine or a bottle of beer?"

"No Southern girl would ever be seen drinking a beer," she whispered softly.

With his right hand, Rossi signaled for the bartender.

"What's your poison, Brother Rossi?"

"A beer for me and a chardonnay for the little lady."

"One soda pop and one chaser . . . right away."

As Rossi handed Terri her glass of wine, he tilted his head in a manner in which no one else could hear what he was about to say.

"Northern girls will drink anything . . . They're not picky."

Just then, the band began to play the song by Chicago titled "Does Anybody Really Know What Time It Is?" Rossi took Terri by the hand and ushered her onto the dance floor.

Moments later, Rossi felt someone tapping him on the shoulder. Instinctively, he turned forty-five degrees to his left. There stood Tom D'Orio, sporting a smile as wide as a carved pumpkin.

"May I cut in?"

"This is our first dance, old boy."

D'Orio was surprised by Rossi's reaction. "Just trying to help you out, bro, remember!"

Rossi politely excused himself from Terri before nudging D'Orio away from the dance floor. "I don't think I'll need your help tonight."

"I'll gladly take her off your hands."

"Not a chance, big guy. Find your own girl."

Rossi found his way back onto the dance floor. "Now, where were we?"

"We were in each other's arms."

Rossi pulled her closer to him. "So we were."

Shortly after the band played its final musical set, Rossi and Terri began their journey back to campus. Within minutes of leaving the fraternity house, Terri remarked about how cold it was outside. Rossi reached for her hand.

"It feels like its ten degrees tonight. But don't worry . . . I'll keep you warm."

As they neared Amos Hall, Bill and Terri raced indoors to escape the cold. Once inside the lobby area, Terri snuggled closer to Rossi.

Rossi was overcome by a volcanic rush of adrenaline; his heart pulsated at five times its normal rate. He directed Terri to an alcove adjacent to the security area; he didn't want to leave her just yet.

"I had a great time tonight," he said.

"So did I."

"I'd like to see you again."

"I'm sure we'll see each other around campus."

That was not the response Rossi wanted to hear. He felt as though he had been zapped with a stun gun. "I meant to say I'd like to date you."

Terri smiled and said, "I know what you meant, Bill. I was only joking. I'd love to go out with you!"

Rossi felt the blood returning to his vital organs once again. "How about Saturday?"

"Next Saturday is fine with me."

Before entering the elevator, Terri removed a pen from her purse and locked eyes with Rossi. Without glancing away, she reached for his hand and scribbled a series of numbers along the crease line.

"That's my private telephone number. Don't lose it because I won't give it to you again."

"Does the pocket protector have this number?"

"I'll never tell."

Rossi then placed his hands on Terri's shoulders and looked into her eyes. "Would it be offensive to kiss a Southern girl on her first date?"

"You'll have to find that out for yourself."

Rossi leaned closer to Terri, wrapped his arms around her, and kissed her gently on the lips. "Did I offend you?"

"If you had, I would have crossed out my telephone number."

CHAPTER 9

Rossi monopolized all of Terri's Saturday nights. He even coerced her to join him once or twice a week for a piece of pizza. The attraction they felt for each other intensified with each passing week, and their relationship blossomed like a rose petal. Rossi desired to take their relationship to the next level and planned to express his feelings to Terri at the Greek Ball.

The Philadelphia Hilton Hotel was selected by the Inter Fraternity Council to host this year's Greek Ball. This black-tie event, regarded as the premier social activity for the entire university student body, followed seven days of fierce competition between fraternities and sororities.

Rossi wanted this to be a special evening for Terri. He approached Rick Murray, president of the Inter Fraternity Council, and asked Rick to use his influence to reserve a choice table for him.

"I'm sure I can do that for you, good buddy," said Murray. "All you need to do is pick up the first two rounds of drinks!"

"Setting terms again, my friend?" asked Rossi.

"Just respectfully requesting, old boy."

"In that case, I'll keep an open tab."

"Who else will be sitting at your table?" asked Murray.

"D'Orio and Lynch."

"You'll have one hell of a good time."

Terri visited several shops in search of an appropriate outfit to wear to the Greek Ball. After an exhaustive day of bouncing from store to store, trying on one dress after another, Terri settled for a full-length black gown with spaghetti straps. The gown was designed to expose much of her shoulders and lower back.

After returning to her dormitory room, Terri telephoned her mother; she couldn't wait to share her excitement with her mother.

"Hello, Mother . . . I called to tell you about this gown I bought today. It's *so* pretty."

"Why would you buy a gown?"

"I was invited to this dance . . . I mean, a formal."

"Who's the lucky guy?"

"Bill Rossi . . . He's the boy I told you about during Christmas break."

"So you two have been dating."

"Yes, Mother. But first, let me tell you about this gown."

"Wait a minute, honey. Let me call your father. I'm sure he'd be interested in hearing what you have to say."

"John!" yelled Sue. "Pick up the telephone . . . It's Terri."

"How's everything going at school?"

"Great. But I called to tell you and Mom about this gown I bought."

"A gown?"

"John, be quiet and let Terri talk," said Sue.

"Sorry, honey."

"I was telling Mom that I bought this gown for the Greek Week Ball. It's so beautiful. It's black and made of a velvetlike material with a satin bow in the back. And it has spaghetti straps."

"It sounds lovely," said Sue.

"When's the dance?" asked her father.

"March 26."

"Who's the lucky guy?"

"Bill Rossi."

"Who's Bill Rossi?"

"He's the boy Terri spoke about when she was home for Christmas."

"Have you two been dating?"

"We started dating shortly after Christmas break."

"Are you seeing anyone else?" asked her father.

"No, Daddy."

"Sounds like you're serious about this boy," said Sue.

John Gullum remained quiet. He wanted to hear what Terri had to say.

"I don't know mother. I know I like him . . . And we enjoy spending time together."

"Is he nice to you?" asked Sue.

"You'd like him . . . He's just like Daddy!"

"It's important that he's nice to you."

"I wish I could talk longer," said Terri, "but I have to go. I just wanted to tell you all about the gown I bought. I'll call back after the ball and tell you everything."

"Goodbye, honey," said Sue.

"Be careful and take care of yourself," cautioned Gullum.

After hanging up the telephone, Gullum joined his wife in the kitchen. "Sounds like Terri's having a good time." Sue didn't respond. She was thinking about what her daughter had said. "Doesn't it sound like Terri's having a good time?" Gullum asked again.

"I'm sorry, John. I was just thinking about Terri."

"What about Terri?"

"I think she's in love with that boy."

"What makes you say that?"

"Just the things she said and by the tone in her voice."

"I think you're overreacting."

"Mark my words. I bet she marries him."

"She's only nineteen . . . She's still a kid."

"I was nineteen when we got married . . . Remember?"

Gullum said nothing.

CHAPTER 10

Advertised to awaken even the soundest of sleepers, the alarm clock blared like a fire station whistle at eight o'clock on the morning of the Greek Ball. Back home in Charleston, Terri needed to be aroused by her mother several times each morning before crawling out of bed. There was no one at Temple to awaken Terri; she needed an alarm clock capable of inducing a heart attack to anyone with a blood pressure above one hundred twenty over eighty.

Terri jumped out of bed and into the shower within minutes of hearing the clock's alarm. She scheduled an early morning appointment with a manicurist to have her fingernails and toenails painted. Afterward, she planned to meet Augie Garganni at 11:00 am. for a haircut.

Although this was Terri's first visit to Garganni's salon, she was not apprehensive. She was confident that her hair would look great! Many of Terri's friends who lived in the Philadelphia area had gone to Garganni's for years for their hair needs. Augie Garganni was regarded as an artist by the girls of Kappa Alpha Theta sorority.

Terri was back on campus in plenty of time to ready herself for the ball. It was four o'clock, and Rossi was not expected to arrive until 6:00 pm. She turned on the water faucet and peppered the bathtub with soap petals. She waited until the soap bubbles reached high into the air before stepping into the tub. Terri immersed her body deeper into the water. Moments later, she imagined Rossi slipping his hand alongside her inner thigh, tantalizing her most sensitive area.

Terri was so engrossed in her imagination that she lost track of time. She glanced at the wall clock and was surprised to learn that it was five o'clock. She couldn't believe she had allowed herself to fantasize about Rossi for nearly an hour. Terri reached for the sponge and began to bathe herself, no longer imaging it was Rossi's hands touching her most sensitive areas.

CHAPTER 11

On the night of the Greek Ball, Rossi and Terri took the Metro to the Center City substation and transferred to the Theatre District stop. From there, they walked across the street to the Philadelphia Hilton Hotel. Once inside the hotel, Rossi handed Terri's coat to the coat-check girl before proceeding to the hors d'oeuvres bar. The hors d'oeuvres table was loaded with shrimp cocktail, stuffed mushrooms, raw vegetables, and an assortment of cheeses. Rossi and Terri nibbled on the shrimp and mushrooms before making their way to their table.

They were surprised to discover they were the last of their friends to arrive. Rossi walked toward the bar, but he was cornered by Murray and D'Orio before having the opportunity to order a drink.

"It's about time you got here," said Murray.

"Did you think I'd be a no-show?"

"Vegas set the line at 2:1," blurted D'Orio.

"At 2:1, you say? If I had known, I would have laid down a hefty wager."

D'Orio shook his head. "It's not that we don't have any faith in you, good buddy. It's just that your track record hasn't been so good!"

"That was the *old me,*" said Rossi.

"The *old you,*" Murray said laughingly. "What's so different now?"

"I'm in love."

"We've heard that before," interjected D'Orio.

"You don't have to believe me, but I really do love her."

"We *don't* believe you," said Murray.

"I'm not going to debate this all evening . . . I got a girl whose waiting for a gin and tonic."

Rossi ordered a gin and tonic for Terri and a scotch and water for himself. Afterward, he turned around and looked at his friends, "At 2:1, you say? Bad bet!"

The seven-piece brass band began to play shortly after the waitresses served the chocolate mousse dessert. Rossi excused himself from the table and made his way to the bar for another round of drinks. While standing at the bar, he heard the band play the song that he and Terri first danced to at the Sweethearts Dance—"Does Anybody Really Know What Time It Is?" He left both drinks on the bar and darted toward his date. He wanted to get Terri onto the dance floor before the song ended.

"Does this song mean anything to you?" asked Rossi.

Terri paused momentarily. "Are you implying that I need to be more conscientious about being on time?"

Rossi couldn't conceal his disappointment. "This song has no special significance for you?"

"Of course, it does, honey . . . We danced to this song at your fraternity house. This is *our* song."

After the song ended, Rossi led Terri to a more private area away from the ballroom. He looked into her eyes and said, "There's something I never shared with you that I hope you won't find offensive."

"What might that be?"

"Do you remember our first date when I asked you to the fraternity's sweethearts party?"

"Yes."

"I almost didn't take you."

"Did you want to invite someone else?"

"Not at all. I wanted to date you from the first time I saw you with the pocket protector. I thought you were drop-dead gorgeous. But as I sat in the tower's lobby that morning, I saw you just as you were about to enter the cafeteria. You looked bad . . . real bad!

You were wearing a rabbit's coat over a sweat suit, and your hair looked like it hadn't been touched in a year. I tried to pawn you off on D'Orio because I knew he was going stag to the party, but he refused to get involved in my predicament. I bribed him with ten Big Macs just to dance with you. I even picked you up forty-five minutes late, hoping you would be so upset with me that you would cancel our date. But when you stepped out of the elevator, all of my apprehensions dissipated, and I remembered why I asked you to the party."

"And what was it that you remembered?"

"How beautiful you were."

Rossi reached for Terri's hand. "I have something special to share with you."

Terri waited with much anticipation. "I've been accepted into medical school."

Terri's eyes filled with tears. "Congratulations, Bill! I'm very happy for you. You've worked hard."

"You're right . . . I have worked hard. And that's why I want you to understand and support my decision."

Terri thought Rossi was going to break up with her. "I understand . . . You need to concentrate on school. You don't need any distractions."

Rossi looked dumfounded. "You got it all wrong, Terri. I told Temple I want to postpone my acceptance for three years. The game plan is for me to support you until you graduate from college. Then you can support me during medical school."

"I don't understand."

Rossi dropped to his knees, reached into the inner pocket of his tuxedo jacket, and presented Terri with a pear-shaped half-carat diamond ring. "Will you marry me?"

The marriage proposal was completely unexpected. Terri tried to conceal her excitement as she considered the proposal. "I can't marry you, Bill . . . I can't stand between you and medical school."

"You're not. I'm only delaying my acceptance for a couple of years. At this moment, all I want is for you to marry me."

"We've only been dating for a few months. We don't really know each other."

"I know we've only been dating for a short while. But there isn't a certain period of time that people have to date before they marry. I know people who have dated for years and got divorced, and I know people who got married three months after meeting each other . . . and they're still together fifteen years later."

Rossi stood up, took a deep breath, and placed both of his hands on Terri's shoulders. "I don't have all the answers . . . All I know is that I love you, and I want to spend the rest of my life with you."

Rossi tilted Terri's head upward. "Will you marry me?"

"When?"

"August."

"This August?"

"Yes . . . this August."

Terri couldn't stop the tears from running down her cheeks. "Yes, I'll marry you, Bill."

"You've made me the happiest person on earth."

Murray noticed that Terri had been crying when she and Rossi returned to the ballroom. He tapped D'Orio on the shoulder and said, "It looks like the Vegas people were right after all . . . It was only a matter of time before Rossi broke up with her."

Rossi escorted Terri to where D'Orio and Murray were standing. "I want you guys to be the first to know that Terri and I are engaged to be married."

D'Orio and Murray were blindsided with this unexpected announcement.

"I think congratulations are in order," said Rossi.

Both Murray and D'Orio congratulated Terri and kissed her on the cheek. Terri and Rossi then excused themselves so to share their excitement with their other friends. Before walking away, Rossi turned toward his friends and said, "Oh, by the way, tell your friends in Vegas that they're not invited to the wedding!"

CHAPTER 12

Terri didn't return to her dormitory until 2:00 am following the Greek Ball. She debated whether she should call her parents now or wait until morning to tell them that Rossi had proposed to her. She decided she couldn't wait until morning.

The sound of the telephone startled Sue Gullum out of a sound sleep. She glanced at her husband lying next to her in bed and realized that he was as motionless as a mime. Sue reached for the telephone handset.

"Mom . . . It's Terri."

Sue shook her husband until he awoke.

"What's the matter?" mumbled Gullum.

"Terri, are you all right?" asked Sue.

"I'm fine, Mother . . . I just needed to call you and Daddy."

"Is Terri all right?" asked Gullum with a concerned tone in his voice.

Sue turned toward her husband and nodded yes.

"What is it, honey?"

"Bill asked me to marry him tonight."

Sue nearly fell out of bed. "Excuse me!"

"I'm getting married!"

"What's going on?" Gullum asked his wife.

Sue placed her hand across her husband's mouth.

"When?" asked Sue.

"In August . . . I can't wait!"

"What's going on?" Gullum asked with more authority.

Sue placed the telephone receiver against her body and looked at her husband. "Terri's getting married."

"What?"

"Don't you think we should discuss this? You don't want to do something which you may later regret."

"I know this is sudden, but we love each other. And when two people love each other, they should commit to each other."

"I'm excited for you, honey . . . I just wish you'd delay the wedding until next year."

"We're getting married in August, Mother . . . Please be supportive of our decision."

"You're old enough to make your own decisions. All I ask is that you look at this from a rational rather than an emotional point of view," said Sue.

"Classes are over in three weeks. We'll talk more about this when I come home. For now, just be happy for me."

"I don't want you to make any life-altering mistakes."

"I'm sorry I woke you."

"You know you can call us anytime, honey."

"Good night, Mom."

"I love you, honey."

Sue hung up the telephone and looked at her husband. "I told you months ago that Terri would marry that boy . . . I just didn't think it would happen so soon."

CHAPTER 13

Three days remained until the end of the semester, and Rossi and Terri had just finished packing the last of their personal items into corrugated paper boxes. Sensing that Terri seemed a little more quiet than usual, Rossi sat down next to her on the twin-size bed.

"Are you all right, hon? You seem a little bummed out today."

Terri hesitated before responding. "It's just that I won't be seeing you again until just before the wedding."

"You'll be so busy preparing for the wedding that the next four months will fly by before you know it." Terri remained silent. "Is there anything else bothering you?"

"Yes, there is. It bothers me that you'll be bartending at the Jersey Shore this summer."

"I've worked at the shore for years now."

"I know that . . . but now we're engaged."

"What does that have to do with my working at the shore?"

"I'm not stupid, Bill. I know all about those girls who kiss up to lifeguards and bartenders."

"The only reason I'm working at the shore is because the job pays good. Where else can I make that kind of money?"

"I'm sure my father could find you a good-paying job?"

"And move to Charleston?"

"Would that be so awful?"

"Terri, you should know that I'm not interested in any other women. If I wanted to date other girls, I wouldn't be getting married."

"I'm still going to miss you."

"I'll miss you too."

CHAPTER 14

Upon arriving in Ocean City, the first thing Rossi did was to look up his former roommate, Chuck Harms. Rossi knew if Harms was in town, he would find him at their favorite watering hole, the Anchorage Bar.

Harms looked up and smiled as Rossi squeezed into the chair next to him. "Look what the cat dragged in."

"It's good to see you too, Chuck!"

"When did you get in?"

"About a half hour ago . . . I haven't even unpacked yet."

"Did you get into doctor school yet?"

"Yes and no."

"What is it? Did you get accepted or didn't you?"

"I was accepted into Temple's medical school for this coming September, but I requested that my acceptance be delayed for a few years."

"Why would you do something like that?"

"Because I'm getting married."

Harms coughed up the beer that he had just swallowed. "Did you say you're getting married, old boy?"

"You heard right. I'm getting married in August."

"Why would you do a thing like that?"

"Because I love her."

"I fall in love every night, but I'm not getting married."

"When you find the right person, you'll settle down."

"I don't know about that."

"Trust me, when you find the person you truly love, you won't want to be with anyone else."

"I hope that doesn't happen to me for quite some time . . . I like waking up to a different girl every morning."

"Not me. Terri has everything I'm looking for in a girl. She's the only girl for me."

"Talking about girls," said Harms. "Maggie stopped at the bar a couple of times. She's been asking about you."

"Tell her I'm getting married."

"Tell her yourself. She plans on coming to Tony Mart's tomorrow night."

"I will. I'll tell her that we had some great times together, but it's time to move on with our lives."

"I have to say I admire you."

"For what?"

"For having the guts to settle down with one girl. Me? I'm much too shallow. I'd rather carve a notch into my bedpost every night."

"Finish up your beer," said Rossi. "I've heard enough of your bullshit for one night."

CHAPTER 15

Terri and her mother stayed awake into the wee hours the day Terri returned to Charleston. They talked about Terri's engagement, and they began to plan for the upcoming wedding.

Sue tried to dissuade Terri from getting married, but Terri kept saying she's in love and that everything will work out. However, Terri confided to her mother that she was uneasy about Rossi working at the Jersey Shore for the summer. She wished her fiancé had come home with her to Charleston. Sue seized the opportunity once again to dissuade her daughter from marrying too soon.

"This is another example of why I have been asking you postpone your wedding date."

"What does this have to do with my getting married?"

"Perhaps Bill isn't ready to settle down. He may still need to sow some wild oats."

"How could you say that, Mother?"

"Because if he's unfaithful, then I'd feel guilty for not warning you about what might happen."

"You're wrong, Mother. He loves me. He doesn't have an interest in any other women."

"I hope you're right, Terri."

"I *know* I'm right."

Later that morning, Terri thought about what her mother had said. She needed to reach out to Bill; she needed to speak with him. Terri picked up the telephone and dialed the number she had committed to memory the day she and Rossi went their separate way for the summer.

Rossi barely heard the ringing telephone. He had softened the ring tone because he didn't want to be disturbed.

"Hello," said Rossi with a crackling voice.

"Bill . . . Is that you?"

"Terri, I wasn't expecting your call."

"You'd rather I not call you?"

"Don't be silly . . . I meant to say I was surprised you called so early in the morning."

"It's eleven o'clock . . . I thought you would have been awake by now."

"I work until 2:00 am. And by the time I clean up the bar and have a few drinks, I don't get home until four o'clock."

"I'm sorry I woke you."

"Don't apologize, babe. I'm glad you called."

"You are?"

"Damn right . . . You're my gal, aren't you?"

"I hope so."

"What do you mean you hope so?"

"I don't know . . . out of sight and out of mind."

"What's that supposed to mean?"

"I'm in South Carolina with my parents, and you're in New Jersey surrounded by scantly clothed girls . . . You figure it out!"

"Like I said, I'm working at the shore because I can't make this kind of money anywhere else . . . I'm doing this for you."

"For me?"

"For us."

"Then why aren't I happy?"

"Because you're letting your imagination run wild."

"I can't help it . . . I love you so much."

"Why don't you come to the shore for the remainder of the summer? I'm sure I can find you a job as a waitress."

"I can't do that. I have a lot to do here to prepare for our wedding."

"I understand."

"But don't be surprised if I come down some weekend."

"I wish you would. I'd love to see you."

After a brief hesitation, Terri said, "I'm sorry to have called you so early. I just needed to hear your voice."

"Call back anytime . . . I enjoyed hearing the sound of your voice."

"I love you, Bill."

"I love you too, Terri."

Terri hung up the telephone, but she still felt tormented. Rossi didn't seem like the same person she knew back at school. She didn't know how or why, but he seemed different.

CHAPTER 16

Rossi encountered more traffic than usual as he made his way across the Ninth Street Bridge to Tony Mart's. He arrived at work ten minutes late, but the manager never addressed his tardiness. There was no need to chastise a valued employee. The manager knew Rossi worked his tail off, and he consistently stuffed the cash register with money night after night.

Immediately after stepping behind the bar, Rossi began to set up his workstation. He washed every single glass on the overhead racks, even though they did not need washing. The glasses are routinely washed at the end of each night. Afterward, he cut up his fruit and prepared the mixers, which would be used for the various fruit drinks.

Sliding open the beer cooler doors, Rossi estimated that two additional cases of beer were needed to sustain this evening's thirsty crowd. He grabbed a two-wheeled dolly from the storage area and transported two cases of America's number one beer, Budweiser, to his bar station.

Rossi was preoccupied with filling the cooler with beer and didn't notice that someone had taken a seat directly in front of his station.

"What does it take to get a drink here?"

Rossi recognized the voice of the bar patron. He looked up from the cooler and smiled. It was Maggie Fitzpatrick, the girl whom he dated last summer.

"You got to know someone to get a drink here," replied Rossi.

"I have connections, young man . . . I know William Rossi!"

"That and a dime will get you a cup of coffee."

Maggie began to laugh.

"How have you been?" asked Rossi.

"Better now that you're back in town."

Rossi sensed that Maggie expected the two of them to begin dating again, even though they broke off their relationship at the end of last summer. "What's your pleasure?"

"How about a late-night date after work?"

Rossi smiled but didn't give in to her temptation. "What can I *fix* for you?"

"How about a complete body massage?"

Rossi leaned across the bar. "I have something to tell you."

"Tell me we can get together after work tonight."

"I'm engaged . . . I'm getting married in August."

Maggie's demeanor turned to rage. "If you don't want to be with me, then just say so. Don't feed me some bullshit story about you getting married. I'm a big girl . . . You don't have to lie to me!"

"I'm really getting married."

"Then why are you here? Why aren't you with your bride-to-be?"

"Because I can make more money working here than working anywhere else."

"You expect me to believe this?"

"I'm telling you the truth, so help me."

Maggie swallowed everything that Rossi shoved down her throat, but she regurgitated the BS as quickly as it went down. "You're working at Tony Mart's because you want to score with the girls, *not* because you can make more money."

"I'm serious," said Rossi.

"I guarantee if some blond-haired bitch starts wagging her ass in your face, you'll take her down in a second . . . even if you *are* engaged."

"You're wrong."

"We'll see."

CHAPTER 17

Terri and her mother were busy the next several weeks finalizing the details for the upcoming wedding. They arranged for the wedding ceremony to be held at St. Matthew's Church, followed by a buffet reception at the VFW.

Since the wedding plans were now etched in stone, there were no pressing details that Terri needed to address. Consequently, she spent much of her day wondering whether her fiancé has been faithful to her. Thoughts of infidelity tormented her. She needed to confirm or dispel her suspicions.

Terri flew to Philadelphia on Thursday and rented a car before continuing her trip to the shore. The drive from Philadelphia to Ocean City took less than an hour and a half. Immediately after arriving in Ocean City, Terri searched for a beauty salon. She wanted to look attractive for her fiancé. She found a quaint little salon on the corner of Asbury and Eighth Avenues; she hoped the salon welcomed walk-ins.

"May I help you?" asked the cosmetologist.

"Is it possible to get my hair styled and have my makeup touched up?"

"No problem . . . I'll be with you in a few moments."

Terri sat down and reached for the *Cosmopolitan* magazine that lay on the coffee table. As she scanned through the table of contents, Terri came upon an article titled "The Tell-Tale Signs of Infidelity." She immediately flipped to the article and began to read the story. The article did nothing to relieve her anxieties.

After leaving the beauty salon, Terri stopped for dinner at Watson's Seafood Restaurant before driving across the Ninth Street Bridge to Somers Point. She parked her rental vehicle down the street from Tony Mart's so not to be seen by her fiancé. Terri wanted to observe how he conducted himself.

Terri passed through the door at 10:00 pm and handed her driver's license to a man with bulging muscles. Since the drinking age in New Jersey was recently lowered to eighteen, the bouncer smiled at Terri and returned the driver's license to her.

Rossi boasted that Tony Mart's was the largest club on the entire East Coast, but Terri failed to comprehend the enormous size of this club. She counted seven differently sized and shaped bars under a single roof. Terri zigzagged her way among the bar patrons like a car swerving in and out of traffic. She spotted Rossi perched behind an oval-shaped bar toward the rear of the building. He was entertaining his patrons by juggling liquor bottles into the air.

Terri took the necessary precautions not to be seen. She felt guilty about spying on her fiancé, but she needed to know if he was someone who could be trusted. For the next two hours, Terri watched as Rossi mixed drinks and worked the customers for tips. He looked happy. She now understood why he preferred to work at the shore!

Terri was about to approach Rossi when she noticed a bleach-blond girl worm her way up to the bar. The girl wore a white miniskirt and a pink halter top that looked two sizes too small. She adjusted her top to accentuate her large breasts and blood-filled nipples.

Rossi drifted toward the blonde while ignoring the raised hands of other people who had been waiting for what seemed like years for a drink. He smiled and gave her a kiss on the cheek. They exchanged a few words and then the blond-haired girl walked away from the bar.

Terri's heart leapt. She couldn't believe what she had just witnessed. All her suspicions appeared to be validated. Rossi was *not* someone who could be trusted!

Terri arose from her seat and maneuvered her way through the crowd as quickly as a mountain lion that had zeroed in on an unsuspecting prey. She positioned herself on the perimeter of the bar and waved her arm just like the blond-haired bitch had done just moments ago.

Rossi was shocked to see that it was Terri who was vying for his attention. He smiled and reached out to touch her.

"It's great to see you, babe . . . I've really missed you."

"It doesn't look like you've missed me."

"What's that supposed to mean?"

"I knew I couldn't trust you. I can't believe I was so naive."

"What are you talking about?"

"What am I talking about? I'm talking about your blonde friend."

"Who?"

"Don't give me who . . . I'm talking about that blonde bimbo you just kissed."

"It's not what it looks like . . . I can explain!"

"Tell it to someone who cares."

"Terri . . . please . . . I can explain!"

Terri fought her way through the crowd as she headed to the nearest exit. Rossi realized that the girl he loved, the girl he planned to marry, was about to walk out of his life.

Rossi sought out the bar manager and asked if he could leave his station for a few minutes. He then fled through the rear exit and caught Terri as she was about to drive away.

"Terri . . . Wait a minute!"

Terri was sobbing uncontrollably. "I thought I could handle you're living at the shore for the summer, but I can't. I've seen too much."

"Are you willing to let our relationship end?"

"It's your fault, not mine!"

"You owe me an opportunity to explain myself."

"I owe you nothing!"

"I'm pleading with you . . . Please let me explain."

Terri didn't say anything. She just continued to cry.

Rossi attempted to put his arm around her shoulder, but she shrugged him off. "Terri, please let me explain. I would never do anything to hurt you . . . I love you."

"Then why did you kiss her?"

"I didn't mean anything by it. She's a waitress at the Italian restaurant down the road. She carries on with all the bartenders at Tony Mart's, not just me."

Terri continued to listen without saying a word.

"If we were an item, then why did she leave?"

Rossi waited for a response from his fiancée, but there was none. He noticed that her sobbing had lessened. "She only stopped by to say hello. As a matter of fact, she dates one of the members of the band."

Terri was embarrassed by what she had said. "I'm sorry, Bill. I'm just having a tough time with everything. And I hate that we're away from each other."

Rossi realized how distressed his fiancée had become. Out of fear of losing the girl whom he loved, he promised Terri that he would leave the shore and move to Charleston for the remainder of the summer. However, he hoped that Terri would not take him up on his suggestion.

Terri was completely caught off guard. "I'd love for you to come home with me to Charleston, but I can't ask you to do that."

Rossi wrapped his arms around her. "I'd rather go to Charleston than do anything to jeopardize our relationship."

"But you make good money here . . . and God knows we'll need the money."

"Screw the money . . . I'm going to Charleston whether you like it or not."

"That would please my parents . . . and me too."

"We'll leave tomorrow."

CHAPTER 18

Sue Gullum had just placed one of her soon-to-be famous pecan pies in the oven when she heard the monotonous ring of the telephone. Before reaching for the receiver, she quickly wiped the flour from her hands. To her surprise, it was Terri who called.

Terri told her mother she would be returning home the following afternoon and that her fiancé would be coming home with her. Sue assured Terri that the guest room would be in tip-top shape by the time they arrived from New Jersey.

After getting off the telephone with Terri, Sue walked out to the garage to speak with her husband. At first, she didn't see him.

"John . . . Where are you?"

Gullum crawled out from beneath the car. "Yes, honey."

"I was just talking with Terri."

"Everything all right?"

"I'm not sure."

"What's going on?"

"Terri's coming home . . . She should be here sometime tomorrow."

"You don't seem excited."

"She's bringing Bill with her."

"We'll finally get to meet him."

When the Gullums heard the approaching car, they rushed outside to greet their daughter and future son-in-law.

"You must be Bill," said Gullum. "I'm John, Terri's father."

"Nice to meet you, sir."

"I'm glad we finally get to meet the person who stole our daughter's heart."

Rossi turned toward his soon-to-be mother-in-law. "I apologize for not being here to help with the wedding arrangements."

"We're glad you're here with us now," said Sue. "Let's go inside. It's hot as hell, and the two of you must be exhausted from the ride."

Sue tapped Terri on the arm. "Take Bill to the guest bedroom. There should be clean towels and a wash cloth on the bed."

Rossi followed Terri up the stairs. "I didn't think I'd have my own bedroom."

"Where did you think you'd sleep?"

"I thought perhaps we would share a bed together."

"I don't *think* so!"

"Maybe later tonight, when your parents are sound asleep, you can come in and wash my back."

Terri smiled and said, "Not until we're married!"

"I hope there's plenty of cold water in the shower!"

Rossi showered and changed clothes before joining the Gullum family downstairs.

"Would you like a glass of lemonade?" asked Sue.

"That would be great, Mrs. Gullum."

"Please call me Sue."

"All right, Sue."

"I understand you want to be a doctor," said John.

"Yes, sir. I've wanted to be a doctor from the time I was a young boy."

"And Terri said you've been accepted into Temple's medical school."

"Yes, but I've postponed my admittance until Terri graduates from college."

"They'll keep a spot open for you?"

"Yes. I have a signed letter from the dean of admissions stating that I can begin medical school anytime within the next three years."

"So you don't *have* to wait three years to begin school."

"No. I can begin school in September if I choose."

"That's great because you never know what tomorrow brings."

"For now, the game plan is for me to get a job and support Terri until she graduates from college. Then she'll get a job and support me until I finish medical school."

"Well, let's hope that everything turns out as planned."

CHAPTER 19

Although the wedding was still three days away, many of the out-of-town guests were beginning to arrive in Charleston. Rossi's relatives, with the exception of his paternal grandfather, Dominic, had already arrived in town to partake in the preceremonial activities. Dominic Rossi was scheduled to arrive this afternoon on Allegheny Airline's five-o'clock flight from Philadelphia. Terri decided to accompany her fiancé to the airport to pick up his grandfather.

The traffic on the two-lane road leading to the airport was exceptionally heavy this day. A section of the road fifteen miles south of the airport was declared impassable. The heavy rains which fell during the past four days caused the road to buckle and collapse.

Rossi glanced at his watch and realized he would be late in picking up his grandfather. This concerned him because Grandfather Dominic had become increasingly more forgetful and disoriented during the past two years. Rossi feared his grandfather may panic and stroll around the airport aimlessly.

Although traffic now flowed at a sustained speed of thirty-five miles per hour, it was still slower than the posted speed of sixty-five. Once again, Rossi glanced at his watch. He calculated that at this rate of speed, he would arrive at the airport fifty minutes late.

Rossi noticed that cars coming from the north were traveling at the normal rate of speed. He extended his head to the left to see if there was a gap between cars approaching from the opposite direction. But he couldn't see anything. His visibility was partially obscured by the Greyhound bus ahead of him.

Rossi continued to follow the bus for several more miles, noting that there were times when the adjacent lane was void of traffic. He again cocked his head outside the window to determine if there was a break in traffic flow. His field of vision was still partially impaired by the bus.

Rossi expressed his concern to Terri about his grandfather becoming disoriented when left alone in an unfamiliar environment. Terri tried to reassure her fiancé that his grandfather would be fine, but he knew differently.

Once again, Rossi attempted to look beyond the Greyhound bus, but his vision was still partially blocked. Since there were no cars in the adjacent lane, he decided to pass the bus. With a sudden turn of the steering wheel, Rossi swerved his vehicle to the left as he pressed the accelerator pedal to the floor. However, he had no time to react to the oncoming cement truck.

The impact was earth moving, the noise deafening. The collision slammed Rossi into the steering wheel and flung Terri out of the passenger door like a projectile. Both Rossi and Terri lay motionless, bleeding from injuries sustained from the accident.

A driver in an eighteen-wheeler who witnessed the accident radioed the South Carolina State Police. Minutes later, emergency vehicles were dispatched to the accident site.

When the emergency personnel arrived at the scene of the accident, they scattered to both accident victims with the speed and precision of a well-rehearsed drill team. An emergency technician searched for a heartbeat by pressing two fingers alongside Rossi's carotid artery. He detected a pulse, although it was irregular and weak. He, along with the help of several other emergency personnel, carefully removed Rossi from behind the steering wheel and placed him onto a stretcher. He was then placed into an ambulance and transported to the hospital.

The other group of technicians focused their attention on Terri. She too was unconscious. However, they believed she may have sustained some internal injuries since she was bleeding from her mouth and nostrils. The technician checked for vital signs, but he was unable to detect a pulse. He immediately started CPR, but he was unable to jump-start her heart. Resuscitation efforts were aborted five minutes later.

Several technicians hoisted Terri onto a stretcher and draped her face and body with a blanket before placing her inside the rear compartment of the second ambulance. However, this ambulance, unlike the other one, would not be taking its occupant to a hospital. The final destination for this ambulance was the county morgue.

CHAPTER 20

A closed casket funeral service was performed by Pastor Toy three days following the automobile accident. The Gullums found it ironic that Terri was buried this day since today was supposed to be their daughter's wedding day.

At the conclusion of the funeral, the Gullums were informed that Rossi had regained consciousness earlier in the day. However, he had no recollection of the accident. Upon hearing the news that his bride-to-be had died as a result of the accident, Rossi became inconsolable. He wished he had perished with his fiancée that fateful day on the highway.

The Gullums visited Rossi at the hospital the following day. They found it extremely difficult to be compassionate. They believed if Rossi had not passed the bus, then their daughter would still be alive. Here was a boy they hardly knew who survived a senseless automobile accident while their precious little daughter, the love of their life, was dead.

"How are you feeling Bill?" asked Gullum.

"I'll be fine, sir."

Gullum stepped around to the side of the bed.

Rossi looked at the Gullums with watering eyes. "Please accept my apology. I'm so sorry for what happened.

"It was a terrible accident," Gullum said with a crackling voice.

Sue Gullum needed some answers. "Do you have any idea why you passed the bus?"

"No, I don't . . . I can't remember anything about the accident."

Sue couldn't determine whether she felt sadness or resentment for Rossi. "You don't remember anything at all?"

"I wish I did, but I don't"

Gullum sensed that his wife was about to say something which she would later regret. "We need to go, honey."

Before leaving the hospital, Gullum placed his hand on Rossi's arm. "We hope you get well and enroll in medical school," said Gullum.

"I'm not sure what my future plans are at this time, sir. I need to get my life in order."

"I know Terri felt guilty about your decision to delay medical school. She would insist you go back to school," said Gullum.

"I'm sure I will . . . but not right now."

Gullum wished him the best of luck, and then he and his wife walked out of the hospital room.

CHAPTER 21

Dr. Rossi graduated summa cum laude from medical school in 1987 and decided to specialize in surgery. He was one of two medical school graduates who were accepted into the surgical residency program at Mount Sinai Hospital in New York City. The surgical residency program at Mount Sinai Hospital was very demanding. Not only were the residents expected to attend lectures, study, and tend to the presurgical and postsurgical needs of patients, but each resident was required to be on call several times each week for medical emergencies.

The most challenging aspect of the residency program was finding time to sleep. Rarely did a night go by without a resident being awakened to address some sort of medical emergency. An appendectomy, a body laceration from an automobile accident, a gunshot wound, a stabbing—these were some of the traumatic injuries treated on a regular basis at an inner city hospital.

Sleep was as rare to a surgical resident as water in a desert. There were many nights when Rossi never reached REM (rapid eye movement) sleep while on call. Just as he burrowed into his cot for a night of much needed rest, the telephone in the doctors' lounge would ring, alerting the young doctor that he was needed for another medical crisis. Rossi would then drag himself out of bed, splash water onto his swollen and irritated eyes, and make his way to the nurses' station.

As he walked down the long dark corridor on sleepless nights, Rossi often second-guessed his decision to become a surgeon. He fantasized how wonderful life would be if he had decided to become a dermatologist, charged with the responsibility of dispensing tetracycline to acne-faced teenagers between the hours of nine and five. Rossi quickly dismissed any thoughts of an alternative career choice. He chose to become a surgeon because he hungered to be in the arena of life and death. It was more than wanting to be a surgeon. He *needed* to be a surgeon, regardless if it meant staying awake for thirty continuous hours.

Following a stressful day in the operating room, the young doctor would strap on his pager and make his way to Central Park. The park had a sedative-like effect on Rossi. However, this one particular day was exceptionally frustrating for Rossi. A five-year-old child was flown to Mount Sinai Hospital from Staten Island, an apparent case of child abuse. The child was nonresponsive when he was evaluated in the ER, and he had multiple contusions on his buttocks and abdomen. Rossi's surgical team was able to stabilize the child's vital signs; however, the child remained comatose.

Rossi vacated the hospital premises as quickly as possible and headed straight to Central Park. He needed to put this unpleasant incident to the back of his mind, if only for a brief moment. However, Rossi would soon realize that this day in Central Park would be different from the others; this would be the day he meets Andrea.

CHAPTER 22

She sat along the lake reading a novel when Rossi first saw her. She was striking, with her long brown hair gently blowing in the breeze. She wore a navy blue turtleneck sweater with matching blue-green watch plaid slacks. Rossi loved that preppy look in a girl. But more importantly, he liked the fact that she was not wearing a ring on her left hand.

"That's a great novel."

The girl looked up to see who was speaking to her. "You've read *A Walk to Remember*?"

"Can't say I have."

The girl redirected her eyes to her book.

Rossi inched closer to the girl. "Do you come to the park often?"

She glanced up once again and closed her book. "I come here when I wish to be alone."

"I thought you might enjoy sharing the afternoon with a nice guy like me."

"Who said you're a nice guy?"

"Lots of people!"

"Like who?"

"My mother for one."

The girl tried not to look amused, but the smile on her face betrayed her. "You're not going to leave me alone, are you?"

"My name is Bill Rossi. What's yours?"

"Andrea."

"Does Andrea have a last name?"

"Andrea."

"I understand . . . Andrea it is."

"You're not a stock broker, are you, Mr. Rossi?"

"No. I'm a doctor."

"A doctor?"

"Actually, I'm a surgical resident."

Andrea was surprised to hear that Rossi was a surgeon. "Well, Dr. Rossi . . ."

"Please call me Bill."

"I'm a third grade teacher at Cathedral Prep, a private school on the Upper West Side."

"Shouldn't you be at school?"

"The school is celebrating 'Take Your Child to Work Day.'"

"So how are your students spending their day?"

"They're probably creating havoc on Wall Street. Most of the parents work in the banking industry."

"Lucky for me you're not working today."

"Why's that?"

"If you were working today, I wouldn't have met you."

Andrea wondered if Rossi was as genuine as he appeared or whether he was another used car salesman.

"I'm starving," said Rossi. "Will you join me for lunch?"

"I can't today. There are a few things I need to do."

"That's a brush off if ever I've heard one."

"I really do have things I need to do. But if you can sneak away from the hospital sometime, then perhaps we can meet for a cup of coffee."

"Sounds great! How can I get in touch with you?"

Andrea reached into her purse and scribbled down her telephone number on a piece of paper. She then handed the paper to Rossi.

"I'll call you soon . . . In fact, don't be surprised if there's a message on your answering machine when you get home."

"Watson," said Andrea.

"Excuse me?"

"My name is Andrea Watson."

Andrea was not as beautiful as Elizabeth Taylor, but Rossi was attracted to her nonetheless. Her high cheekbones, flawless facial skin, and warm brown eyes accentuated her natural beauty. Her only imperfection was the tiny space between her upper two front teeth.

Andrea's parents wanted to correct the diastema when she was younger, but she felt if Lauren Hutton didn't have a problem with the space between her front teeth, then why should she? Besides, Andrea believed this space gave her character.

Andrea was the only child of Andrew Watson, the CEO of Watson Pharmaceuticals, and Allison Clinton-Watson, the only surviving heir of the Colgate fortune. She attended the Winston-Chambers Academy in Boston, Massachusetts, a boarding school for the crème de la crème. Not only did this prestigious preparatory institution afford Andrea an education which equaled or exceeded every other institution in North America, it also instilled in her the proper social graces expected from the privileged few. Yearbooks from past years looked like editions of *Who's Who* among corporate America.

Although Andrea enjoyed a privileged lifestyle, she didn't let the spoils of life turn her into a self-centered arrogant woman. Andrea studied sociology at Radcliff College, and she became sympathetic to the needs of others. Her hunger for helping people steered her onto a pathway opposite the one laid out for her by her father, and this angered Andrew Watson. Andrea preferred to donate her time and money to organizations such as the Children's Hospital Fund, the Make-A-Wish Foundation, and the Women Society for Battered Women rather than devour adversarial rivals in the corporate world.

CHAPTER 23

Andrea was intrigued by the young doctor, and she hoped he would keep his promise to call her. Although her encounter with Rossi was brief, she was extremely careful not to disclose any personal information to him. Under no circumstances did she want this man, or any man she may date, to know that she was the daughter of wealthy parents. If someone knew she came from money, she would never be able to ascertain his true feelings for her; and this uncertainty would be too unimaginable for her.

It was several days before Andrea received the telephone call she had wanted to receive. She picked up the telephone handset on the third ring. "This is Andrea."

"Andrea, this is Bill Rossi."

"Who is this?"

Rossi was disappointed that Andrea didn't remember him. "Bill Rossi. I met you at the park the other day."

"You're the good-looking doctor."

"I'm sorry for not calling sooner, but things got really hectic at the hospital."

"Saving a few lives, were you?"

"A few."

"What do I owe the pleasure of this call?"

"I have a few days off beginning Sunday and thought perhaps we could get together."

"What do you have in mind?"

"It's a surprise."

"A surprise?"

"Trust me . . . I'm sure you'll enjoy yourself."

The pause in the conversation alerted Rossi to the fact that Andrea was becoming cautious. "I know we just met, and you don't know anything about me. But I really *am* a nice guy."

The silence was nerve-racking.

"Who said you're a nice guy?"

"Would you like a list of references?"

"One will do."

"My mother!"

Andrea started to laugh. "Then I'm certain I'll be safe."

"Is that a yes for Sunday?"

"That's a yes."

"Great! Wear casual clothing. And bring a jacket or a sweater because it will cool down in the evening."

"What time shall I expect you?"

"Is one o'clock all right?"

"One o'clock is perfect."

"Great . . . that will give me time to get home from the hospital and sleep for a few hours."

"Get your rest. I don't want you falling asleep on me."

"That won't happen . . . I promise you."

"We'll see."

"Where shall I meet you?"

"In front of Cathedral Prep. I have a few errands to run near the school Sunday morning."

"Cathedral Prep it will be. I'll see you at one."

"I'll be there."

The sun's rays peeked through the partially drawn curtain and danced across Andrea's face. It was eight thirty on Sunday morning, and Andrea was awakening. Normally, she would have slept a bit longer, but she was too excited to sleep.

Andrea didn't know what excited her more—her spending the day with Dr. Rossi or the anticipation of what activity Rossi had planned for their date.

Andrea wished she knew what was planned. All he told her was to wear casual clothing. But Andrea knew all too well that a man's idea of casual clothing can vary greatly from a woman's. Andrea struggled over whether to wear jeans or sportswear. Considering Rossi suggested she wear casual clothing, Andrea chose to wear the sportswear pant and jacket combination.

Rossi pulled up to the front entrance of Cathedral Prep Grade School shortly before one o'clock, driving a late model Fiat convertible.

"Have you been waiting long?"

"No . . . I got here a few minutes ago."

"I received a telephone call from a nurse at the hospital asking for permission to administer a narcotic to a patient. I apologize for being late."

"No apologies are necessary, Doc."

Rossi opened the passenger side car door. "Are you ready to go?"

"I'm as ready as I'll ever be."

Andrea slipped inside the sports car and immediately reached for her sunglasses. "Where are we going?"

"I thought I'd take you to the Jersey Shore for the day."

"That sounds like fun."

While driving down the Garden State Parkway from New York City, Rossi spoke of the things he did during his summers in Ocean City. Much of the conversation pertained to his experiences while bartending at Tony Mart's.

"What's the first thing that pops into your mind when you think about Tony Mart's?" asked Andrea.

"There was this band called the Bob Shoo Bops who played songs from the fifties and sixties."

"I thought you would say the suntanned babes wearing tight-fitting halter tops!"

"If you had asked me what comes to mind when I think about working at the beach, I would have said the suntanned girls wearing bikinis made from leftover dental floss."

"You also worked as a lifeguard?"

"A medic."

"Did you save a few lives that summer?"

"No . . . but I pulled a few splinters from barefooted people running along the boardwalk."

"And you collected a paycheck for that?"

"I was paid to be available just in case some middle-aged want-to-be jock overdid it and ended up in cardiac arrest."

"Sounds like you were overworked?"

"It was a lousy job, but somebody had to do it."

Rossi exited the Garden State Parkway and headed east for Ocean City. As he drove across the Ninth Street Bridge connecting Somers Point to Ocean City, he was overcome by an aromatic sensation that was as exhilarating as a batch of freshly baked chocolate chip cookies.

"Can you smell that?" asked Rossi.

"Smell what?"

"The salt air. I know I'm near the shore when I can smell it."

Rossi continued to drive along Ninth Street until it intersected with Central Avenue. When Rossi reached the intersection of Eleventh and Central, he pointed to the top floor of the yellow-wood-framed house. "I lived up there with four other roommates."

"The house looks just like the one featured in last month's *Architectural Digest*," Andrea said sarcastically.

"What do you expect for $350?"

"That's $350 a month?"

"That's $350 for the entire summer . . . including utilities."

"Isn't there a law against taking advantage of unsuspecting college students?"

"No one ever complained," said Rossi. "In fact, we had a waiting list of people who wanted to bunk with us."

"You wouldn't find my name on that list."

Andrea and Bill spent the entire afternoon at the beach; but as the sunlight gave way to moonlight, they decided to head back to the city. It was 11:00 pm by the time they arrived in New York.

"I had a great time today," said Rossi.

"So did I. It was a lot of fun."

Andrea snuggled closer to Rossi. "I can understand why you enjoyed your summers in Ocean City."

Rossi nodded as he turned onto Sixty-First Street. "Where can I drop you off?"

"I live at 4522 Park Avenue."

"Park Avenue?"

"Just one of the perks for working at Cathedral Prep."

"Would the prep provide me with an apartment on Park Avenue if I were the school's physician?"

"I don't think so."

"Why not?"

"Because everyone knows doctors are rich!"

"Tell them I'm still a resident. I haven't made my first million yet."

"I'll do that first thing in the morning."

"So you're suggesting I keep my second floor apartment in the Village?"

"I would if I were you."

Rossi inched closer to Andrea. "I'd like to see you again?"

"You would."

"Very much."

"I think that can be arranged."

CHAPTER 24

The first half of the work week was exceptionally busy for Dr. Rossi. Not only was he scheduled to work twelve-hour shifts on Monday, Tuesday, and Wednesday, he also had on-call responsibilities for Tuesday night. However, after completing his shift on Friday, he wasn't expected back at the hospital until 7:00 am Monday.

Rossi telephoned Andrea Tuesday with hopes of getting together with her on Friday evening, but he failed to reach her. Instead of trying to contact her by telephone again, Rossi sent two dozen long-stemmed yellow roses to her workplace.

On the card he wrote, *Hope you're free Friday night. If so, meet me at the doctors' lounge on the third floor, 7:00 pm. Bill. P.S. Business attire suggested.*

Rossi was concerned that he had not heard from Andrea regarding Friday night; however, he realized there was no reason to expect a confirmation from her. The card did not ask for an RSVP. Rossi purchased two orchestra seats, third row center section, for Andrew Lloyd Webber's production of *The Phantom of the Opera*. Following the show, he made reservations at the Casa Bella Restaurant in Little Italy for a late dinner.

Andrea arrived at Mount Sinai Hospital at six forty-five and slipped into the elevator nearest the registration desk. As she stepped out of the elevator on the third floor, she turned right and followed the signs directing her to the nurses' station. Andrea waited until the nurse finished her task before interrupting her.

"Excuse me . . . Can you page Dr. Rossi please? He's expecting me."

"And what is your name?" asked the nurse.

"Andrea Watson."

"He's with a patient right now," said the nurse. "He'll soon be finished with his examination."

Moments later, Andrea saw the young Dr. Kildare walk out of the hospital room with a patient's medical record in hand.

Rossi scribbled his notes on the chart and gave the nurse a few instructions as to how he wanted the patient to be treated before turning his attention to Andrea.

"You're a sight for sore eyes."

"Are you flirting with me, Doctor?"

"Just making an observation."

"Your note suggested that I wear business attire. Am I dressed appropriately?"

"You couldn't have looked any better even if I had laid out your clothes."

"What have you planned for this evening?"

"Have you seen the *Phantom*?"

"Not in the United States."

"What does that mean?"

"My mother and I saw *The Phantom of the Opera* in London."

"What's that saying about best-laid plans? Oh well . . . I guess we can see a movie and then get a bite to eat."

"Don't be silly. The *Phantom* is a production that you can see over and over."

"Great! I'll be right back . . . I just need to get out of my doctor uniform."

Their relationship blossomed during the next several months. With the Christmas holiday approaching, Rossi believed this was as good a time as any to meet the families. He introduced the subject to Andrea while the two of them were having lunch one afternoon at Saul's deli.

Andrea longed to meet Bill's mother and father, but she was less than enthusiastic about Rossi meeting her parents. She had managed to conceal the fact that she came from a family of means;

however, she realized Rossi needed to know everything if she hoped to have the trusting relationship she so badly coveted. However, the main reason for Andrea's reluctance to having Rossi meet her parents was because she was uncertain about her father's reaction. It was irrelevant that Rossi was a physician with a promising future; what mattered most to Andrew Watson was that Dr. Rossi was not a WASP.

CHAPTER 25

Andrea and Bill drove to Philadelphia on December 20 to visit the Rossi family for a few days. Upon seeing her son stroll up the walkway arm in arm with his girl, Mrs. Rossi raced outside to greet them.

"I'ma glad you here," said Mrs. Rossi in broken English.

"Mother, this is Andrea."

Mrs. Rossi wrapped her arms around Andrea. "I'ma happy to meet you."

"I'm pleased to meet you too."

"You musta be special because my Billy never before bring a girl home for Christmas."

Andrea let out a sigh of relief as she felt her unfounded apprehensions dissipate.

"Comma inside," said Mary Rossi. "Makea yourself at home." Mary Rossi opened the door and ushered her son and Andrea into her home.

A feeling of warmth engulfed Andrea immediately upon entering the house. Unlike her parents' home where a Picasso hung above the fireplace, a portrait of the Rossi family was centered over the sofa. And the scent of garlic, rather than the smell of stale air peppered with a lilac fragrance, permeated throughout the home.

"Whatever you're cooking, it smells great!"

"I make linguini with calamari."

"I can smell the garlic," said Andrea.

"I usea garlic for everything."

Andrea learned how to prepare calamari and several other Italian food dishes while visiting with Bill's parents.

"Hopefully my cooking will be as good as yours, Mama Rossi."

"Bill no comma home too much because he work all the time," said Mrs. Rossi. "You now know how to cook his favorite food."

"Thanks to you."

"People say first you learn how to cook the food somebody like, then they marry you."

Andrea felt her cheeks take on a rosy color when Mrs. Rossi talked about marriage.

"I'll make sure your son doesn't starve."

The dinner menu was simple yet delightful. Mama Rossi prepared a classic Caesar salad with anchovies, calamari in Sunday gravy served over a bed of linguini, and freshly baked Italian bread. When Andrea and Mama Rossi excused themselves to get the cookie tray and coffee, Joseph Rossi signaled for his son to join him in the adjacent room.

"Andrea seems like a nice girl. Do you love her?"

"I don't know . . . maybe."

"She loves you."

"You think so?"

"I can see it in her eyes . . . Don't let her get away."

Andrea viewed life at the Rossis as uncomplicated in a complicated world. In a world filled with pretentious people, the Rossi family seemed as genuine as a sermon given by a newly ordained priest. Everything seemed as perfect as a Norman Rockwell portrait.

Andrea carried the cookie tray into the dining room and then returned to the kitchen to help Mrs. Rossi with the dishes. As Andrea rinsed the soiled dishes and silverware, she was blindsided by Mary Rossi.

"Do you love my Billy?"

Andrea hesitated before answering. "I think so."

"Don't push him . . . He real busy at the hospital."

"I would never do that."

Mary smiled at Andrea and said, "My Billy find himself a nice girl. You are good for our family."

CHAPTER 26

Their drive to the Hamptons was uneventful. Andrea spent four wonderful fun-filled days at the Rossis, the kind of Christmas she read about in romance novels. Andrea told Bill she found his parents refreshing. From the time she arrived at their home and until the day she left, Andrea said she felt as though she was a member of their family. Rossi reassured her that they were not just being polite, they truly liked her.

Andrea tried to imagine what their visit with the Watsons would be like. How could she ever begin to prepare Rossi for what lay ahead? How could she explain that the home she grew up in was as cold and as sterile as a half-filled ballroom?

"Bill, I need to explain a few things to you."

"I'm all ears."

"I've never spoken very much about my parents. However, after spending these past few days with your family, I now realize how very different your childhood was from mine.

"I know. You never learned how to cook calamari!"

"I'm trying to be serious, and you're making jokes."

"I'm sorry, honey."

Andrea gathered her thoughts once again. "Your father worked very hard to provide for his family. And you were not denied any necessities, regardless of cost. However, there were things you wished you had but were not given because of finances."

"Isn't that true of everyone?"

"Please don't interrupt me, Bill."

"I'm sorry."

"I'm not being critical or condescending. I'm just trying to explain that I grew up differently from you."

"And the point of all this is what?"

Andrea hesitated momentarily. "You know my last name is Watson. My father is Andrew Watson . . . as in Watson Pharmaceuticals. My mother is wealthy in her own right. She is the only surviving heir to the Colgate fortune." Rossi felt like he had just been zapped by a stun gun. "I'm telling you this because I love you, and I believe you love me."

Rossi appeared to have recovered from the fifty thousand volts of electricity that Andrea shot through his body just moments ago.

"Why were you so secretive about everything?"

"There was no other way for me to determine whether you were in love with me or in love with my money."

"I don't know what to say."

"I'm sorry for not being honest with you, but I had to be certain of your feelings."

Rossi tried to comprehend everything he had been told.

"This is all overwhelming. The way you dressed, the way you conducted yourself at various functions, I knew you were culturally educated. But not even in my wildest dreams could I have imagined that you *are* Watson Pharmaceuticals!"

"Are you angry with me?" asked Andrea.

"Not at all . . . I'm just trying to put everything into proper perspective. What should I expect this weekend?"

"Just be yourself. My parents will love you. What's important to them is that I'm happy. But please understand they're not as affectionate as your family. They're more reserved. That's just the way they are."

Andrea instructed Rossi to turn right at the next entrance. On the two brick pillars securing the entrance gate were the words private drive inscribed on brass plaques.

Rossi must have driven a half mile before seeing the Watson residence, an impressive two-story twenty-room colonial mansion. Four circular columns extending from the roof to the ground outlined the entrance to the home.

Rossi parked his Fiat on the governor's circle in front of the home. Two male servants, dressed in butlerlike uniforms, greeted Bill and Andrea as they climbed out of the car. Unlike Mr. and Mrs. Rossi who came outside to greet their son, the Watsons waited inside their home for their daughter.

"Merry Christmas, Andrea," said Allison Watson.

Mrs. Watson then turned to greet Rossi. "Bill, would you like to freshen up before dinner?"

"Yes, I would."

The butler escorted Dr. Rossi to his room.

Rossi's room, or more appropriately described as his suite, was nearly as large as his entire apartment in New York. A screened fireplace, nestled between two high-backed overstuffed chairs, was positioned opposite the large king-size bed. A door at the far end of the bedroom led to the private bathroom which was equipped with a Jacuzzi and a walk-in two-header shower.

After freshening himself, Rossi slipped into his navy blue slacks and blue and white stripped sweater before joining the Watsons for cocktails and appetizers in the library.

"Bill, can I fix you a drink?" asked Andrew Watson.

Rossi thought about ordering a cocktail since both Mr. and Mrs. Watson were having mixed drinks, but he remembered Andrea said don't try to impress anyone, just be yourself.

"A beer please," said Rossi.

"I'm sorry, but I didn't stock any beer," said Watson in an unapologetic manner.

Andrea spoke up in defense of her boyfriend. "Bill also likes scotch, Daddy."

"Johnnie Walker Red with a splash of water would be great," said Rossi.

Andrea asked for another chardonnay.

Rossi groped for something to say. He looked around the room and noticed that books written by Shakespeare, Byron, Twain, Dickens, Elizabeth Barrett Browning, Frost Elliot, and Crane lined the walls. Books from more contemporary authors such as Stephen King, John Grisham, and Tom Clancy were also found on the walls of the library.

"You have an impressive collection of books," said Rossi.

"So I've been told," replied Andrew Watson.

The maid announced that Christmas Eve dinner was being served. Andrew stood and asked that everyone join him in the dining room. The dining room was enormously large, as was every other room in the mansion. The table, with its four evenly spaced gold candelabras, was large enough to accommodate thirty people comfortably. A gold chandelier containing three hundred miniature lightbulbs hung above the dining room table. Six oil paintings were strategically positioned about the room.

Rossi didn't believe Andrea when she said her lifestyle was very different from his. However, he now realized that she had understated their dissimilarities. In fact, her lifestyle was probably different from most people. Rossi didn't know any other family that could accommodate an entire football team at the dinner table.

Allison took one look at the dinner table and immediately chastised the butler. "Henry, the table looks so impersonal. This is Christmas Eve. We should be seated closer to one another rather than at opposite ends of the table."

"Right away, madam. Whatever you say."

Henry repositioned the place settings before helping the women with their chairs.

"That's much better," said Allison.

"Yes, madam."

"You may carry on."

Henry placed linen napkins on everyone's lap before excusing himself from the dining room.

"One moment, Henry," said Andrew Watson. "What are we having for dinner?"

"Pheasant, sir."

"I thought we were having goose!"

"I thought pheasant would be more appropriate this evening," interrupted Allison.

Andrea attempted to soften the tone of the conversation. "Bill, have you ever eaten pheasant?"

"No, I haven't. But I heard it's delicious."

Watson said grace with the same insincerity as the speeches he delivered to nonprofit organizations. After dinner, Allison asked Henry to serve the coffee and dessert in the family room.

Andrea took the young doctor by the arm and directed him toward the family room. As Rossi walked down the hallway, he couldn't help but wonder why Andrew Watson was silent for much of the evening. Rossi enjoyed conversing with Andrea and her mother, but Mr. Watson seemed reluctant to join in on the conversation. He just sat at the table, pushing the food from one side of his plate to the other.

Before retiring for the night, Andrea and Bill strolled around the Watson estate. Andrea couldn't help but notice that Rossi seemed exceptionally quiet as they walked.

"I think you impressed my family," said Andrea.

"Maybe your mother, but I'm uncertain about your father."

"Why would you say that?"

Rossi hesitated for a moment before answering. "Because my name isn't William Kennedy or William Eisenhower."

"You're wrong, Bill."

"Then why did your father ignore me all evening?"

"I think you're being overly sensitive."

"I hope you're right."

"Besides, it's me you're dating, not my family."

"We'll see."

Everyone had eaten breakfast by the time Rossi woke up the following morning. He quickly showered and dressed before making his way to the sun room for coffee.

"Bill, shall I have Maria prepare breakfast for you?" asked Allison.

"No, thank you, Mrs. Watson. I'll just fix myself some toast and orange juice."

"Nonsense. Maria will get the toast and juice . . . That's what she's paid to do," said Andrew Watson.

"Did you sleep well?" asked Mrs. Watson.

"I did until I heard the reindeer tap dancing on the roof."

"That's what I must have heard last night," said Allison. Allison then turned toward her husband. "Did you hear anything last night, honey?"

"I didn't hear a thing," Mr. Watson responded tersely. "And we need to hurry if we're going to make the eleven-o'clock church service."

"Since we're pressed for time, why don't we exchange gifts after church," said Allison.

"After we return from the club," Andrew blurted back.

Following church service, the Watsons and Dr. Rossi went to the Manhattan Golf and Tennis Club for brunch. The clubhouse was extraordinary. Portraits and busts of successful and influential members lined the hallway leading to the dining room.

"The club is phenomenal," Rossi said to Mr. Watson.

"We enjoy it."

"How long have you been a member?"

"My grandfather was a charter member."

A man dressed in a black tuxedo with a red bow tie and cummerbund greeted the Watson party as they entered the dining room. "Merry Christmas, Mr. Watson."

"Merry Christmas, Arnold. Did your family enjoy themselves?"

"Yes, sir, thank you. Santa was very good to our children."

"That's great, Arnold."

Arnold assisted the women with their chairs. "I'll be back momentarily for your drink order," he said.

As Mrs. Watson waited for Arnold to return, she noticed that they were the only ones in the dining room. "Have no other families made reservations for today's brunch?" asked Allison Watson.

"One other family, madam," responded Arnold. "The Standish family is seated in the informal dining room."

Allison turned toward Andrew and suggested they leave so the workers can return home to be with their families.

"Nonsense. We're having brunch *here* today."

From the lox and bagels to the chocolate mousse cake, Rossi found everything delicious. However, he was disappointed with the ambiance of the club; it seemed as sterile to him as an operating room. He believed everyone, with the possible exception of Andrew Watson, felt uncomfortable knowing they were the only people in the club. Rossi enjoyed country club dining but not on Christmas. He believed holidays should be celebrated at home with family and friends.

Everyone returned to the Watson home following brunch. Uncharacteristically, Andrew donned a Santa Clause outfit and distributed gifts to family members. Mrs. Watson served eggnog as Christmas music, sung by Frank Sinatra, Dean Martin, and Bing Crosby, played in the background.

As they enjoyed the warmth of the fireplace later that evening, Andrea snuggled closer to Rossi.

"I bet you're wishing you were back at your apartment."

"Only if you were there with me."

"I may have made a mistake bringing you here."

"I'm glad I came."

"You seem tense . . . What's bothering you?"

"I don't think I can make you happy. I'm in *way* over my head. My friends are Harris, Wilson, and Casey, not Vanderbilt and Rockefeller."

"I don't need things to make me happy. I'm happy just being with you."

"If only I could believe that."

"That's the truth."

Rossi drove back to the city the following day; he needed to be back at the hospital by noon. Andrea, on the other hand, stayed in Long Island a few more days. She wanted to spend time with her parents before returning to the city, but her father needed to fly to Chicago the next morning for business. So Andrea shopped and visited with her mother for the remainder of her stay.

Andrea thought it peculiar that her mother never spoke of Bill after he left their home. It was as though she had never met him. Andrea was beginning to believe that Rossi's assumption that her parents disliked him had merit, and she couldn't understand why. It's not as if Bill was an uneducated gigolo without a promising future. He was a white-collared professional, soon-to-be surgeon. Andrea hoped that Bill was wrong to infer that her parents disliked him because his surname was Rossi and not Mellon. Regardless, she would not let her parents influence her feelings about the man she loved. She knew Bill was a kindhearted person, and to her, that was more important than his nationality.

When Andrea returned to her apartment following the holiday break, she found an unstamped envelope in her mailbox. She immediately recognized the handwriting on the note. The note read, *Glad you're back. I missed you. I spent six fantastic days with you. Eager to get together with you soon. Bill.*

Andrea felt a tingle reverberate throughout her entire body. She realized she loved this man and wanted to spend the rest of her life with him. However, she knew a storm as unsettling as a percolating pot of coffee loomed east of the city. Andrea prayed that their love for each other was strong enough to withstand the fury of this category 5 hurricane named Andrew Watson.

CHAPTER 27

Dr. Rossi set the standard of excellence for the other surgical residents at Mount Sinai Hospital. His work ethic, combined with his technical and diagnostic expertise, was second to none.

The head of the Surgical Department recognized that Rossi had been blessed with exceptional surgical skills, and he submitted his recommendation to the hospital hierarchy that Rossi be appointed chief surgical resident. This recommendation was unprecedented since the chief surgical resident had always been the most senior resident. After much deliberation and with little fanfare, the board members broke tradition and selected Dr. William Rossi as its chief surgical resident.

Rossi was thrilled with this vote of confidence from his superiors; however, he was concerned about the additional workload that was demanded of the chief resident. He would now be responsible for overseeing the other residents, and he would be required to make himself available for countless staff meetings. These additional responsibilities translated into having less time to spend with Andrea.

As the days evolved into weeks, and the weeks into months, Rossi became frustrated with not seeing Andrea as often as he would have liked. He needed to find a way to fulfill his hospital obligations and still have time to spend with Andrea.

Eight months after that fateful day at Central Park, Rossi decided he wanted to marry Andrea. He wrestled with several options before deciding the manner in which he would ask Andrea to marry him. His only concern was that his decision required that he take a short leave from his hospital responsibilities.

Upon learning that the surgical director had approved his request for a four-day leave, Rossi visited a travel agency on Forty-Second Street and booked their excursion. He then telephoned Andrea and asked that she meet him at DeBlasio's for dinner. Although Andrea had several errands to run after work, she promised to meet him at the restaurant by 6:00 pm.

Rossi gulped down two beers while waiting for Andrea. She finally walked into the restaurant at six fifteen.

"Sorry, I'm late," apologized Andrea. "I had a difficult time hailing a cab."

"What would you like to drink?"

"A chardonnay," said Andrea as she slid into the booth opposite Rossi.

Rossi signaled for the waiter. "A chardonnay for the little lady and a beer for myself."

"Would you like an appetizer?" asked the waiter.

"An order of fried zucchini," said Andrea.

"Right away, madam."

Rossi turned his attention to Andrea. "How was school today?"

"Frankie and Eddie got into a fight, and Eddie ended up with a bloody nose."

"What were they fighting about?"

"Who was going to carry Christine's books home from school . . . Can you imagine fighting over a girl in third grade?"

"That proves that women are the root of all evil, regardless of age."

"Is that how you feel about me?"

"Not you, my dear. You're just what the doctor ordered."

The waiter returned with their drinks before reciting the day's dinner specials. Rossi ordered Linguini Don DeBlasio, his favorite dish, and Andrea ordered Veal Romano.

"You ordered spaghetti again?"

"I like spaghetti."

"You've probably eaten spaghetti every week for the last twenty-some years."

"So what?"

"You should try something else for a change."

"What should I have ordered?"

"Whatever you like to eat."

"I thought that's what I did."

"You don't understand."

"What was it I said? Something about girls being the root of all evil."

"Forget it. I shouldn't have said anything."

Rossi swallowed a mouthful of beer. "What are you doing May 25?"

"What day is May 25?"

"A Thursday."

"Probably teaching school. Why do you ask?"

"I've arranged some time off from the hospital and wanted to know if you'd like to get away for a few days?"

"What do you have in mind?"

"A dinner and a show."

"Where?"

"It's a surprise!"

"You and your surprises."

"Can you get away?"

"I suppose so. I have a few personal days left."

"Great!"

"Should I bring anything special?"

"Only a valid passport."

"A what?"

"A passport . . . Trust me."

CHAPTER 28

Andrea couldn't stop from wondering where Bill planned to take her. She thought Europe but realized that it was difficult to do Europe in a few days. Andrea also considered the Caribbean or the Bahamas, but she knew that passports were not required in those countries. Mexico seemed the most logical destination to Andrea since Mexico was doable in a few days. Although passports were not required in Mexico, Rossi may not have known this.

Rossi called Andrea on the eve of their trip and informed her that they would be taking a taxi to the airport. Andrea begged Bill to reveal where they were going, but he refused to give in to her pleas. He wanted everything to be a surprise.

Rossi arrived at work earlier than usual on the twenty-fifth to address any unexpected problems. Fortunately, the day was uneventful for the young doctor; there were no medical crisis and no departmental issues which required his attention. Rossi was reassured by the head of the Surgical Department that the other residents were more than qualified to handle any medical issues and not to concern himself with anything other than having a great time.

The taxi cab idled outside Andrea's apartment. She had not yet finished packing, but Rossi was not concerned. He knew the flight did not depart until 7:10 pm, and it was only a one hour drive to JFK airport. Unless the traffic to the airport was heavier than expected, Rossi knew they would arrive at the airport in plenty of time to board the flight.

Andrea stepped out from her apartment twenty minutes later, carrying a single piece of luggage. She apologized for being late, stating her mother telephoned her just as she was preparing to leave the apartment. Andrea tried to end the telephone conversation with her mother because she knew the cab driver was waiting outside for her. However, Allison, being her normal difficult self, wouldn't get off the telephone until all her questions were answered. She really became agitated when Andrea mentioned that she was going away with Bill for several days.

"And where are the two of you going?" asked Allison.

"To tell you the truth, Mother, I really don't know. Bill said he wanted to surprise me."

"You're planning to go away with a person you hardly know, and you have no idea where he's taking you. Are you crazy?"

"I think it's exciting, Mother."

"Andrea, why would you agree to go away with anyone without knowing where you're going?"

"Mother, I'm not concerned about Bill. I've known him for nearly nine months now, and he has never given me any reason not to trust him. He just wants this trip to be something special."

"I can't understand how he would expect you to go away with him and not give you any indication as to where you'll be going."

"He did tell me to bring a passport."

"A passport!"

"Mother, I have to go. I just wanted to let you know that I'll be away until Sunday night."

"Be very careful, Andrea."

"I love you, Mother."

"I love you too."

It was approximately 5:30 pm when the cab pulled alongside the airport terminal. Rossi handed the baggage handler the trip itinerary in such a way that Andrea could not read their destination city.

Bill and Andrea entered the international terminal at JFK Airport and passed several gates where passengers were boarding flights to Tokyo and to Istanbul. Just ahead, on the left side of the terminal, Andrea spotted side by side gates. Passengers traveling to Cancun, Mexico, were boarding the plane at gate 34, and passengers traveling to Montreal, Canada, waited patiently in their seats at gate 36. Believing Mexico to be their destination, Andrea drifted toward gate number 34. Bill tugged at Andrea's arm to indicate that she was going the wrong way. They continued to walk down the corridor, passing several more gates along the way. As they approached gate 53, Andrea read the placard that was posted on the wall adjacent to the gate. The placard indicated the flight to Paris, France, was scheduled to depart at 7:10 pm.

Andrea squeezed Bill's arm upon discovering they were going to Paris. Andrea loved Paris. Although she visited Paris several times in the past years, Andrea knew this trip would be memorable for her. She was about to visit the City of Lights, the most romantic city in the world, with the person she loved.

Rossi asked Andrea to remain seated while he approached the airline employee for seat assignments.

"May I help you, sir?" asked the woman at the boarding area.

"I hope so. My girlfriend and I are on this flight to Paris, and we have been assigned seats 17A and 17C."

The employee looked at the travel record and confirmed that they indeed were assigned those particular seats.

"Yes, sir. Everything is in order . . . We'll be boarding the flight shortly."

Rossi inched closer to the gate agent. "Sometime during the next several days I plan on asking my girlfriend to marry me."

"Congratulations," said the boarding agent.

"Thank you. But I would really like to make this trip as memorable as possible for her. What would be the cost if I upgraded our seats to first class?"

The airline employee pounded the keys on her computer as skillfully as a concert pianist. She clicked into the site that displayed international tariffs. The boarding agent informed Dr. Rossi that the cost of a one-way first-class ticket upgrade from New York to Paris is $425 per person.

"That's more than the ticket itself costs!"

"I realize that."

"That's too expensive for me."

"I'm sorry, sir."

Rossi sat down next to Andrea and waited for the boarding process to begin. As Andrea told Rossi what she would like to do in Paris, she was interrupted by an announcement from the lounge area. The gentleman nearest the Jetway announced they were about to begin boarding the aircraft. Anyone with small children or anyone needing special assistance was permitted to board the plane. Bill and Andrea gathered their belongings and began to make their way toward the aircraft. Before exiting the terminal, Rossi turned backward to make certain they had not left anything behind. To his surprise, he realized the airline employee whom he spoke with earlier was walking toward him.

"Sir, may I look at your boarding tickets please?"

Rossi handed the tickets to the agent.

"I'm sorry, sir, but there has been a mistake with your seating assignment. The computer inadvertently assigned these seats to two other people. Here are your new boarding tickets. I apologize for this mishap."

Rossi looked at the airline employee after examining his tickets. The smile on her face said, "You're welcome." Rossi handed the tickets to Andrea. Her eyes grew to the size of golf balls; her smile extended from ear to ear. Andrea immediately recognized what this woman did for them. Andrea and Bill then boarded the aircraft with the other first-class passengers.

Rossi enjoyed the first-class ambiance from the moment he stepped into the plane in New York and was handed a crystal-fluted goblet of Dom Pérignon champagne. Rossi immediately realized that there were advantages to sitting in the first-class cabin other than sitting in wider seats. The passengers in the forward section of the aircraft nibbled on an assortment of cheeses, fruits, and nuts before feasting on Caesar salad and beef tenderloin. Passengers in the rear section of the airplane dined on coleslaw and Salisbury steak.

The plane began its descent into the Charles de Gaulle Airport at 7:28 am. The Eiffel Tower, lit up like a decorated Christmas tree, was visible from the left side of the aircraft. After clearing customs,

Andrea and Bill hailed a taxi to take them to the Le Grande InterContinental Hotel in the heart of Paris.

The Le Grande InterContinental, a four-star hotel, had been impeccably preserved throughout the years. The hotel was spectacular, from the mahogany reception counter to the white orchids which were artistically arranged in a large Waterford vase. A four-foot diameter round mahogany table with a polished marble tabletop sat beneath an enormous crystal chandelier in the hotel foyer.

The Le Grande InterContinental hotel is located across the street from the Opera House and a block away from the Metro, a network of subway trains. The Metro is a convenient way to access the places of interest in Paris. In a short period, one could navigate his way to the Eiffel Tower, the Arc de Triomphe, the Louvre, the Notre Dame, the Sacré Cœur, the Invalides, Montmartre, and Pigalle.

Bill and Andrea walked the streets of Paris in search of a place to eat. They found a charming café overlooking the river Seine and asked the hostess to seat them at a table along the sidewalk. They snacked on cheese and crackers while they waited for the waiter to bring them a crock of French onion soup. Afterward, they took the blue line Metro to Montmartre.

Montmartre is recognized as the mecca for art studies by people from around the world. With their easels tucked under their arms and their canvas bags filled with paints, charcoals, and brushes, students made their daily trek to Montmartre Square and patiently waited for the tourists to arrive. Then, like a pack of wolves in a hen house, they pounced on the unsuspecting prey with a collective goal of separating them from their money.

"You like if I paint your picture?" asked one of the artists.

Bill nodded at Andrea before responding. "Can you sketch a portrait of the two of us in charcoal?"

"Yes, sir."

"Great."

Andrea and Bill sat motionless for fifteen minutes while the Korean student skillfully outlined and shaded the likeness of his subjects. Upon inspecting the sketch, they marveled at how much the portrait looked like themselves. They paid the artist three hundred francs before retreating from the heights of Montmartre.

Bill and Andrea spent the remainder of the afternoon and evening visiting the many attractions of Paris. After enjoying a late dinner along the left bank of the Seine, they returned to their hotel room. There they shared a carafe of wine on the balcony as they admired the panoramic view of the City of Lights.

CHAPTER 29

The following morning Rossi called the concierge and requested that an order of croissants and coffee be delivered to his room. As they dined on the balcony overlooking the Opera House, Andrea asked Rossi if there was anything special he wanted to do today.

"As a matter of fact, I have our entire day planned out," he said.

"A penny for your thoughts."

"Do you remember my promising you a dinner and a show?"

"Yes."

"Since this is our last day in Paris, I made dinner reservations at Maxim's, and I have tickets for the midnight show at the Lido."

"Really?"

"I want tonight to be special."

"That's awfully nice of you . . . and I appreciate your wanting to do this for me. But that's just too much money."

"Like I said, I want this to be a special evening. Next week, we'll eat at McDonald's."

"What time is dinner?"

"We have a seven-thirty reservation."

"Let's take a cab to Champs Élysées . . . I need a dress for tonight."

They arrived at Maxim's at precisely 7:30 pm. Upon arriving at the restaurant, the maître d' escorted them to a table for two. The décor of the restaurant was exquisite. Oil paintings of renowned artists were strategically positioned on the walls while small lamps rested on each tabletop. An extravagant Waterford crystal chandelier hung in the center of the dining room.

A waiter, donning a white linen napkin over his left arm, approached Andrea and Bill.

"Bonjour, mademoiselle et monsieur."

"Bonjour."

"Voulez-vous un cocktail?"

"I'm sorry, but we don't speak French," replied Dr. Rossi.

The waiter looked at them with a slight hint of disgust. "Would you care for a cocktail?"

"We would like a bottle of merlot, please."

"Oui, monsieur."

The waiter returned shortly and poured each of them a glass of wine. "Do you have any questions about the menu, or are you ready to order?"

"I believe we're ready," said Rossi.

"Mademoiselle?"

"I'd like the escargot appetizer."

"And for your entrée?"

"The lobster tail, please."

"Et vous, monsieur?"

"I'll have the clams on the half shell and the duck l'orange."

"Tres bien."

After placing his dinner order, Rossi raised his wine goblet. "The best day of my life is when I met you in Central Park. I love you, Andrea."

"I love you too."

Rossi then removed a small rectangular-shaped box from his sport jacket and pushed it across the table. Andrea's eyes filled with tears in anticipation of what lay inside the box. She opened the box and found a two-karat marquis-shaped diamond neatly packaged inside the box. The ring had exceptional color and clarity. With tears flowing down her cheeks, Andrea held the ring with her right hand. She wanted to speak but found herself incapable of doing so.

Rossi then reached for her hands from across the table. "Andrea, this ring represents the love I have for you. Will you do me the honor of marrying me?"

"I hoped you would ask me to marry you," said Andrea as she wiped the tears away from her eyes.

"Is that a yes?"

"Yes, I'll marry you."

They finished their dinner before making their way to the Lido for a late performance. After the show, they returned to the hotel and packed their belongings for their next-day flight to New York.

CHAPTER 30

Andrea and Bill cast aside their earphones and inched closer to each other. They couldn't care less what movie the airline chose to air on their return flight to New York. Choosing a date and location for their upcoming wedding was a topic of greater interest for them than watching the full-length motion picture.

Rossi suggested they have a Christian wedding ceremony in Central Park since that is where they met. However, Andrea said her father would be heartbroken if they did not marry at the family estate. Ever since she was a young girl, Mr. Watson remarked about how their home would serve as an excellent venue for a wedding. Rossi agreed to be married at the Watson residence.

Rossi asked Andrea if she preferred a smaller, more intimate reception or a "go all out" event befitting a royal couple. Without hesitation, Andrea said her father only does things in the grandest of ways. The most discussed topic on the flight from Paris to New York was when they would exchange their vows. Andrea suggested they marry in August, before the beginning of the new school year. Rossi's only objection to being married in August was that he would not be able to separate himself from his hospital responsibilities on such short notice; there was no way he could take time off for a honeymoon. Andrea said a honeymoon was not all that important to her, and as far as she was concerned, they could go away later in the year.

After their arrival in New York, Bill and Andrea shared their desire to marry each other with their parents. Mr. and Mrs. Rossi were thrilled with the news of the upcoming wedding. However, the

Watsons, as expected, were less than enthusiastic. They suggested postponing the wedding for a year since they needed time to secure a location for the reception. Andrea reminded her father that he had said more than once that his home would be a wonderful place to host a wedding reception. Realizing his daughter would marry this man with or without his consent, Andrew Watson reluctantly agreed to host the affair.

The nurses on the surgical floor waited patiently for Dr. Rossi to report to work. They were dying to hear all about his weekend in Paris. When Rossi nonchalantly mentioned that he asked Andrea to marry him while dining at Maxim's, the nurses screamed with excitement. They approved of his marrying the beautiful school teacher and demanded that they be invited to the wedding.

CHAPTER 31

Andrea believed three months was more than enough time to plan a wedding since she didn't have to concern herself with securing a ballroom for the reception. However, she soon discovered that there were more details than just finding a place to party that required her attention to properly host a wedding. Mrs. Watson suggested that Andrea hire a wedding coordinator to assist them with the ceremonial obligations. Andrea and her mother only wanted to concern themselves with the dinner menu, the floral arrangements, and the hiring of a band.

Mrs. Watson wanted everything to be perfect for her daughter's wedding. Knowing that her home was large enough to accommodate twenty overnight guests, she invited Andrea's grandparents, aunts, and uncles to stay at her home as houseguests. She also reserved rooms at several of the bed-and-breakfast establishments for the remaining out-of-town guests. Allison Watson entrusted the responsibility of securing tee times for anyone who wished to play golf to her husband.

The tension at the Watson home escalated throughout the week preceding the weeding. Mrs. Watson rode the domestic help as sternly as a Marine Corps drill sergeant. She demanded they polish the gold place settings and shampoo the carpets throughout the entire home.

The first out-of-town guests to arrive were Andrea's paternal grandparents, Phillip and Nancy Watson. They too hailed from New York. They bought a home in the Hamptons when Mr. Watson Sr. first founded the Watson Pharmaceutical Company forty-three years ago. However, they had since sold their Long Island estate and moved to a more temperate climate when Mr. Watson Sr. retired in 1985. They now make their home in Palm Beach, Florida.

Phillip and Nancy Watson returned to New York twice a year since relocating to Florida. They came to the city in December to attend the annual Christmas Spectacular Show at Radio City Music Hall, and they returned to the Hamptons the third weekend in July to participate in the annual member-guest golf tournament at the Manhattan Golf and Tennis Club.

Dr. Rossi's parents arrived in New York three days prior to the wedding. The Watsons had extended an invitation for the Rossis to stay at their home as houseguests; however, Joseph and Mary Rossi declined their invitation in favor of staying at a bed-and-breakfast inn. They had never traveled to New York City, and they wanted to visit the Empire State Building, the Statue of Liberty, Ellis Island, and other points of interest.

CHAPTER 32

The day of the wedding was surprisingly serene at the Watson residence. Mrs. Watson placed the responsibility of handling any last-minute glitches with the wedding coordinator. She made it understood she wanted to spend the day with her daughter and did not want disturbed.

Dr. Rossi, to his surprise, seemed calm the morning of the wedding. His friends said he would eventually succumb to nervousness; but he felt as relaxed as a swan on water. However, Dr. Rossi sensed that something was not quite right with himself because he was having difficulty memorizing his wedding vows. He blamed Andrea for his inability to learn the phrases because she gave him a copy of the vows just hours before the ceremony. He later admitted to being nervous because his friends, who assisted him with the vows, were able to regurgitate the phrases at will.

The maid of honor, along with the other bridesmaids, gathered at the Watson home for breakfast. Afterward, they were directed to Mrs. Watson's master bathroom where two beauticians from the Waldorf Astoria set up workstations to shampoo and style the girls' hair.

The wedding ceremony proceeded uneventfully until it was time for Bill to recite his marriage vows. As the minister cued Rossi that it was time for him to deliver his declaration of affection, his mind went blank; he had forgotten his lines. He felt like an entertainer with stage fright on opening night. Without hesitation, Rossi reached within himself and recited in sonnetlike fashion the words which reflected his feelings for Andrea.

Andrea glanced at her fiancé in astonishment, knowing these were not the phrases which she wrote for him that morning. She listened intently to his words, realizing the man she loves was speaking from his heart and not from some handwritten piece of paper.

The area of the estate designated for the reception was outlined by an enormous white canvas tent supported by Roman-like columns. Beneath the covering adjacent to the swimming pool stood the hors d'oeuvres table layered with clams, oysters, shrimp, and caviar. An ice sculpture shaped like a marlin sat in the center of the food display. A strolling violinist played as Bill and Andrea received congratulatory wishes from their guests.

Following dinner, the guests danced to the sounds of an eight-piece band. A husband-and-wife team entertained everyone by singing songs from Frank Sinatra, Billy Joel, Britney Spears, 'N Sync, Whitney Houston, and Diana Ross. When the duo began to play a tune which was easily recognized by the wedding guests, everyone began to move their arms in rhythmic fashion as they spelled out the letters to the YMCA song popularized by the Village People. As the guests continued to spell out YMCA, Dr. and Mrs. Rossi slipped away from the wedding reception and made their way to the Flanders Hotel in Ocean City, New Jersey.

CHAPTER 33

As per Dr. Rossi's request at check-in the previous night, a hotel bellman wheeled a breakfast cart into the honeymoon suite at 10:00 am. Andrea nibbled on a strawberry as her husband poured the coffee. After breakfast, Andrea and Bill changed into their beach attire and walked to Twelfth Street where they claimed their piece of the beach near the lifeguard station. For three wonderful days, they basked in the sun and dined at Watson's Seafood Restaurant, the Crab Trap, and Gregory's restaurant in Somers Point. They partied at Tony Mart's their final night in town before returning to New York.

Rossi's first day back at the hospital was like most other days since he began his medical career at Mount Sinai Hospital; twenty-four hours of work were crammed into an eighteen-hour day. However, he no longer cared that he worked long hours because he knew that, at the end of the day, he would be going home to his wife and not to an empty apartment. Rossi maintained the same work intensity the next several months that he displayed prior to getting married, and his work ethic did not go unnoticed. Several days later, the chief of the Surgical Department invited Rossi to dinner at Randazzo's Restaurant in the Little Italy section of Manhattan. Randazzo's Restaurant was one of Rossi's favorite restaurants. He met the owner, Mark Randazzo, an ex-professional boxer from Chicago, years ago at his original restaurant in Coral Gables, Florida.

During dinner, the department chief made Rossi a proposition. He told Rossi he was a remarkable surgeon and that he and the other partners liked the way he interacted with his patients. He offered Rossi a full-time position with a salary of $100,000 a year for three years. Afterward, he would have the opportunity to become a full partner with a salary commiserate with the other partners. He hoped this offer would dissuade the gifted Dr. Rossi from seeking offers from other surgical corporations. He believed Rossi would someday become a world-renowned surgeon.

"I'm flattered, sir . . . I had hoped to remain at Mount Sinai."

"We don't want to lose you, Bill . . . You're *one fine* surgeon!"

"Would you mind if I discuss this offer with my wife before giving you an answer?"

"Not at all . . . Take all the time you need. We want you to be certain of your decision."

"I'll give you my decision in a few days. Thank you, sir."

That evening, Rossi discussed the opportunity with his wife. Andrea said this was his decision to make and that she would support him regardless of what he decided to do. Rossi appreciated Andrea's unconditional support, but he wanted to know her true wishes.

"Do you think we should stay here in New York, or would you prefer that I look for a surgical opportunity elsewhere?" he asked.

"I think they *really* want to keep you here with them," said Andrea. "They're making you an unbelievable offer. Besides, if you stay at Mount Sinai, we wouldn't have to leave New York."

Rossi informed the chief surgeon the following morning that he would accept their offer to remain at Mount Sinai. The chief said he would have the corporate attorney draw up a contract for him to sign immediately.

Several months later, while strolling through Central Park, Andrea snuggled closer to her husband.

"Honey"—Andrea used this affectionate term whenever she needed a special favor from her husband—"since you're now making a good income, would you mind very much if I quit teaching?"

"Don't think for one minute I'll allow you to stay home and watch soap operas all day while I'm working my butt off!"

"I'm serious, Bill."

"I thought you enjoyed teaching?"

"I love teaching . . . but I'd rather stay home and take care of our family."

"You what?"

"I said I'd rather stay home and take care of our child." Rossi stood as rigidly as a person in a state of suspended animation. "You're not disappointed that I'm pregnant, are you?"

"Heavens, no! This is the best news that you could have ever given me. When will the baby be born?"

"The doctor said the due date is December 23."

"I can't believe I'm going to be a father."

Rossi grew more excited about Andrea's pregnancy with each passing day. He often wondered about what it would be like having a son or a daughter and doing the kinds of things that fathers do with their children.

"Have you thought about a name for the baby?" asked Bill.

"If it's a girl, I thought about naming her Ashley or Courtney. What are your feelings?"

"I'm partial to Courtney."

"And if it's a boy, I thought about naming him Jon-Michael or Trevor. Do these names do anything for you?"

"I was thinking about Tadd."

"Perhaps we should table the boy's name until later."

As summer gave way to autumn, it became more apparent that Andrea was pregnant. She now wore maternity clothing, and her stomach looked as though she had swallowed a basketball. Dr. Sheffey, Andrea's obstetrician and gynecologist for the past ten years, reviewed the most recent sonogram. He was about to divulge the sex of the fetus when Andrea stopped him; she preferred not knowing the baby's gender. Dr. Sheffey respected her wishes and said that the baby was developing nicely.

Rossi was exceptionally quiet during dinner. Ever since Andrea told him she was pregnant, he second-guessed his decision to remain in New York. He liked the hospital staff, and it was advantageous for him, from a professional stand point, to remain at Mount Sinai. However, Rossi realized he would soon be responsible for the safety of a child.

When Andrea returned home from work that evening, she was surprised to find her husband at home, looking as though he was deep in thought.

"What are you doing home so early?" asked Andrea.

"I told the chief that I needed to leave early today."

"Are you all right?"

"I've been rethinking our decision about living in New York. I think its best that we move to another city."

This announcement was completely unexpected. "I thought you loved New York."

"I do . . . I did."

"What are you concerned about?"

"The dangers associated with living here in the city. I continuously treat people who have been victimized with every imaginable type of weapon, and the growing numbers of people with communicable diseases are escalating at crisis levels. So I began to think, why not move to a city where life is simpler and where you can walk without the fear of being mugged or killed."

"What about your appointment at the hospital? You signed a contract."

"The contract states that I have the opportunity to become a partner after three years; it doesn't obligate me to *become* a partner. I'll tell them I changed my mind about remaining in New York. I'm sure they'll release me from my obligation to the corporation once they hire another associate."

"Where would we go?"

"I don't know. I'll start looking at the classified section in the medical journals. I'll make inquiries as to who may be in need of a surgeon."

"I'll do whatever you think is best for us."

"I'm convinced that relocating to a small town is the right move."

Rossi informed the surgical associates that he had changed his mind about becoming a partner and that he and Andrea decided to leave the city. He explained that his decision to leave the city had nothing to do with them personally or with the hospital. Rossi said he preferred to raise his family in an environment different from New York.

The associates reluctantly agreed to release him from his contract; however, they asked that he remain on staff until they hire another physician. Rossi agreed to remain at the hospital for as long as it took to find a qualified associate.

Rossi reviewed the medical journals in hopes of finding an available surgical position. He was surprised to find that there were numerous positions available; however, most opportunities were in larger cities such as Boston, Chicago, Pittsburgh, and Los Angeles. Of these cities, Pittsburgh was the only one that Rossi seriously considered because he read in the *New York Times* that Rand McNally had rated Pittsburgh the most livable city in the U.S. Rossi then conducted his own study and discovered that Pittsburgh, even though it enjoyed a great reputation as a medical and research center, was still considered a large metropolitan city. After much deliberation, Rossi decided against coming to Pittsburgh. He wanted to move to a more rural community.

With painstaking effort, Rossi continued to plow through the medical journals for a surgical position. Most cities advertising for a surgeon had a population greater than one million people. After hours of skimming through countless journals, Rossi came upon an advertisement that caught his eye.

SURGICAL POSITION AVAILABLE
DERRY, PENNSYLVANIA
POPULATION 3,000
Send Resume to:
Dr. Benjamin Hetfeld
c/o Derry Suburban Hospital
386 Main Street
Derry, Pennsylvania 17143

The first thing Rossi did upon returning home from work was to unfold his map of Pennsylvania and search for the town of Derry. He was surprised to find that Derry is located in Eastern

Pennsylvania, not far from Philadelphia. During dinner that evening, Rossi shared the information he found about the available surgical position in Derry with his wife. Andrea could hear the excitement in Rossi's voice, but she had no desire to leave New York. Rossi said he planned to drive to Derry this coming weekend to get a feel for the community and asked Andrea if she would like to come along. Without hesitation, Andrea said most definitely!

It took them nearly two and a half hours to drive from New York to Derry. A roadside billboard boasting Derry as *A Wonderful Place to Raise Children* stood on the east side of the two-lane road. As they continued their drive down the road, they passed a nondenominational Christian church, a two-story school building housing children from grades 7-12, and a municipal building with the fire department facing Main Street and the police department accessible from the rear of the building. Rossi stopped at the police station and asked for directions to Derry Suburban Hospital. The police lieutenant told Rossi to continue along Main Street for three more blocks and then turn right onto Broad Street. The hospital is on the corner of Broad and Beaver.

Andrea's impression of Derry differed from her husband's. She perceived Derry as a culturally deprived community which lacked the sophistication of nineteenth-century Paris. Rossi regarded Derry as a small intimate community that could have been used as the movie set for *It's a Wonderful Life*.

Derry Suburban Hospital looked unlike any other hospital that Bill or Andrea had ever seen. The two-story red brick building more closely resembled a high school than a hospital. In fact, the image that popped into Andrea's mind when she first laid her eyes on the hospital was the scene in the movie *Grease*, when John Travolta and the other T-Birds and Pink Ladies burst through the high school's front doors on their way to the carnival.

Bill and Andrea entered the hospital and proceeded directly to the administration office.

"May I help you?" asked the secretary.

"I hope so," responded Rossi. "I would like to meet with Dr. Benjamin Hetfeld regarding the surgical position at the hospital."

"Do you have an appointment with Dr. Hetfeld?"

"No, I don't. But I would like to speak with him if at all possible. I just drove in from New York City."

The receptionist looked at Dr. Hetfeld's schedule. "Dr. Hetfeld has three more surgeries scheduled for today . . . I can page him for you."

"I would appreciate it, thank you."

Dr. Hetfeld answered the page ten minutes later and said he would be available to meet with Dr. Rossi between surgeries in the cafeteria. Bill and Andrea found their way to the cafeteria and ordered coffee and a slice of apple pie while they waited for Dr. Hetfeld. A man wearing surgical scrubs with matching cap and booties approached Bill and his wife.

"Dr. and Mrs. Rossi?"

"Yes."

"I'm Ben Hetfeld."

"Nice to meet you," said Rossi.

"What can I do for you?"

"I recently completed a surgical residency at Mount Sinai Hospital, and I'm thinking about relocating to Derry."

"Isn't there a hospital in New York where you can work?"

"I had the opportunity to become a partner with the surgical group at Mount Sinai."

"New York is a fabulous city . . . What would possess you to leave New York for our little town?"

"We both love New York. However, my wife is pregnant, and we believe our child will be safer in a small town like Derry."

"We do live in a safe community. In fact, I can't remember the last time we had to deal with a serious crime."

"That's precisely why we want to relocate here."

"You'll find that your work day will be quite different from what you're accustomed. In New York, you were able to limit your practice to surgery. Not so in Derry. Most days, you'll work as a surgeon, other days you'll be asked to function as a pediatrician, a rheumatologist, a dermatologist, or even an obstetrician should Dr. Wilson become overwhelmed with deliveries on a particular day."

"It sounds like I better reread my medical books."

"There's just one more thing we need to discuss," said Hetfeld. "I can appreciate your wanting to raise your children in a place where you believe they'll be safe. And fortunately, we haven't had to endure any serious problems here in Derry. However, I do have concerns whether you and Andrea will be happy living here."

"And why's that?"

"Derry is a rural community comprised primarily of blue-collared workers. Our lifestyle, or should I say lack of a lifestyle, is fine for people like myself who grew up here. But for those people who have been exposed to the smorgasbord of activities that large cities can offer, they may find living in a town like Derry too simplistic and too boring.

"Andrea and I have already discussed those things, and we believe we're up for the challenge!"

"If this is what you truly want, then the job is yours. When would you be available to start?"

"Probably within a month. I have to tie up some loose ends back in New York."

"That's fine. That will give me some time to do the customary background check. I'm sure everything will check out, but I'm still required to do the search."

"Everything will check out fine."

"Call me when you're available to start."

"Will do."

On their drive back to New York, Andrea again voiced her concerns about moving to Derry. Rossi reassured her that if she truly hated living in Derry after giving herself a reasonable amount of time to adjust to small town living, then he would move the family to another city.

Rossi informed his associates that he had accepted a position in Derry, Pennsylvania, and asked to be released from his obligations with them as soon as possible. The associates said they anticipate hiring another associate within the next two or three weeks.

Andrea and Bill returned to Derry the following weekend to search for a place to live. There were only a handful of houses listed for sale in the realtor section of the *Derry Gazette*; most of the people in town were born in Derry, and they planned to remain in Derry. The homes which were available for sale were not the style of home that Andrea dreamed of owning. These were the typical three-bedroom wood-framed homes that were built in the 1940s. However, they did find a house which was architecturally different from the others. This home belonged to a former physician who moved to Fort Lauderdale, Florida. The English tutor home boasts four bedrooms, three full baths, one powder room, a spacious living room, and a cozy family room. The dining room walls were covered with wainscoting. Sculptured oak wood outlined the floor to ceiling fireplaces in both the living room and the family room. The French doors in the kitchen served as a portal to the glass-enclosed Florida room and the inground swimming pool.

Andrea loved the house. Of all the amenities this home offered, what convinced Andrea that this was truly the house for her was the built-in swimming pool. She believed the pool will provide her family many hours of enjoyment and quality time together.

Realizing this was the first time his wife had shown excitement about anything associated with Derry, Rossi agreed to purchase the home. The home was structurally sound, but in need of some redecorating. The wallpaper was dated, and the crown molding and baseboard were in need of a fresh coat of paint. Andrea drove to their new home often during the next several weeks because she wanted to be certain that the redecorating was being completed to her satisfaction. To her surprise, the redecorating was completed when promised; and it looked better than either she or her husband had imagined. In fact, Andrea could have petitioned the *Home and Garden* magazine to feature her home in an upcoming edition.

The telephone rang at 10:30 am. A man with a raspy voice from Mayflower Movers said he would be at the house within an hour. A tractor trailer truck with green and yellow markings drove up the Rossi driveway shortly before eleven fifteen. The driver parked his truck alongside the front porch and began transferring furniture from the truck into the house. Andrea picked up a midsized box earmarked for the kitchen and began emptying its contents onto the Formica countertop.

"What do you think you're doing?" asked Rossi in a concerned tone of voice. "You're eight months pregnant."

"I'll be fine."

"They're being paid to move everything."

"I'll be careful, honey."

"Just amuse me, will you please."

"Whatever you say."

Rossi and Andrea worked together hand in hand; he unpacked the boxes, and she placed the items in their designated places. It took Andrea the better part of a week to complete the unpacking. She celebrated her emptying the last of the boxes by opening a bottle of cabernet sauvignon. Andrea was just beginning to feel a slight buzz from consuming too much alcohol in a short period when she heard a knock on the door. Standing on the front porch cradling several baskets of food were a gaggle of women representing the local Welcome Wagon organization.

"Mrs. Rossi?" asked one of the women.

"Yes."

"We're with the Welcome Wagon . . . May we come in?"

"Please."

One by one, the women presented Andrea an assortment of items, including a pan of lasagna, dinner rolls, blueberry pie, a fruit basket, and a horseshoe to hang above the doorway for good luck. Andrea was touched by the sincerity of the women. These ladies were not as sophisticated nor as educated as the women she socialized with in New York, but they were genuine. Andrea didn't know these ladies, yet she felt very relaxed in their presence; and more importantly, she believed she could trust them. She thought if the other women in town were as cordial and as considerate as these ladies, then living in Derry may not be so unimaginable.

When Rossi arrived home from his first day at work, Andrea shared her experiences of the day with him, including the visit from the Welcome Wagon representatives. She then asked her husband how his day was. He initially said it was great, that his day was every bit as exciting as his days at Mount Sinai. However, he later retracted his comment and confessed that his day was boring. Other than performing an emergency appendectomy on a forty-five-year-old man, the remainder of his workday entailed stitching the forehead of a boy who fell off a tree, sterilizing and bandaging the lacerations on the lower right leg of a six-year-old girl who was involved in a head-on bicycle accident, and injecting penicillin into the arm of a sixteen-year-old girl who entered the emergency room with pneumonia-like symptoms. His first day on the job was unfulfilling; it lacked the rush of adrenaline he experienced at Mount Sinai Hospital. He hoped he could adapt to his new role as the town's multidimensional physician. But he was uncertain.

CHAPTER 34

The morning of December 21 started out just like all other mornings for Bill and Andrea; he went to work, and Andrea cleared the breakfast dishes from the table. However, shortly after her husband left home, Andrea began to experience several minor contractions as she finished wrapping the last of her Christmas gifts. She telephoned her husband, believing she was going into labor; but Rossi tried to lessen her fears by explaining that she was experiencing false labor contractions. When the contractions intensified, she again paged her husband. Rossi immediately called for an ambulance to transport his wife to the hospital.

Andrea's gynecologist, Dr. Wilson, happened to be in the hospital tending to another expectant mother when Andrea arrived at the emergency room. He quickly evaluated her condition and instructed the nurse to prepare a room for her immediately. The admitting nurse assigned her a room in the maternity wing without first requiring her to fill out the obligatory paperwork.

Twelve hours later, after a very difficult labor, Andrea gave birth to an eight-pound-seven-ounce brown-eyed baby girl. Andrea was exhausted after twelve hours of labor, yet she felt exhilarated for having given birth to such a beautiful little girl. The editor of the *Derry Record* listed the birth announcement in the morning's edition.

> Courtney Theresa Rossi, daughter of Dr. William and Andrea Rossi, was born at 9:28 pm. on December 21, 1992. She weighed eight pounds and seven ounces. The entire community of Derry wishes the best for the Rossi family!

Needing to recuperate from the birthing process and to familiarize herself with her new role as a mother, Andrea remained an inpatient at the hospital for several days following Courtney's birth. Rossi fastened the unisex Mickey Mouse bumper pads to the rails of the crib and laid a white thermal blanket embroidered with the likeness of "Big Bird" over the mattress the night before his wife and daughter would be discharged from the hospital.

Rossi brought his family home the morning of Christmas Eve. Realizing Mrs. Rossi would not be up to the task of preparing a Holiday meal, three neighbors stopped by the Rossi home with gifts in hand. Unlike the "Three Kings" bearing gifts of gold, frankincense, and myrrh, these neighbors brought a turkey, whipped potatoes, and broccoli.

After dinner, Andrea removed the dinner plates from the dining room table before joining her husband in the family room. Andrea sat down in one of the two high-backed chairs that faced the fireplace.

Rossi stirred the fire with a wrought iron poker, causing the flames to reach high into the cold air. No longer concerned that the fire was incapable of sustaining itself, he removed a bottle of merlot from the wine rack and poured two glasses of wine. As he handed Andrea her drink, Rossi acknowledged that Courtney's birth was the most precious gift she could ever have given him.

CHAPTER 35

After an exceptionally cold and snowy winter, the people of Derry welcomed the coming of spring. They emerged from their insulated abodes upon seeing their shadows and began to spruce up their yards and wash their outer windowpanes. Several industrious people even decided to whitewash their faded picket fences in preparation of the coming summer season.

The town came alive on Memorial Day. Up and down the streets, children pedaled their two-wheeled Schwinn racers, which they decorated earlier that morning with multicolored crepe paper. Many of the children customized their bicycles by placing miniature flags on their handlebar grips and attaching playing cards between the spokes of the wheels to create the *tat, tat, tat* sound.

Andrea fed and bathed Courtney the morning of May 30 while Bill drove to the hospital to check on his patients. After lunch, she dressed her daughter in a pretty sky blue sunsuit and waited for her husband to return from the hospital. The Rossi family then strolled to the city hall, where they laid claim to their piece of the sidewalk on Main Street and waited for the parade to begin.

Although Courtney was only six months old, she seemed quite attentive. She listened to the bands as they played selections from John Phillip Sousa's compositions, such as "The Stars and Stripes Forever" and "The Washington Post." At the conclusion of the parade, performers and spectators gathered at the VFW fairgrounds for a community picnic; Derry's Chamber of Commerce provided the hot dogs and hamburgers, and each family was asked to bring a side dish or dessert. The highlight of the day was a reenactment of a World War II battle staged by men who had actually fought in the war.

Following church service one Sunday morning in August, Andrea mentioned to her husband that she had been experiencing bouts of nausea. Rossi, thinking his wife may again be pregnant, asked Andrea when she last menstruated. Andrea said she hadn't had a period in two months. However, she didn't believe she was pregnant because her menstrual cycle had been irregular since giving birth. Rossi insisted that she be examined by Dr. Wilson.

Wilson asked Andrea several questions related to her nausea before instructing his nurse to obtain urine and blood samples. Andrea asked Dr. Wilson if he had any idea what may be causing her periodic episodes of nausea, but he said it would be unprofessional of him to make a guess. He promised to call her within the next two days to discuss the findings.

Andrea was shocked to hear that she was pregnant. Rossi, on the other hand, was elated to hear that his wife was with child. He always wanted two children; he only wished that the children would have been spaced a little further apart.

Andrea struggled with morning sickness her entire first trimester of pregnancy. She was so nauseous most days that she didn't even bother getting dressed. Knowing Andrea had not been feeling well, her friend, Cindy Rae, stopped by the Rossi home and offered to help care for Courtney. Andrea told Cindy she appreciated her support but insisted she was quite capable of caring for her daughter.

Although Andrea was able to provide basic care for Courtney, she was remiss in not recognizing that Courtney was not as playful as she should have been. When her husband arrived home from the hospital that evening, Andrea shared her concerns regarding Courtney's lethargic behavior.

"Perhaps she's teething," said Rossi.

"Why don't you ask Dr. Harris to take a look at her?"

"I'll talk to him first thing in the morning."

Rossi knocked on Dr. Harris's door at eight fifteen the following morning. "Jeffrey, if you have a free moment today, I'd appreciate if you'd take a peek at Courtney."

"What's wrong with Courtney?"

"Probably nothing . . . But Andrea says Courtney hasn't been herself lately."

"Have Andrea bring her to the office at 11:00 am."

"Thanks, Jeff. I really appreciate this."

Rossi called his wife and advised her that Dr. Harris wanted to see Courtney at his office at 11:00 am.

Andrea was at the office before eleven o'clock, but Dr. Harris didn't walk into the examination room until eleven twenty.

"I'm sorry for keeping you waiting," said Harris.

"No apologies necessary . . . I'm just appreciative that you're able to see Courtney on such short notice."

"What seems to be the problem with Courtney?"

"She's not as peppy as usual, her appetite is poor, and it seems like she's had a cold forever."

"How long has she had these symptoms?"

"I'm not sure . . . perhaps a couple of months . . . I haven't been well myself."

"Let me run some tests on Courtney. Afterward, I'll discuss the findings with both you and Bill."

"Thanks for everything, Dr. Harris."

Harris called Rossi three days later and asked if he were available for lunch. Rossi told him he would make himself available.

Rossi arrived at the cafeteria at twelve thirty and immediately spotted Harris seated near the back of the room. After exchanging pleasantries, Harris reached into his briefcase and removed a piece of paper.

"I received Courtney's test results this morning. The blood tests show a decrease in production of oxygen carrying protein in red blood cells."

"What does that mean?"

"I'd like to run more tests before making a diagnosis."

"Jeff, I'm not going to crucify you for a misdiagnosis."

Harris hesitated momentarily before responding. "I think Courtney has thalassemia."

"That's impossible. The only way thalassemia can be symptomatic is if Courtney received the gene from both Andrea and myself. I'm Mediterranean, but Andrea is English."

"I know that, Bill. That's why I didn't want to make a diagnosis with such limited information. However, I still believe that we're dealing with thalassemia major."

"Would you like to run more tests?"

"I'd really like Courtney to be examined by this hematologist at the Children's Hospital of Philadelphia . . . Dr. John Gaffney. He's well respected, and he is extremely knowledgeable about thalassemia. He's the man you need to see!"

"Thanks, Jeff."

Rossi went back to his office and immediately telephoned Dr. Gaffney.

A woman with a pleasant voice answered the telephone. "Dr. Gaffney's office . . . May I help you?"

"I'd like to schedule an appointment for my daughter Courtney. My name is William Rossi."

"How old is Courtney?"

"She's nine months old. She was born on December 21."

"What's the reason for the examination?"

"Courtney was recently examined by Dr. Harris in Derry, Pennsylvania. He believes she may have a blood disorder."

"The first available appointment is on Tuesday, November 3 . . ."

"That's five weeks from now. If one of my patients had a serious illness, I wouldn't keep him waiting five weeks for an appointment!"

"Are you a physician?" asked the receptionist.

"Yes. I'm a surgeon."

"Let me call you back, Dr. Rossi. I'm sure I'll be able to find an appointment for your daughter sooner than November 3. I just have to check with Dr. Gaffney first."

"I understand. Tell Dr. Gaffney I would appreciate any courtesies he could extend to me."

"What's your telephone number, Dr. Rossi?"

"It's best to call me at work—215-775-5400."

"I'll call you as soon as I speak with Dr. Gaffney."

"Thanks very much."

At the end of the day, Rossi went home without first checking on his hospitalized patients. He struggled with how to tell his wife that Courtney may have a serious blood disorder, and he feared Andrea's pregnancy could be adversely affected if she became depressed.

When Rossi entered the house that evening, he kissed his wife and sampled what was cooking on the stovetop. After dinner, Rossi helped his wife clear the dishes from the table before pouring himself and Andrea a drink.

"I had lunch with Dr. Harris today," said Rossi. "He received Courtney's test results, but he wasn't certain what to make of them. He recommended that we take Courtney to the Children's Hospital of Philadelphia and have her examined by a hematologist named Dr. Gaffney."

"What did Harris say?"

"He was hesitant to say anything, but he suspects Courtney has a blood disorder named thalassemia."

"What in the world is thalassemia?"

"In layman's terms, thalassemia is a blood disorder similar to leukemia. It's associated with people of Mediterranean ancestry."

"Do you think Dr. Harris is correct?"

"I can't understand how it's possible . . . The only way to be seriously affected with this disease is if the person acquires a gene from each parent.

"Do you have the gene for this disease?" asked Andrea.

"I do, but I'm recessive . . . I'm not symptomatic in any way whatsoever."

"But you said this disease is associated with people of Mediterranean ancestry?"

"That's right."

"I'm not Mediterranean."

"I know. That's why I told Dr. Harris that it's impossible for Courtney to have this disease. But he insists that the test results are consistent with a diagnosis of thalassemia."

"Perhaps the test results are wrong."

"That's why Dr. Harris wants Courtney to be examined by Dr. Gaffney. He'll be able to confirm or refute the diagnosis."

"Did you make an appointment for Courtney?"

"I called the office today, but there was nothing available for five weeks. However, I'm expecting a call tomorrow from Gaffney's office about moving up the appointment."

CHAPTER 36

Dr. Gaffney telephoned Rossi himself the next morning and asked him to bring Courtney to the office first thing Monday morning. The next several days seemed to like an eternity for Rossi. He became more anxious with each passing day as he grappled with the fact that his daughter may have a life-threatening disease. Even though he told himself it was impossible for Courtney to have thalassemia, he couldn't dismiss the fact that Harris seemed confident with his diagnosis.

Andrea found it difficult to digest the information that Rossi fed her regarding Courtney's medical condition. In fact, she told her husband she believed Courtney displayed more energy recently than she had in the previous month. Rossi knew differently, but he didn't want to strip away the last bits of hope that Andrea clung to so desperately. Rossi realized this was Andrea's way of dealing with an unimaginable situation.

Early Monday morning, Rossi made his rounds at the hospital before meeting Dr. Hetfeld for breakfast. Hetfeld agreed to cover for Rossi while he was away in Philadelphia provided Rossi brought him up to date on the medical status of his patients. Afterward, Rossi returned home to pick up his wife and daughter before making the forty-five-minute drive to Philadelphia.

Upon entering Dr. Gaffney's office, Rossi was given so many medical forms to fill out that it took him the better part of an hour to complete. Gaffney entered the consultation room just as Rossi completed his last medical questionnaire. He introduced himself to Bill and Andrea before discussing Dr. Harris's assessment of Courtney's medical condition. When Rossi told Gaffney he questioned Harris's diagnosis, Gaffney suggested he retest Courtney.

Gaffney pushed himself away from his desk and opened the door leading to the reception room.

"It will take an hour or so to complete the tests," he said. "Why don't the two of you get a cup of coffee or something to eat. The cafeteria is on the second floor."

"I'd prefer to wait in the lounge if you don't mind," said Andrea.

"Whatever you prefer," said Gaffney. "I thought you'd find the cafeteria a more comfortable place to wait."

Andrea turned the television dial to *Good Morning America*, but she was unable to focus on any news stories. She continually got up from her chair and walked down the aisle toward Dr. Gaffney's office.

Rossi also became more anxious while waiting for Gaffney's return, but he forced himself to remain seated. He knew Andrea would become even more agitated if she were to see him pacing up and down the hallway.

Gaffney returned to the visitors' lounge at ten thirty and told Bill and Andrea that there were two additional tests that still needed to be performed on Courtney. Gaffney said the laboratory promised to have all the results available for his review by 2:00 pm. Gaffney insisted they get away from the hospital and suggested they go to the Society Hill area of Philadelphia for lunch.

Andrea remembered reading that the streets of Society Hill were littered with restaurants and unique boutique shops. She thought browsing through the various shops could possibly stop her from focusing on Courtney, even if only for a few minutes.

They drifted into and out of the different shops, admiring the many gift items which were unavailable back home in Derry. They eventually made their way to Smokey Joe's Café, where they each ordered a Philly cheese steak and a diet soda.

Upon returning to Gaffney's office, Bill and Andrea were directed to a conference room, where they waited for Dr. Gaffney to brief them about Courtney's medical status. Gaffney laid the report on his desktop, pushed his high-back leather chair away from the desk, and walked toward Bill and Andrea.

"The tests are conclusive," said Gaffney. "The results are consistent with those reported by Dr. Harris. Courtney has thalassemia major."

Andrea began to cry. She understood this was a serious illness, but she had no concept about the overall severity of the disease.

Bill wrapped his arms around Andrea and held her tightly while trying to fight back his own tears. He knew quite well what this diagnosis meant; he knew Courtney's remaining few years of life would be compromised.

Bill turned away from Andrea and focused his attention on Gaffney.

"I thought the only way someone can become afflicted with thalassemia major is to receive genetic information from both parents."

"That's correct."

"I know I'm recessive for this disease, but Andrea is English. She's not of Mediterranean ancestry."

"Andrea *must* have the genetic trait," said Gaffney.

The room became uncomfortably quiet. Moments later, Gaffney turned toward Andrea and said, "Let me take a sample of your blood . . . This will confirm whether or not you have the gene for this disease."

Andrea waited anxiously for the test results. She understood that if she were recessive for this gene, then she must have inherited the gene from one of her parents. But how was that possible? Both of her parents are English.

Gaffney had just finished examining his last patient for the day when his fax machine suddenly came to life and started to print. It was the laboratory report he was expecting.

Gaffney quickly reviewed the report before calling Bill and Andrea into his private office. He removed the eyeglasses which sat upon the tip of his nose and looked directly at Andrea.

"My intuition was correct," said Gaffney. "You're recessive for thalassemia."

Andrea's stomach felt as though she had been kicked by a martial arts expert.

Looking at Gaffney, Rossi asked, "Where do we go from here? What do we do?"

"First, we need to get Courtney some fresh blood. That's our most immediate concern. There is less oxygen flowing through Courtney's body because of her lower blood count. Less oxygenated blood results in less energy. That's why she's been lethargic lately."

"Will she only need one transfusion?" asked Andrea.

"She'll need to receive blood for the rest of her life. In fact, as she grows older, she'll need to be transfused more often."

"Will she be able to play like other children?"

"Yes and no. You'll notice that Courtney will be as energetic as the other children after receiving blood. However, as her red blood count decreases, her activity level will taper off."

"What else can we expect?"

"As Courtney ages, she will acquire more mongoloid-like features."

Andrea felt like she was being pummeled by a series of right hooks from Mike Tyson, but she couldn't throw her towel into the ring. She had to stand toe to toe with her assailant because she needed to know everything about this disease.

"If Courtney receives blood regularly, and she doesn't over exert herself, will she be able to marry and have children someday?"

Gaffney glanced at Rossi momentarily before redirecting his attention toward Andrea.

"Children with thalassemia do not live into their adult years."

Andrea's legs wobbled with the intensity of a 3.8 earthquake. Lowering herself onto the sofa, Andrea burst into tears. Rossi tried to comfort his wife, but his efforts were futile. Andrea continued to sob uncontrollably.

Rossi extended his hand toward Gaffney.

"This is a difficult moment for us, John. Let's get some blood into Courtney . . . I'd like to take my family home as soon as possible."

Gaffney called the Hematology Department to arrange a transfusion for Courtney. The technician told Dr. Gaffney that she was about to leave for the day and asked if the transfusion could wait until morning. With a tone of voice reserved for the most contemptuous person, Gaffney informed the technician that the patient will be at the clinic within the next ten minutes.

"Thanks, John. I know my daughter is in good hands."

"I'll give her the same care as if she were one of my own children."

Following Courtney's transfusion, the Rossi family returned to Derry. Few words were spoken during their drive home. Their lack of communication was not out of concern for awakening Courtney, who had fallen asleep following an exhaustive day of testing; they just wanted to comprehend everything they were told.

CHAPTER 37

Bill and Andrea reacted differently to the disturbing findings. Rossi approached the problem logically, searching for answers from a medical perspective. Due to advances in the field of medicine, Rossi realized that finding a cure for thalassemia was always a possibility.

Andrea reacted emotionally to the information she was told by Dr. Gaffney. She didn't understand the medical jargon associated with this disease, but she clearly understood that her daughter would soon die. And she understood that her dreams of seeing her daughter twirling a baton as a majorette or seeing her walk down the aisle wearing a wedding gown would remain unfulfilled.

Although it was early evening when the Rossi family returned home, Courtney was not ready for bed. The blood transfusion had invigorated Courtney to the heights that Andrea had not witnessed in months.

After placing Courtney in her crib for the night, Rossi sat down on the sofa next to his wife and reached for her hand.

"I realize it's difficult for you to accept the fact that Courtney is seriously ill."

Andrea pulled her hand away from her husband. "Don't you mean terminally ill?"

"Andrea, I'm struggling with this myself. I wish Courtney wasn't sick . . . I wish this was just a terrible nightmare. But that's not the case. Courtney *does* have a blood disorder and unfortunately it *is* fatal." Rossi knew he needed to be strong for his wife. "I understand what you're going through, honey. Honestly, I do. But let's not focus on the negatives. Let's enjoy the time we have with her."

"Maybe they'll find a vaccine or an antidote."

"Who knows what tomorrow brings? Advances in medicine happen every day. Perhaps there *will* be a cure for this disease one day!"

Rossi didn't believe everything he told his wife, but he knew the health of their unborn child could be compromised if Andrea became more stressed or depressed.

CHAPTER 38

Later that night, long after Courtney had fallen asleep, Andrea kept rehashing all that was said during the course of the day. She was troubled by many of the things that Dr. Gaffney had said, and she needed to discuss these things with her husband before going to bed. Andrea made her way to the family room, believing she would find her husband engrossed in the most recent episode of *Star Trek*. Instead, she found him sitting on the sofa in the dimly lit room, holding a tumbler of scotch and water in his hand.

"Bill . . . I need to speak with you."

Rossi raised the tumbler to his lips and sipped on the single-malt scotch. "What do you want to talk about?"

"How is it possible for me to have this genetic defect?"

"It's possible because it's what it is!"

"You're a doctor . . . Give me the courtesy of an explanation!"

Rossi gulped down another mouthful of scotch before addressing his wife. "Do the math . . . You should be able to add two and two."

"What's that supposed to mean?"

"That apparently you're not English."

"Both of my parents are English," said Andrea.

"I'm telling you things are what they are, not what you were led to believe."

Andrea didn't appreciate what her husband implied. "There has to be a logical explanation for all of this."

"There is . . . You just don't want to accept the explanation."

Andrea paced back and forth. "I need to speak with my parents."

"I think that's a great idea."

"I'll drive to New York first thing tomorrow morning."

Andrea strapped Courtney into her car seat before embarking on her journey to the Watson estate. She encountered no delays as she maneuvered her vehicle along the interstate, yet Andrea felt as stressed as if she had battled five lanes of bumper-to-bumper traffic during rush hour.

Andrea steered her vehicle onto the driveway and proceeded to the gated entrance. She punched the six numbers on the security keypad which allowed her access to the estate. She patiently waited for the gate to swing open.

Allison Watson ran down the steps of her home upon seeing Andrea climb out of her vehicle.

"Welcome home, darling."

"It's good to be home."

Allison lifted Courtney out of her car seat and held her lovingly. With her granddaughter clinging to her shoulders, Allison escorted Andrea to her bedroom and waited while her daughter unpacked her overnight bag. Allison was delighted to see Courtney; however, she wondered why Andrea made the two-hour drive without first taking the time to verify if she were home. Andrea said there was an issue she needed to discuss with both her and her father. When Allison pressed her daughter for more information, Andrea insisted that she discuss the issue when both parents were together.

Andrea decided to freshen up before proceeding to the library. The library was her favorite room. This was the only room in the house where she was permitted to play as a child. Upon entering the library, Andrea was surprised to find her father sitting in one of the four overstuffed chairs.

"Daddy . . . I didn't realize you were home!"

"I came home just a few minutes ago. Is Courtney with you?"

"She's with Mom."

"And how is my little princess?"

"She's the reason I'm here."

"What do you mean?"

"We'll discuss this later . . . Mom said Maria is waiting to serve lunch."

Andrew assisted his daughter and wife with their chairs before sitting at his customary seat at the head of the table. They dined on New England clam chowder and pecan-crusted salmon salad. Following lunch, Andrew suggested they retreat to the library to discuss whatever was troubling Andrea.

"I'd prefer talking in the family room if you don't mind, Father," said Andrea. She didn't want her favorite room littered with dirty laundry.

"The family room it is."

Andrea began the conversation by discussing what she and Bill had been doing back in Derry. She didn't feel the need to smack her parents with a two-by-four at the onset of the conversation. A few minutes later, Andrea began to explain the reason for her unexpected visit.

"I have a personal matter I need to discuss with you."

"Are you getting divorced?" asked Mr. Watson in a flippant tone of voice.

"Courtney has been diagnosed with a life-threatening disease."

"What's wrong with Courtney?" asked Andrew.

"She has a blood disease . . . a genetic disorder."

"Leukemia?" asked Allison.

"Thalassemia."

Allison reached for her husband's arm. "We'll get Courtney the best medical care available."

"There *are* no cures for this disease," blurted Andrea.

"I'll search out the most qualified doctor," said Andrew. "Money won't be an issue."

"Bill and I are making the necessary arrangements for Courtney's care."

"We're only trying to help," explained Allison.

"You said this is a genetic disease?" asked Mr. Watson.

"Yes . . . and that's why I came home. I need some answers."

Andrew and Allison said nothing.

"What I don't understand . . . how is it possible for Courtney to have a disease associated with people of Mediterranean descent if I'm English as I've been led to believe?"

Andrew and Allison looked at each other without uttering a single word. They knew the time had come to divulge a familial secret which they hoped would have remained buried.

"I can explain," said Andrew.

Andrea looked inquisitively at her father.

"As you know, your mother and I lived in Philadelphia years ago. My father had just introduced Watson Pharmaceuticals to the nation, and I was working eighty-hour weeks to kickstart the business. We lived in a modest home, and we didn't employ any live-in help. However, I did hire a woman to help your mother around the house. She would arrive shortly after breakfast and would return home before dinner. Her responsibilities were to clean the house, help with the laundry, and prepare dinner. Her name was Carla.

"Carla was at the house preparing dinner one afternoon when she received a telephone call informing her that her husband had been killed in an automobile accident. She was devastated. She had very little money and not much of anything else. Carla was totally dependent on her husband for financial support. When he died, Carla was left with nothing. There were no insurance policies or retirement benefits. Your mother and I paid the funeral expenses.

"To prevent Carla from becoming homeless, we invited her to move in with us as a live-in maid. She was extremely grateful for the opportunity. Shortly after moving into our home, Carla learned that she was pregnant. Your mother and I decided to pay all of Carla's medical expenses, and she was provided the best prenatal care available. Her pregnancy was uneventful until her thirty-ninth week when she began to experience severe headaches. She met with her obstetrician, Dr. Knisley, who discovered that Carla's blood pressure was elevated. He also detected a presence of protein in her urine. Knisley asked Carla to collect urine samples for a twenty-four-hour period and then return to the office for reevaluation.

"When Carla returned to the office, Dr. Knisley noticed that she was more swollen than the previous day, that her weight had increased by six pounds, and that there was an increased amount of protein in her urine. He immediately strapped a blood pressure cuff around her left bicep and discovered that her blood pressure was elevated.

"Dr. Knisley instructed Carla to go to the hospital immediately. Sensing urgency in his tone of voice, Carla asked him if there was anything to worry about. Knisley hurriedly explained that she had a severe case of pre-eclampsia and that she needed to go to the hospital immediately. He also informed her that he must deliver the baby by caesarian section. Carla asked the doctor if her baby's health was in jeopardy. Dr. Knisley reassured Carla that she was very ill, but he believed the baby would be fine.

"When Carla arrived at the hospital, her blood pressure was very high. The emergency personnel wheeled Carla into an operating room and inserted intravenous lines into her arms. They had to order blood from the blood bank. Anesthesia doctors hooked her up to several monitors. The nurses said the baby seemed good.

"Carla knew that something was terribly wrong. She asked Dr. Knisley if everything was okay with her baby. Knisley told her the baby was fine, but he was having difficulty stabilizing her condition. Carla asked Dr. Knisley if she could speak with me. Initially, Knisley said no. However, moments later, he reconsidered and agreed to permit me in the operating room. Carla was concerned that her baby would be given up for adoption if she died. She begged me to care for her baby should something go terribly wrong during the birthing process. I promised I would, but I assured her that she would be able to care for the baby herself.

"In the operating room, Carla's blood pressure moved to critical. Dr. Knisley needed to act immediately. He knew he could not delay the caesarean section as that would jeopardize Carla's life. Knisley alerted his team that he was ready to operate. As the operation began, the circulating nurse went to the computer to check the emergency admission blood work. Knisley listened to the report in horror. The numbers from the coagulation panel were critically depressed. The proteins that made Carla's blood able to clot were severely compromised. Knisley immediately realized that Carla had developed the coagulation problem known as disseminated intravascular coagulation or DIC for short. He also knew his chances of controlling the bleeding were rapidly slipping away.

"Knisley delivered the baby without difficulty. The baby girl was fine, but Carla's blood pressure began to fall precipitously. Knisley worked hard to control the bleeding uterus, but nothing worked. Sponge after sponge filled immediately with blood. It would not clot. Medication did nothing. The doctor was helpless. The blood and clotting factors which were infused into her veins flowed as rapidly as the Niagara River just before running down the falls, but he was losing the patient. Carla was in fulminant DIC and could not be saved. She died on the operating table."

Andrew Watson poured himself another scotch before continuing with his story. "Your mother and I honored Carla's request to raise her child as our own." Mr. Watson turned and stood directly in front of Andrea. "You were that baby."

Andrea sat motionless on the sofa. She thought perhaps one of her parents had an extramarital affair resulting in an illegitimate child or one or both of her parents were of Mediterranean descent. Never in her wildest dreams had she considered the possibility that she was adopted.

"We adopted you, raised you, and loved you as though you were our birth child," interjected Allison. "We then moved to New York so no one would know you were not our daughter."

"Did you honestly believe the truth would never come out?" asked Andrea.

"We decided to wait until you were older to tell you the truth. However, with each passing year, we no longer regarded you as an adopted child. We thought of you as our daughter."

Andrea stared at the people she had believed to be her biologic parents until moments ago. She got up from her chair and walked toward the doorway. Mrs. Watson stopped Andrea before she had the opportunity to leave the room.

"You're not angry with us, are you, honey?" asked Mrs. Watson.

"Mother, I don't know what I'm feeling at this moment."

"We never meant to hurt you," said Andrew. "We love you, honey!"

"I got to go . . . I need time to gather my thoughts."

Andrea shared what she learned from her parents with her husband.

"It makes sense," said Rossi.

"What makes sense"?

"How you acquired the gene for thalassemia."

Andrea paused momentarily before speaking. "It's *our* fault that Courtney's going to die."

"It's no one's fault . . . Sometimes bad things just happen."

"Where do we go from here"?

"We need to cherish the time we have with her and enable her to live as normal a life as possible."

"I'll try," said Andrea, fighting back tears.

"And it's important that you stay healthy . . . for the baby's sake."

A frightened expression replaced Andrea's somber appearance. "The baby!" cried Andrea. "What if he's born with this disease"?

"It's possible but unlikely."

CHAPTER 39

Rossi returned to his daily ten-hour work schedule shortly after Andrea's return from New York. Realizing there was a finite number of years until his daughter would succumb to her blood disease, Rossi set a priority of spending time with Courtney every single day.

Andrea, on the other hand, did not have a job to divert her attention from her daughter's illness. However, she discovered that if she kept herself busy during the day, there was less time for her to become depressed. Taking Courtney to the playground or to the duck pond was now as much a daily routine for the two of them as eating breakfast. And they especially enjoyed their Wednesday trips to the library, listening to the librarian recite tales such as *Little Red Riding Hood* and the *Three Little Pigs*.

Andrea found it increasingly more difficult to take Courtney to the playground as her pregnancy progressed into the thirty-fourth week. And with Christmas just two weeks away, Andrea scheduled an appointment with Dr. Wilson prior to traveling to Bill's parents for the holiday.

Dr. Wilson recommended that Andrea not travel far from home this holiday season because he was concerned that she may suddenly go into labor. So Andrea and Bill decided to invite both immediate families to their home for Christmas dinner this year.

To everyone's surprise, Andrew Watson was not his usual obnoxious self. He was rather charming to the in-laws, even though he regarded them as inferior people. Mr. Watson even sang Christmas carols with the other family members while Bill and Andrea decorated the Christmas tree. Bill didn't understand why Mr. Watson was in such a festive mood. Was it possible that Andrew realized he had been unfairly critical of Bill and his parents? No, he didn't believe that for a single moment. He believed a more probable explanation for Andrew portraying himself as a nice man was that he received a six-figure year-end bonus by the board of directors of Watson Pharmaceuticals. Humbug!

Following dinner and dessert, both Bill's and Andrea's parents decided to begin their journey back home before the driving conditions worsened. A fresh blanket of snow had already covered the grass, and the snow was now beginning to stick to the pavement. The weather bureau predicted four inches of snow before tapering off to flurries at daybreak.

Bill tucked Courtney into bed before snuggling next to his wife on the sofa. Shortly afterward, they heard laughter and screaming from outside their home. They peered out the window and saw a group of children sliding down the hill on their Flexible Flyer snow sleds. They looked at each other, neither speaking a word. They were consumed with thoughts of Courtney not being able to play like the other children. Bill turned away from the window and sauntered toward the fireplace.

"Would you like another glass of wine?"

"No, thanks," said Andrea. "I'm feeling a little tired."

"You've had a long day."

"I've had a great day."

Bill put his arms around his wife. "There will be two children in our home this time next year."

"Courtney and Michael Joseph," Andrea whispered softly. She then folded the blanket and placed it on the sofa. "If you don't mind, I'd like to go to bed. I'm really tired."

"Whatever you wish."

"Good night, Bill."

"Merry Christmas, Andrea."

Rossi tossed another log into the fireplace and poured himself a vodka martini. He sat on the hearth of the fireplace with his back to the fire, enjoying the heat as it radiated along his back. He thought about the emotions he experienced this past year—the jubilation over the birth of his daughter and the agony of discovering that she had a fatal blood disorder. He prayed that his soon-to-be born son be spared from any life-threatening illnesses.

CHAPTER 40

Michael Joseph Rossi was born on January 12, 1994, weighing eight pounds thirteen ounces. Dr. Wilson drew several vials of blood from Michael immediately after his arrival into this world and had it tested for thalassemia. The following day Dr. Wilson informed Andrea and Bill that Michael had no evidence of thalassemia in his genetic makeup.

Bill and Andrea became more involved with their children's activities as the years passed. Andrea volunteered as a Brownie leader for Courtney's troop no. 126, and she assisted with the coaching responsibilities for her daughter's kickball team. Courtney enjoyed playing kickball, but her participation was restricted because of her blood disorder. Rossi volunteered to participate in one activity at a time; unlike his wife, he needed to work.

Michael enjoyed playing baseball, but he had difficulty catching fly balls. To enhance Michael's baseball skills, Rossi took him to the ball field and hit fly balls to him. After weeks of catching fly balls, Michael became as proficient an outfielder as any of his teammates. In fact, Michael received "the most improved ballplayer award" at the baseball banquet.

Michael also excelled in football, playing running back on offense and inside linebacker on defense. Rossi would have enjoyed being the position coach for his son, but he asked to coach the offensive and defensive linemen. He didn't want anyone accusing him of showing favoritism to his son.

Derry's first football game of the season was against rival Moon Township. With the score tied at 13 near the end of the third quarter, Dr. Rossi felt a vibration on the left side of his hip. He walked to a more quiet area beneath the stadium steps and called his answering service. He was informed by an emergency medical technician that a critically injured patient was being transported to the hospital and that he was needed in surgery.

Dr. Rossi walked through the emergency room doors ten minutes later and was met by Officer Druzak of the Derry Police Department. Druzak informed Rossi that a Caucasian in his early twenties was brought to the hospital with a knife would in his abdomen.

Rossi entered the doctors' lounge, changed into his scrubs, and walked into the operating room. He positioned himself alongside the young man lying on the gurney. A member of the surgical team applied pressure to the wound in hopes of limiting the amount of blood loss.

Dr. Rossi then turned toward the lead nurse and asked for the patient's vital signs.

"One hundred over seventy," replied the nurse.

Rossi removed the gauze, examined the area surrounding the laceration, and palpated the adjacent organs to determine whether any organs were damaged. There were no other problems associated with the knife wound. Rossi then cleaned the surgical site with sterile saline solution and sutured the wound. Afterward, the nurse bathed the tissue surrounding the wound site with an antiseptic before bandaging the patient.

After leaving the operating room, Rossi looked for Officer Druzak. As he made his way down the corridor, Rossi noticed that Druzak was talking to an orderly near the doctors' lounge.

Rossi walked up to Druzak and asked, "What do you know about this guy?"

"Not much, Doc. I was at the station when the call came in that a man was lying facedown on the sidewalk near the edge of town. I jumped into my cruiser and drove south toward the bridge. As I turned onto Hidden Acres Drive, there he was, sprawled out on the ground. I first thought he might be drunk. When I got closer to him, I noticed blood had collected beneath his body. I then believed he was dead. I turned him over and placed my fingers on his carotid artery. I felt a pulse and immediately radioed for an ambulance."

"Do you have any idea where he's from?"

"Nope . . . he was unconscious when I got there. After the nurses removed his clothes, I searched for a wallet. But I didn't find anything . . . not even a dollar."

"He's probably a homeless person. I used to see people like him all the time in New York."

"Is he going to make it, Doc?"

"He'll be all right. He lost quite a bit of blood, but fortunately, none of his organs were damaged. He'll require several weeks of hospitalization."

"Be sure to call me before you discharge him. I have a few questions I need to ask him."

"I'll call you as soon as he's well enough to be discharged."

"Thanks, Doc."

When Rossi told Andrea about leaving the football game to perform surgery on some homeless man, she expressed concern about the safety of her children. She had not witnessed any acts of crime since moving to Derry. She, along with the other people in town, was lulled into a false sense of security. But things were different now. A stranger had crossed the boundary separating Derry from the rest of civilization. And the stranger was stabbed and left for dead.

Newspaper reporters from surrounding communities, with hopes of uncovering information about the stabbing victim, swooped into town with the same fanfare that precedes the arrival of the Barnum & Bailey Circus caravan.

The Derry police chief called the Pennsylvania State Police Bureau to ask for assistance in identifying the homeless man. Detective Carrigan, a twenty-year veteran of the state police corps of officers, was assigned to the case. Carrigan cross matched the fingerprints he obtained from the victim with the fingerprints in the police database. A match was not found—the identity of the man was still a mystery.

Detective Carrigan, along with Officer Druzak of the Derry Police Department, drove to the hospital to interrogate the stabbing victim.

"How are you feeling?" asked Carrigan.

"I'm a little weak, but I'm kickin'."

"I'm Detective Carrigan, and this is Officer Druzak."

The stranger nodded.

"What's your name and where do live?" asked Carrigan.

"My name is John Walker . . . and I'm from Philadelphia."

"What's your address in Philadelphia?"

"Well, I actually live underneath the Walt Whitman Bridge."

"Do you know who stabbed you?" asked Druzak.

"No."

"No idea whatsoever?"

"Not at all . . . I was hitchhiking on the Jersey side of the Walt Whitman Bridge, trying to catch a ride to Atlantic City, when two white guys pulled up beside me."

"Was it one of those guys who stabbed you?" asked Carrigan.

"No."

"What happened next?" asked Druzak.

"I asked if they were heading anywhere near Atlantic City."

"Go on," said Druzak.

"The taller guy said they were going to the Tropicana Casino, but they had to pick up a friend along the way."

Walker hesitated before continuing with his statement.

"Go on," said Druzak.

"I didn't sense any danger. They seemed friendly enough. They even shared their cigarettes and whiskey with me." Walker's voice began to crack.

"I know this is difficult for you," said Carrigan, "but we need to know what happened."

"They then drove along the Atlantic City Expressway to the Black Horse Pike where they pulled onto a side street. A dark blue van with Illinois license plates was parked along the side of the road. The driver of the van came over to where we were parked."

"Can you describe him?" asked Druzak.

"He was about six feet two inches tall, two hundred eighty pounds. His head was shaved, and he had a goatee. He looked intimidating."

"What was he wearing"? asked Carrigan.

"A white tee shirt with a black leather vest . . . and denim pants."

"Did he get into the car?" asked Hudson.

"No. He walked to the passenger side of the car and handed the shorter guy some money. He then pulled out a gun and told me to get out of the car."

Walker again paused momentarily before continuing with his statement. "I was frightened and confused, but I did what he said. He forced me into the back of the van, tied my hands and feet, and covered my mouth with duct tape."

"What did the other guys do?" asked Druzak.

"They told me to have fun, and then they drove away."

"What happened next?" asked Carrigan.

"He drove away. At first, I wasn't sure which direction he was going because I couldn't see anything from the back of the van. However, I heard the toll booth operator ask him for $3. I then knew he was heading to Philadelphia."

"What was the significance of $3?" asked Carrigan.

"If he was driving to Atlantic City, the toll would have only been $2."

"Then what happened?" asked Druzak.

"After about a half hour, he stopped the van and opened the rear door. He looked at me, smiled, and said he wouldn't hurt me if I did what he told me to do."

"I'm sure this is difficult for you, but we must know all the details," said Carrigan.

"I didn't resist his advances."

"And what was that?" asked Druzak.

"I don't think it's necessary to spell everything out. When he finished raping me, he said he couldn't take a chance of my identifying him. He then pulled out a knife, stuck it in my stomach, and tossed me out of the van. The next thing I remembered, I was in a hospital bed with tubes connected to my arm."

"You're free to go," said Carrigan. "I'll issue an all-points bulletin for the police to be on the lookout for the man and the vehicle matching your description."

Although Walker felt well enough to leave the hospital, he wished he could have remained in the hospital for a few more days; he couldn't remember the last time he ate as well. But Walker was now on the streets again in a town which was totally unfamiliar to him. Unlike Philadelphia, where a smorgasbord of uneaten food scraps filled the trash containers surrounding the many sports and concert facilities, there were no such places in Derry where Walker could satisfy his need for food.

He walked into the Catholic Church and pleaded for some money to buy food. The priest, having heard of this man's misfortune, brought him into the rectory and served him a plate of last night's rigatoni and meatballs. He also gave Walker $50 to help sustain him during his time of need. The priest apologized for not being able to provide him with more money; he told Walker he gave $50 to another homeless man asking for assistance who came to the church just yesterday. Walker thanked the priest for his kindness and then headed to the grocery store to purchase some nonperishable food items.

After leaving the A&P Supermarket with a bag of groceries and several cardboard boxes, Walker navigated his way along Main Street in search of a place to spend the night. Near the edge of town, Walker came upon a park with picnic shelters and charcoal grills. On the sign adjacent to the park entrance read Derry Community Park. He believed this park was the perfect place to build his cardboard hut.

Rumors that an unwanted guest had claimed a parcel of land at the park as his own circulated around town with the speed of a runaway train. Walker was spotted at football practices, band rehearsals, and community activities. He was extremely visible. He didn't believe there was a need to conceal his presence. The women of Derry viewed him as being brash and arrogant; and his lack of humility angered them. They didn't want a man without the means to support himself, especially a homeless man, to litter *their* community with his presence. These women, with the support of their husbands, demanded that the mayor force Walker to leave town. Although sympathetic to Walker's plight, the mayor instructed the police chief to escort Walker out of town.

Walker became enraged when told that he must leave Derry. He pleaded with the police chief to be allowed to stay in town because he didn't do anything wrong. The police chief said his hands were tied, and if he didn't comply with his request, then he would be arrested for vagrancy. Walker agreed to leave without incident.

The mayor inspected the area where Walker had established residency to verify that he left town. All that remained were several banana peels, an empty box of Ritz crackers, and a discarded cardboard box. Walker was nowhere to be found; he apparently took the police chief's suggestion to relocate to another community.

CHAPTER 41

A woman approached the mayor the following day and said she had seen the homeless man hiding among the trees beyond the clearing in the park. Officer Druzak was dispatched to the location to search for Walker. But after an exhaustive two-hour search of the area, Druzak informed the mayor that he did not see Walker. The mayor discounted the woman's sighting.

The city's workers decorated the park for the eighteenth annual harvest festival. Orange and black crepe paper dangled from the picnic shelter and witches and goblins were painted on the apple bobbing washtub. Horse-drawn carts used for hayrides were positioned on the dirt road adjacent to shelter number 15.

Families gathered at the park by early afternoon for a day of fun and games. The men and teenaged boys competed against one another with bocce and horseshoes, while the women and young children went on hayrides. The girls entertained themselves by playing badminton, croquet, and jumping rope.

Courtney didn't participate in any of the activities because she felt tired. It had been three weeks since she last received a transfusion, and her blood count was low. For much of the day, Courtney busied herself by sketching pictures of trees, flowers, and birds. Whenever she became bored from spending so much time in the shelter, Courtney strolled along the creek adjacent to the back edge of the park.

Early that evening, as the townspeople were preoccupied with dinner preparations, Courtney decided to take another walk along the creek. As she approached the section of the creek where an embedded bolder caused the water to flow around the north and south edges of the rock, Courtney heard the sound of what she believed to be a distressed kitten. Using the moss covered rocks as stepping stones, Courtney crossed over to the other side of the creek. There, tangled inside a bed of vines, lay a black spotted white kitten covered with burs.

As Courtney bent over to free the kitten, she became startled when someone slid a hand over her mouth and wrapped the opposing arm around her waist. Courtney tried to scream as she was lifted off the ground, but she was unable to do so. She was terrified.

In less than a minute, Courtney was carried across the field and through the thickened brush before disappearing into the trees. Lacking the energy to fight, she lay lifeless within the arms of her abductor.

CHAPTER 42

When the women finished arranging the food trays, they lit the two candles which were positioned equidistant from the ends of each picnic table. The lighting of the candles indicated that it was time for dinner.

Dr. Rossi and Michael navigated their way toward the picnic table where Andrea stood watch. Rossi glanced around the shelter for Courtney before asking his wife the whereabouts of their daughter. Andrea told him she was busy arranging the food on the buffet table and had not spoken with Courtney within the last fifteen minutes. However, she assured her husband that Courtney must be somewhere nearby.

Rossi called out Courtney's name, but there was no response. Bill and Andrea searched the outer perimeter of the picnic shelter in hopes that Courtney had grown tired and fallen asleep. But she was nowhere to be found. They rushed to the creek in fear that Courtney may have fallen and hurt herself, but again, they left the area disappointed. Panic overcame Bill and Andrea.

Officer Druzak radioed the police station and reported the Rossi girl missing. Two patrolmen, who were assigned station duty, responded immediately and assisted in the search for Courtney. Officer Druzak called the Pennsylvania State Police Headquarters in Philadelphia and requested additional manpower. A group of five officers, headed by Detective Richard Monti, arrived before 10:00 pm. These troupers assisted the Derry police by securing all roads leading into and out of town. Monti's only concern was whether the abductor escaped prior to their establishing a perimeter around town.

Everyone at the park joined in the search for Courtney. They walked to the edge of the wooded area and spread out in fanlike formation. They were confident they would soon find the missing girl.

The townspeople scoured the park for Courtney until Detective Monti suspended the search at 11:00 pm. However, Monti maintained the roadblocks throughout the night. He asked everyone to return to the park at dawn to resume the search for the missing Rossi girl.

Monti approached Rossi and asked for a few minutes of his time. "I'll be right with you sir," said Rossi before turning to his wife and suggesting that she and Michael return home. Rossi then directed his attention toward Monti. "You want to speak with me, Detective?"

"Yes, I do." Monti gave some last-minute instructions to one of his officers before focusing his thoughts on Rossi. "I hope you don't mind, but I have to ask you a few questions."

"Anything you need, Detective."

"Do you have any idea who may have kidnapped your daughter?"

"Not at all."

"Has anyone threatened you or been angry with you lately?"

"Not that I can think of."

"Any disgruntled patients?"

"Not really . . . but there was this one patient."

"What patient?"

"Someone I performed surgery on a couple of weeks ago."

"Did something go wrong with the surgery?"

"No . . . Everything went well."

"Then what's so special about this guy?"

"He's homeless . . . and the people chased him away."

"What's his name?"

"I doubt if he had anything to do with Courtney's disappearance. He was very appreciative of my saving his life."

"It's possible this may be a random act of violence, but I doubt it. We need to keep an open mind and follow all leads."

"I understand," said Rossi.

What's his name?"

"John Walker."

The kidnapper carried Courtney deep into the woods until he could no longer hear the commotion coming from the shelter. He lowered Courtney to the ground and promised to remove his hand from her mouth if she wouldn't scream. She indicated that she would not scream by nodding. After the man removed his hand from Courtney's mouth, she turned and faced him. Courtney stared at the man standing before her.

"I know you . . . My father saved your life!"

Walker didn't say anything.

"Why do you want to hurt me?"

"I won't hurt you."

"Then why are you doing this?"

"Because everyone in your precious little town treated me like scum . . . like I wasn't good enough for them."

"Please let me go."

"Soon."

"I don't believe you."

"Let's go . . . We can't stay here."

Walker led Courtney deeper into the woods, increasing the distance between themselves and the park. It was late at night, and it was becoming increasingly more difficult to see. In fact, if it were not for the moonlight, Walker would not have been able to see anything at all. As Walker continued to distance himself from the park, he heard the sound of an oncoming train. Realizing this train may be his means of escape, Walker continued his march toward the sound of the approaching train. The train tracks were approximately two hundred yards ahead, and Walker knew he couldn't take the girl with him; the police would be looking for a man traveling with a young girl. But what was he going to do with her. If he left her there, she would identify him as her abductor, and he would be hunted down and charged with kidnapping. There was no way he would allow himself to be incarcerated.

"This is as far as we go," said Walker. "I can't take you with me."

"Can I go back now?" asked Courtney.

"I can't let you go . . . You'll tell the police."

"I won't tell anyone."

"I don't believe you. Besides, I can't take the chance."

Courtney began to cry uncontrollably. Walker then shoved her face down to the ground. "Forgive me for doing what I have to do."

As Walker ran toward the train, he wondered how long it would be before someone found Courtney; he hoped he'd be long gone by then. He thought if he changed his name and moved far away from here, then not even Sherlock Holmes would be able to track him down.

CHAPTER 43

Courtney stood up and brushed the leaves off her clothing. She was wobbling as badly as an unaligned wheel on an automobile. The trembling was partly due to the cold night air; but mostly it was due to her near death experience.

Courtney started running towards the park, but she soon became fatigued. She rested momentarily before continuing with a slower paced walk.

As Courtney navigated her way through the woods, a man jumped out from behind the massive oak tree which stood directly in front of her. She tried to scream, but her voice was inaudible.

"Relax," said the man. "Don't be scared.... I won't hurt you."

She was too frightened to speak.

"Let me help you, little girl... I saw what happened to you back there."

"If you saw that, why didn't you do anything?"

"I was keeping a close eye on you. If I thought you were in any real danger, I would have come running."

"Will you help me?"

"Sure I will...I'll help you take off those clothes."

Courtney screamed as loudly as her small lungs would permit.

"Shut up!"

Courtney continued to scream.

The man slapped her with the back of his hand, causing her to fall to the ground. He leaned over her and cocked his arm in anticipation of striking her again.

"Please don't hit me," she pleaded.

"Then you better do what I say!" He starred at her with piercing eyes. "Take your clothes off."

Not wanting to anger the man, Courtney reluctantly obeyed his command. Minutes following the assault, Courtney perceived an opportunity to escape captivity. She darted toward the picnic shelter knowing that her father would be there to protect her. Realizing that the little girl was attempting to flee the area, the man reached for the girl with his right arm. Courtney was able to avoid being grabbed by the man by shrugging her left shoulder away from him. However his sweeping arm contacted Courtney's right ankle, causing her to lose her balance. As Courtney fell toward the ground, her head careened off an oblong shaped rock that lay adjacent to an oak tree. She immediately became quiet and motionless.

The man positioned his face adjacent to Courtney's nose and mouth with the hope of detecting an exchange of carbon dioxide for oxygen. But Courtney was not breathing. She was dead. He stood up and looked both left and right, making certain that no one was in his vicinity. He then began to run. He wanted to get as far away from this place as he possibly could.

CHAPTER 44

The Rossi family was devastated by Courtney's disappearance. They never imagined anything like this would ever happen to them. They moved away from New York to protect their children from senseless brutal crimes. What other reason would they have had to abandon promising careers in a city they both loved? Derry was supposed to be the kind of place where Andrea and Bill could raise their children and protect them from the decadence commonly found in larger cities. Crimes such as kidnapping were not supposed to occur in Derry!

Officer Druzak told Andrea and Bill to remain optimistic. However, they could not prevent themselves from imagining the worst. They feared their daughter may have been tortured, abused, or even murdered. But what they feared most was not ever finding their daughter and wondering if their little girl was used as a human sacrifice for some satanic cult.

Realizing that Andrea would have a difficult time falling asleep, Bill gave her a valium tablet. He refused to take one himself; he wanted to remain alert just in case information pertaining to Courtney's whereabouts became available. He lay in bed, but he was unable to fall asleep. He tossed and turned all night, thinking how frightened Courtney must be.

The search for Courtney resumed at daybreak. The policemen who manned the roadblocks throughout the night reported no sightings of the Rossi girl, and they were relieved from duty. The remainder of the police force, along with many of the townspeople, entered the wooded area where Courtney was last seen.

A gunshot indicating that a discovery had been made was heard at 9:43 am. The police chief was summoned to a location in the woods approximately two miles from where Courtney was last seen. There, lying facedown on the ground was the lifeless body of a little girl. Officer Druzak turned the girl over so to make a positive identification. The dead girl was indeed Courtney Rossi.

Officer Druzak informed Monti that Courtney was found murdered. Monti asked Druzak to compile a list of suspects. Unfortunately, only one name popped into Druzak's mind. That name was John Walker. Druzak told Monti that he received numerous telephone calls the past several days stating that Walker was seen near the park. Monti issued an all-points bulletin for Walker's arrest.

CHAPTER 45

Walker hopped on the first train that passed through Derry. He didn't care which direction the train was traveling. He needed to get as far away from Derry as possible. Walker had no idea what time of the day it was or how far the train had traveled; hours seemed like days when hiding out in a cold uncomfortable boxcar. However, Walker believed he was somewhere in the Midwest because he witnessed two sunrises and two sunsets since jumping on the train.

As the train slowed to negotiate the horseshoe curve up ahead, Walker realized this may be his best opportunity to jump off the train without risking serious injury. Like a trained paratrooper, Walker jettisoned himself off the train and tumbled down the hillside. He then walked east toward the rising sun in search of a road or pathway that would lead him to an unknown destination.

He walked approximately two miles before finding a three-foot wide grass walkway. Walker followed the path in a northern direction for a distance of twenty football fields before hearing the sound which he believed to be diesel engines. With the sun reaching it maximum height in the sky, Walker drifted toward the noise. He soon discovered that his intuition was correct; the sound he heard came from two monstrous pieces of farm equipment.

Walker treaded cautiously along the pathway to avoid being detected by the two sumo-looking farmers driving the tractors. He continued to walk north until the matted pathway became indistinguishable from the surrounding landscape. There, on the unpaved road, he waited for a car or truck to drive by with the hope of hitching a ride to the nearest town.

The road was not heavily traveled. Forty-five minutes must have passed since Walker first stepped onto the road. Waiting for a passing vehicle conjured up memories of a time when he waited for his father to return home from work to take him to a Philadelphia baseball game. The wait was tortuous; minutes seemed like hours and hours like days.

A truck filled with hay approached from the east. Walker stood in the middle of the dusty road and signaled for the driver to stop. When the vehicle came to a halt, he walked toward the driver and asked if he could hitch a ride to town. The driver was reluctant to allow the hitchhiker to enter the cab of his truck and considered having him ride in the back. However, the driver relented and told Walker to come onboard.

The driver shifted the transmission from first gear to third gear before glancing toward Walker.

"Where ya from?" asked the driver.

"Los Angeles," said Walker, carefully choosing the words which would not connect him with Derry.

"You're a long way from LA," said the driver. "What brings you out here?"

"Los Angeles was becoming too dangerous with all the gangs and stuff."

"If you're looking for a safe and quiet place, then Omaha is the place for you."

"What do people do for fun here?" asked Walker.

"You're in cornhusker country!"

"What does that mean?"

"You sure you're not from Mars?" asked the driver sarcastically. "Cornhusker country means Nebraska football . . . cornhusker football."

"I guess football is big here?"

"Cornhusker football is everything here!"

As the driver entered the outskirts of town, he asked the stranger if he wished to be dropped off anywhere special."

"Not really. I just need to find a job. I don't have any money."

"Why don't you see if Jim Dumbrowski has any work for you at the livery stable. He usually has more work than a centipede has legs. And if you work for him, he'll probably let you throw down a blanket in the stable."

"I'll do that. Thanks for the advice."

"See ya around."

Walker hopped out of the truck and made a bee's line to the livery stable. As he stepped across the threshold, he saw a middle-aged man forging horseshoes over an open flame. His biceps appeared to be stressing his short-sleeved tee shirt. Walker approached the Hulk Hogan look-alike and introduced himself as Jack Armor. He then asked the proprietor if he needed a helper.

Mr. Dumbrowski gave the stranger a once over.

"Have you ever worked in a livery stable?"

"No, but I'm a fast learner."

"I need help, but I wanted someone with experience."

"I would really appreciate your giving me a chance . . . I need the money."

"Where are you bunking down?"

"A man who drives a brown pickup said I might be able to stay in the barn."

Dumbrowski shook his head from side to side. "This is against my better judgment, but I'll give you a shot . . . Don't make me regret this."

"You won't be sorry!"

CHAPTER 46

Bill and Andrea struggled psychologically with the murder of their daughter. They knew they would have had to endure Courtney's death someday, but *today* was not supposed to be the day! And her passing should have been uneventful and not the frightening, tortuous death she experienced. However, Courtney *is* dead and funeral decisions needed to be made.

Andrea and Bill chose an ivory-colored casket with matching pillow and padding for their daughter. Brenda Mattausch, the funeral director's wife, offered to embroider Courtney's name into the padding adjacent to the pillow.

Andrea knew Courtney loved wearing her white communion gown and veil and insisted that her husband take this garment to Mattausch's Funeral Home for the viewing. She wanted Courtney dressed in her favorite outfit.

The Rossi family returned to the funeral home the following day at 1:00 pm for a private viewing. Courtney looked like a bride dressed in her white gown and veil.

Andrea burst into tears upon first seeing Courtney. She realized she would never again have the opportunity to prepare blueberry pancakes with whipped cream for her daughter.

Rossi too was saddened. As he looked at his daughter lying peacefully in her casket, he realized she will never need another blood transfusion and her frail tiny arms will never again be pricked with another needle.

Most of the people living in Derry came to Mattausch's during the next several days to show respect for Courtney and to provide support to the Rossi family. Bill appreciated their thoughtfulness, but he had no desire to speak with anyone. He only wanted to be left alone so that he could reflect on his memories of Courtney.

However, Rossi became distracted upon seeing a man whom he had never met enter the funeral parlor. The man, wearing a custom-tailored gray pinstriped suit, appeared to be in his seventies by the number of crease lines on his suntanned leathery-looking face. As the man sauntered toward the casket, Rossi couldn't help but notice that he dragged his right foot. Rossi wondered whether the man's physical condition was a result of some sort of birth defect or injury.

After reciting a prayer for the deceased young girl, the man walked over to Dr. Rossi and nodded as if to say *I'm sorry for the loss of your daughter*. He extended his right hand and introduced himself.

"Dr. Rossi. My name is Tony Strampello."

The gentleman then scribbled down his name and telephone number on a piece of paper before handing the card to Rossi. Strampello then leaned closer to Rossi and whispered into his ear, "Now is not the appropriate time, but call me whenever you finish grieving. I may be able to help you find the person responsible for your daughter's death." Strampello then walked away.

However, before leaving the funeral home, Strampello approached Dr. Rossi's father and the two of them embraced.

Rossi was bewildered by this demonstration of affection. He thought he knew all of his father's friends, but he was certain he had never met nor seen this man prior to today. However, it was quite evident that his father and Tony Strampello knew each other.

Later that evening, after friends and family had retired for the night, Rossi sat down on the chair next to his father.

"Who was that man you were talking to at the funeral parlor?"

"Anthony Strampello . . . He was a friend of your grandfather, Dominic."

"He handed me a note with his name and telephone number and said he may be able to find the person who killed Courtney. What's his story?"

"He's connected to the mob."

Rossi couldn't believe what he was hearing. "What's the association between him and granddad?"

"What do you remember about your grandfather?"

"Not much . . . I was pretty young when he died. But I remember he always gave me a silver dollar when I visited him."

"Do you remember anything else?"

"I remember he wore dark-colored suits most of the time."

"When your grandfather came to this country in the early 1930s, he came alone. He left his wife and family back in Italy. Things were difficult for him. He didn't speak English, and he only knew a handful of people who came to the United States before him. All he was told was to go to Philadelphia and connect with the other Italian families after he left Ellis Island.

"Your grandfather contacted an Italian family he knew from his hometown. The patriarch told him he could live with them until he found a job and was able to support himself. However, finding work was not easy. The United States was just beginning to recover from the Great Depression, and jobs were scarce. Those Italian immigrants who were fortunate enough to find jobs worked for pennies.

"Your grandfather found a job working as a fruit vendor, making $4 a day. He was grateful for the job, but he soon discovered that $4 a day would not enable him to save enough money to have his wife and family join him in the United States. Your grandfather became more and more frustrated with his inability to save money. Out of desperation, he turned to a life of crime."

Joseph Rossi poured himself a stiff drink before continuing. "Now don't misunderstand me," said the elder Rossi. "He wasn't a bank robber or anything like that. I never knew what your grandfather actually did. He never discussed business at home, and I was forbidden to associate with any of his cronies. However, I suppose he was no different from the mob guys you see on television. I'm sure he was involved in theft, gambling, racketeering, and prostitution. And he probably acted as an enforcer at times, physically punishing or perhaps even killing people when ordered to do so by his superiors. Murder and death were as much a part of organized crime as are books and encyclopedias to a library."

Dr. Rossi felt like he was sucker punched when told of his grandfather's involvement with organized crime. "Did you know what your father did to put food on the table?"

"Not at first . . . But when I got older, I noticed people acted differently when they were in his presence. People opened doors for him, they waited for him to enter a room before entering the room themselves, and they walked alongside or behind your grandfather, never in front of him."

"Didn't that seem strange to you?"

"Not really. I guess I got used to people acting like that. But there was one thing I thought was odd. People always bowed their heads when your grandfather walked passed them."

"Did Granddad have any bodyguards like you see in the movies?"

"There were two men who always shadowed your grandfather. One of the men, Sammy, was your grandfather's associate for many years. Everyone called him Sunshine, but I never understood how he got his nickname. He never smiled, and he was always in a bad mood. The scars on his left cheek and the crease lines on his forehead made Sammy look much older than his true age of fifty-two."

"He must have been a sight to see," mumbled Rossi.

"The other man, Tony Strampello, was glued to your grandfather's side. He was much younger in age. I'd guess he was in his early twenties by the smoothness of his skin and by the way he styled his hair. But what I remember most about Slick—that's what everyone called him—was that he was always impeccably dressed. He wore expensive suits with black and white winged-tipped alligator shoes. And people gravitated toward Tony because of his bubbly personality. But every now and then, someone would mistake his friendly demeanor as a sign of weakness. Then Tony would come down on him like an F-5 tornado, turning into a heartless adversary with very little provocation."

"What did Tony and Sammy do for Granddad?"

"They were lieutenants in the organized crime family. Whenever they were in the presence of your grandfather, very few words were spoken. But they were completely loyal to him. Their main responsibility was to protect your grandfather. They acted like Secret Service agents who were charged with protecting the president.

"Sammy and Slick continuously scanned the area where they walked, looking for anything out of the ordinary. Although my father trusted them both with his life, he favored Tony. I think Tony reminded your grandfather of himself when he was a young lieutenant in the 'family.' They were both arrogant and fearless young men, not concerned with stepping on anyone's toes to get what they wanted. And they believed they were invincible, not thinking for a moment they could be harmed.

Over the years, your grandfather introduced Strampello to anyone who was in a position to move him along the ranks in the 'family.'"

"What does this have to do with me?"

"I'm sure Strampello believes if he can help you find the person who murdered Courtney, then he would be repaying a debt to your grandfather for all of his support throughout the years."

"The police are confident they'll soon find Walker. I'll let them handle it."

"I agree with you, son. I'm sure the police will find him before long."

With the Thanksgiving and Christmas holidays approaching, Andrea and Bill decided to decorate their home as they did in past years; they realized it was important to resume as normal a lifestyle as possible for Michael's sake. In fact, Andrea decided to take Michael to Manhattan on the Saturday following Thanksgiving to view the window displays at Lord and Taylor's and Macy's.

Rossi told his wife he wouldn't be able to accompany her and Michael to New York because he needed to address some unfinished work at the hospital. However, the real reason for his not wanting to go to New York was because he wanted to sit face to face with Officer Druzak and find out what the police have been doing to find Walker.

When Rossi confronted Druzak about the whereabouts of Walker, he was told there was nothing new to report. Druzak reaffirmed his promise to find this man. However, Rossi sensed that Druzak's confidence in apprehending Walker was deteriorating faster than the concrete walls of Alcatraz.

With each passing week, Rossi became more frustrated with the Derry Police Department. They assured him that immediately following Courtney's death, Walker's arrest was imminent. However, four months later, the police were no closer to apprehending Walker than they were on the night of the murder.

Rossi wanted to search for Walker himself, but he knew he was needed at the hospital. However, with each passing week, Rossi found it increasingly more difficult to concentrate on medicine. Images of his daughter lying facedown in a puddle of blood flooded his thought processes. He imagined how frightened she must have been when removed from her protective womb and taken to unfamiliar surroundings. Although Courtney was naked when found in the woods by Officer Druzak, Rossi prayed that she had not been molested. An autopsy would have revealed whether Courtney had been sexually assaulted. However, neither Rossi nor Andrea wanted to know the results of the autopsy. Knowing their daughter had been raped would have been too unimaginable for them.

Rossi questioned the effectiveness of the roadblock manned by the Derry Police Department because he couldn't imagine how Walker managed to evade being captured. He wondered whether the Derry policemen were any more qualified than Officer Barney Fife from *The Andy Griffith Show* in securing roadblocks.

All information obtained by the Derry Police Department pertaining to the whereabouts of John Walker proved unreliable. As the months passed, Rossi became less tolerant of people, including his own family.

Michael begged his father on numerous occasions to come outside and play baseball with him, but Rossi always said he was too busy. Without turning his head, he promised to come out later; but later never came. He just sat in his chair and read from his medical journals. However, neither Andrea nor Michael ever saw him turn a single page. He just continued to stare at the same page.

For hours at a time, Rossi sat in his chair, thinking about what he would do to Walker when he finds him. He fantasized about taking a baseball bat across the back of Walker's knees, listening to his painful cries as he dropped to the ground. Then with another swing of the bat, he would strike Walker's forehead as though it were a baseball. This second blow would quiet any lingering cries as the blood from his cracked skull would fall onto the ground, painting an asymmetrical silhouette around his head.

Andrea was concerned for her husband's mental state. During the past month, he had withdrawn emotionally from his family and friends. However, when Rossi began disassociating himself from his hospital responsibilities, Andrea became alarmed. At first, Rossi made excuses for not being able to serve on hospital committees; but as time passed, he responded in a more offensive and disrespectful manner when asked to serve on a committee. He just wanted to be left alone to do what he wanted to do which was to sit in a chair and obsess about what he planned to do to Walker.

On the evening of March 3, Officer Druzak drove to the Rossi home to meet with both Andrea and Bill. He wanted to brief them on the ongoing investigation into their daughter's death. When Officer Druzak told them there were no new developments to report and that all of their leads were cold, Rossi exploded verbally.

"You mean to tell me that after months of investigation, you have no clues as to where Walker has gone?"

"I'm sorry, Dr. Rossi. We followed up with every lead we had, but nothing came of them. It's like he vanished into thin air."

"It's hard to believe, with all the manpower between the Derry and the Pennsylvania State Police Departments, no one has been able to find out where Walker is hiding."

"There are only two of us handling this investigation, Dr. Rossi."

"I was told every available man was being used to solve this case."

"At first, there were eight officers assigned to this case. However, the state police can't keep eight policemen on this particular case indefinitely . . . There are other crimes that need to be investigated."

"How many men are assigned to this case?"

"Two, sir. Myself and Detective Monti."

"That's great! The man who murdered my daughter is running around free, probably searching for another innocent child to victimize, and the police are only able to assign two men to hunt down this predator."

"I know things seem hopeless right now, but one little clue can often give us the information we need to put all the pieces of the puzzle together. Please be patient, Dr. Rossi. We'll find this guy."

"I've run out of patience! And I'm pissed off!"

"We'll find him, Dr. Rossi. I promise!"

"Do you have anything else to report, Officer Druzak?"

"No, sir."

"Then I'll walk you to the door. I hope, the next time we get together, you'll have some information for me."

"Yes, sir."

"Goodbye, Officer Druzak."

After escorting Druzak to the front door, Rossi walked into his living room and spoke with Andrea.

"Can you believe they still have no idea where Walker is?"

"I'm sure they're doing the best they can, Bill."

"That's not good enough. I want Walker found. I want him dead. In fact, I'd like to kill him myself!"

"Please don't talk like that, Bill. You're frightening me."

"Well, that's how I feel."

"What's happening to you? I know you're upset with what happened to Courtney, and you're upset that the police haven't been able to find Walker, but please get a grip on yourself."

Andrea looked at her husband, waiting patiently for some sort of response. However, Rossi continued to gaze out the window, acting as if he hadn't heard a word she said.

After a few moments, Andrea said, "I know you've been extremely affected by this ordeal. In fact, your entire demeanor has been negatively affected. You used to be a compassionate and loving husband and father. You're now full of hate. You're even talking about wanting to *kill* someone. I think you should schedule an appointment with the hospital psychologist . . . Maybe he can help you repress some of your anger."

Bill cocked his head slightly to the right and stared directly at Andrea with daggerlike eyes.

"I'm not making any appointments with any psychologist. There is nothing abnormal about the way I feel. And there is nothing wrong with my wanting to see Walker dead for doing what he did to Courtney. In fact, everyone would agree that it was justifiable homicide if I were to kill him! If you can't understand what I've said, then perhaps I should schedule an appointment for you with the psychologist!"

"You need help, Bill"

"What I need is for you to leave me alone so that I can do what I need to do."

"And what is that?"

"*Whatever I have to do!*"

"Perhaps Michael and I should move in with my parents until you get a hold of your emotions."

"Perhaps you should do whatever the hell you want to do. Just leave me alone!"

Andrea ran out of the living room and into the bedroom, crying hysterically as she locked the door behind her.

"Leave me alone!" screamed Bill. "Just leave me alone!"

CHAPTER 47

Even though Dumbrowski was pleased with Armor's work ethic, he had an uncomfortable feeling about him. He didn't know why he felt the way he did. Perhaps the reasons for his uneasiness were because he came to town with only the clothes he was wearing and because he had no money in his pocket. However, after further analysis, Dumbrowski believed his greatest concern pertained to Armor's reluctance to talk about his past.

Armor told Dumbrowski he left Los Angeles because it was becoming increasingly more dangerous to live there due to the escalating drug trade and gang-related activities. But Dumbrowski wasn't buying that story. If Armor had in fact left Los Angeles for good, then he would have been toting a suitcase. Dumbrowski wanted to know everything there was to know about his employee. He wanted to know if Armor had a criminal past.

Later that day, Dumbrowski dropped by the police station to talk with his longtime friend, Sheriff George Manning. Dumbrowski related his concerns about Armor to Sheriff Manning, and the sheriff said he would run a profile on Armor to determine if there were any outstanding warrants for his arrest.

Sheriff Manning did not look like the prototypical law enforcement officer. If you were asked to choose the person from a lineup of five men whom you believed most resembled a policeman, you would not select him. Manning was nearly as wide as he was tall, standing five feet nine inches and weighing two hundred forty-eight pounds. And his belly, which was supported by the large three-inch wide black gun belt, oscillated up and down like a Jell-O mold when he walked.

Dumbrowski had the utmost respect for Manning as a police officer. The sheriff always made it a practice of being extremely thorough with his investigations, never dismissing any singular piece of information which could prove helpful during the course of his investigation. He would uncover all stones while searching for information to solidify his case. If there were a hint of any criminal activity in someone's background, the sheriff would find it.

To his surprise, Manning didn't find any information to suggest that Armor was anything other than the drifter he appeared to be. There were no outstanding warrants for his arrest and there were no positive matches to the set of fingerprints he lifted from a beer bottle belonging to Armor. However, Manning felt there was something about Armor that wasn't quite on the up and up. This feeling, commonly referred to as a "sixth sense" by fellow law enforcement officers, is a sensation which cannot be identified by using the other five senses of sound, sight, smell, touch, or taste. This extrasensory perception ability enabled Manning to solve cases subconsciously by allowing his mind to sift through and piece together all the available investigative information.

Manning, like Dumbrowski, didn't believe that Armor moved to Omaha from Los Angeles because of the increased presence of drugs and gangs. Armor appeared too "street smart" to prefer living in the Midwest. He was definitely a "big city" kind of guy.

Manning drove to the livery stable the following day to confront Armor. As he walked into the stable, Manning spotted Armor molding horseshoes over the fire.

"How's it going, Jack?"
"All right, I guess."
"Is Jim here?"
"No. He's having lunch at the diner."
"Don't you eat lunch?"
"I pack my lunch."
"Has Jim been keeping you busy?"
"It's been a little slow lately."
"That's too bad . . . What do you think of our little town?"

"Seems nice enough."

Manning walked to the bench and picked up a horseshoe. "It's a lot different here than Los Angeles, wouldn't you say?"

"I guess."

"Why would a person from a big city like Los Angeles want to move to a little town like this?"

"I wanted to get away from the violence and drugs."

"Dumbrowski said that when you came to town, all you had were the clothes on your back. You didn't even have a penny."

"So what?"

"That would make it seem like you came here in a hurry."

"I told you LA is getting crazy."

"So you said, but I don't believe you."

"Then why do *you* think I came here?"

"To hide out."

"Is that right?"

"Yep. I have a feeling you're running away from someone or something. Am I right?"

"Why are you badgering me?"

"Because there's something about you that stinks, and it's not your clothes."

"Man, just leave me alone. I'm not bothering anyone . . . and I'm not running away from anything or anyone."

"We'll see. Just know that I'll be keeping an eye on you!"

CHAPTER 48

When Rossi arrived home from work the following day, he noticed that Andrea's car was not in the driveway. He initially thought Andrea and Michael were at the department store because he remembered Andrea say just the other week that Michael needed new clothes.

Rossi walked into the kitchen and noticed a note dangling from a magnet on the refrigerator door. He reached for his eyeglasses before reading the note. *Dear Bill, Michael and I will be staying with my parents for the time being. I love you, but I can no longer tolerate your behavior. You must understand that you're not the only one who has been affected by this ordeal. I too grieve for Courtney, but I'm not projecting my frustrations or sorrow onto you or anyone else. Please seek psychological counseling before it's too late. Love, Andrea.*

Bill thought, *before it's too late. What does she mean by before it's too late? Too late for me? Too late for us? Too late to find the scum who killed my daughter? Too late for what? She's right. If I don't do something now, it's going to be too late. If I don't take matters into my own hands, then it's going to be too late to find John Walker.*

Rossi became incensed as he reread Andrea's letter. "How dare she say I need help . . . that I need psychological counseling because I can't control my emotions," Rossi mumbled to himself as he paced throughout the house. *You better get some help before it's too late.*

Before long, the anger that Rossi harbored within himself was replaced with a feeling of tranquility. His frown gave way to a smile as he muttered, "I will get some help Andrea. It's not too late.

Thanks for helping me realize what I need to do to make things better."

Rossi stepped into his automobile and drove to the cemetery. He knelt down in front of Courtney's gravesite and recited a prayer. He then stood up, looked down upon the headstone, and spoke a few words to his daughter.

"Hello, honey . . . How are you today? I'm sure you're fine because you're with Jesus in Heaven! I miss you, baby. I know you wouldn't have lived many more years because of your illness, but I wish you were still here with me. Your mother and Michael left me because of the way I've been behaving. She thinks I'm a hateful person. She doesn't understand how I feel. She wants me to get some help. And thanks to her, I plan on getting some help. I now know what I have to do to make things better. And I will make things better for both you and me. I promise!"

Rossi returned home, walked into the bedroom, and opened the top drawer of his nightstand. There, buried underneath the most recent medical journal, was the note that Tony Strampello had given him at the funeral home. Rossi sat down on the corner of the bed and studied the card. After a few moments, he picked up the telephone and punched in the ten-digit number.

"Strampello residence."

"Hello. This is Bill Rossi from Pennsylvania. May I speak with Mr. Strampello?"

"One moment, Mr. Rossi."

Moments later, with the telephone receiver resting against his ear, Rossi heard what sounded like an object being dragged across the floor.

"This is Tony Strampello."

"Mr. Strampello, this is Bill Rossi. We met at my daughter's funeral. You said you may be able to—"

Strampello interrupted Rossi's comment. "Let's not talk over the telephone. I remember who you are. I'd like to spend some time with you. Come to Fort Lauderdale . . . We'll talk then. You can stay at my home."

"I'd like that, sir. I can catch the first flight Saturday morning, if that's okay with you."

"That's fine with me. I'll have a man waiting for you at the boarding area. He'll introduce himself to you."

"I appreciate you're seeing me, Mr. Strampello."

"We'll talk on Saturday."

CHAPTER 49

The car inched its way to the entrance gate of the Watson mansion. Moments later, the voice of the security guard could be heard from the intercom. "State your name and the reason why you're here."

"This is Andrea Watson Rossi. I would like to see my parents."

"Right away, Ms. Watson."

The gates separated, and Andrea drove her Buick through the opening. As Andrea approached the home, she saw her mother walking down the driveway to greet her.

"Hello, darling," said Allison. "How are you?"

"I'm fine, Mother. How are you?"

"Some days are better than others. Today is a good day for me."

"I'm glad to hear that, Mother."

"And how are you, Michael?"

"I'm great, Grandmother."

As they entered the home, Allison turned toward her grandson. "Are you hungry, honey? I can have Maria fix you and your mother something to eat?"

"We're fine, Mother. We stopped for a bite to eat along the way."

"If you get hungry later, just let me know. I can always have Maria whip something up for you."

"We'll be fine, Mother."

When they entered the house, Michael raced to the family room and connected his Atari game system to the television. He couldn't wait to play the Daytona 500 race car game. Andrea and Allison slipped into the library and became reacquainted with each other. They sipped on hot tea and nibbled on the cheese and crackers which Maria prepared for them.

"And how is Bill?" asked Allison.

"I don't know, Mother."

"Are the two of you quarreling?"

Andrea was unable to hold back her emotions. She began to cry uncontrollably. Allison got up from her chair and sat down next to her daughter. "What's wrong, Andrea?"

Andrea wiped the tears from her eyes. "I'm concerned about Bill . . . I'm afraid he's having an emotional breakdown."

"*Really?*"

"Courtney's death affected him more than I would have believed. When Courtney first passed away, Bill became depressed.

Then afterward, he seemed to snap out of it. He returned to work, and he behaved like a father again, making certain he spent quality time with Michael every day. But as the months passed, and there was no new information about Courtney's murderer, Bill grew increasingly more impatient. He's not the same person I married, Mother. He'll sit in a chair for hours and stare out the window without saying a word. And when he begins talking about Walker, the words that come out of his mouth . . . let's just say those are not the words of a Christian person."

"Has Bill been abusive to you?"

"No, Mother . . . not physically. However, he's beginning to frighten me with the way he looks at me at times. If he's not pleased with something I did or said, he'll stare at me with those piercing daggerlike eyes of his and not say a word. And he'll continue to stare at me until I walk away."

"He needs some help, Andrea."

"I know that, Mother, but he refuses to get counseling. He says it's absolutely normal to want to kill the person who murdered Courtney."

"I'm concerned about *your* safety. Why don't you and Michael move back home with us for a while? I know your father would love having you here with us."

"Thank you, Mother. I didn't know where else to go."

"You and Michael can stay with us for as long as you wish."

Rossi looked forward to meeting Strampello, and he hoped Strampello could deliver on his promise of finding Walker. He no longer believed the police were capable of finding Walker in the foreseeable future, and he no longer had the patience to wait for the law enforcement community to do its job. He needed to find this man and to bring him to justice before he lost all sense of rationality.

Rossi boarded TWA's 9:00 am flight from Philadelphia to Fort Lauderdale on Saturday. Before sliding into his assigned seat on the aircraft, he reached into the overhead compartment and removed a pillow and a navy blue flannel blanket. Rossi had difficulty sleeping the night before. He tossed and turned for much of the night, mentally rehearsing what he planned to do to Walker when the two of them finally meet. But for now, all he wanted to do was to prop his head against the window and sleep for the next two and a half hours.

The woman seated next to Dr. Rossi had a fear of flying. She was told the best way to take her mind off flying was to engage in a conversation with another passenger. The woman surmised that the passenger seated next to her had no fear of flying because he looked warm and cozy wrapped up in a blanket with his eyes closed. She reasoned this man had *no* fear of flying.

As the airplane taxied away from the terminal, she tapped Dr. Rossi on the shoulder.

"Excuse me, sir. Do you fly much?"

"Occasionally."

"Does flying make you nervous?"

"No."

"Flying scares the bee-je-bees out of me, but I don't have a choice. You see, my daughter is pregnant with her first child, and she'll be giving birth any day now . . . and I want to be there with her. It would take me too long to drive to Florida."

Rossi nodded, but he didn't say a word. He had no desire to speak with anyone, especially someone he doesn't know.

"My name is Pamela, but you can call me Pam. What's your name?"

"I'm Dr. Rossi."

Rossi immediately realized he made a mistake telling her he was a doctor. He hoped his comment about being a doctor flew over her head.

"I hope nothing happens which would require you to render medical treatment!"

Rossi looked at Pamela and smiled at her in a pathetic manner. *She heard me all right!* Rossi tried to smile at Pamela, but only the left side of his mouth moved; the right side of his face reacted as if he had Bell's palsy.

"I'm sure everything will be all right," he said. "Just relax and try to sleep."

"I'm too nervous to sleep."

Rossi turned his head away from Pamela and glanced out the window, trying to avoid the conversation which he feared would soon begin.

"They say there's a greater chance of being killed in an automobile accident than from a plane crash. Do you believe that, Dr. Rossi?"

"Yes, Pam. I believe planes are safer than cars."

"Then why do planes make me nervous and cars don't?"

"Because when you're driving a car, you feel like you're in control of everything. When you're in a plane, you must rely on the pilot to make the proper decisions."

"Are you a psychiatrist, Dr. Rossi?"

"No. I'm a surgeon."

"Will you be vacationing in Florida or will you be attending a medical seminar?"

"Neither, actually. I'm meeting a gentleman to discuss a personal matter."

"I'm sorry, Dr. Rossi. I don't mean to pry. I become this way when I get nervous."

"I understand, Pam. That's why you should try to sleep so that the trip will seem much shorter for you."

"I wish I could sleep, but I can't."

Rossi reached into the seat pocket in front of him and removed TWA's most recent inflight magazine. He read the CEO's article addressing the ongoing mergers in the airline industry. Shortly after beginning the article, Rossi felt a tap on his shoulder. He again turned toward Pamela.

"Excuse me, Dr. Rossi. May I ask you a medical question?"

Rossi nodded.

"My husband had a bunion removed from his left foot two months ago. I asked him to come with me to Florida, but he said his foot hurts too much to travel that far. Is it possible for his foot to hurt two months later, or do you think he's lying to me?"

"There's no way I can answer that question for you, Pam. Bunion surgery can sometimes take longer to heal than you think. You should ask this question to whomever performed the surgery."

Pamela sat quietly for a few moments, pondering which question she should ask next. However, before she had the opportunity to ask another question, Rossi said, "I hope you'll excuse me, Pam, but I need to get some rest. I was up very late last night performing emergency surgery on a man who was injured in an automobile accident. I need to be rested for my meeting this afternoon."

"Go right ahead and get some shut eye, Dr. Rossi. I won't disturb you."

Rossi turned off his overhead light, pulled down the shade over the window, and leaned his head against the window.

Moments later, Pamela tapped his shoulder once again. "Do you want me to wake you when breakfast is served?"

"No, thanks. I just want to rest."

"Sorry for bothering you, Dr. Rossi."

The airplane landed at 11:28 am. Rossi exited the aircraft and looked for the person whom Strampello said would be there to meet him.

Rossi noticed a man standing at the far corner of the arrival gate who was dressed differently than the other people who had gathered to meet their loved ones. This man wore a white silk shirt, black pants, and black wing-tipped shoes. He appeared to be in his fifties because of the gray hair that highlighted the temples of his head. Unlike the other people who smiled as they greeted their friends and family members, this man remained expressionless.

The man walked toward Rossi. "Are you Dr. Rossi?"

"Yes."

"My name is Marcello. Mr. Strampello has been looking forward to your visit. Let's get out of here."

Marcello and Rossi made their way down the concourse. "Did you check any luggage, Doc?"

"No. I only have this garment bag."

"That's great. It always seems to take longer than it should to get your luggage here."

Rossi and Marcello exited the terminal and stepped into a black Cadillac that was parked along the curb.

"I would like to express my condolences for the death of your daughter," said Marcello. "I heard the police haven't arrested anyone yet."

"That's right. In fact, the police don't even know where he is. That's why I came to Florida. I'm hoping Mr. Strampello can help me find this guy."

"If he's alive, Mr. Strampello will find him."

Rossi arrived at the Strampello residence ten minutes later.

"Welcome to Florida, Dr. Rossi. Did you have a pleasant flight?"

"Somewhat. There was a woman seated next to me who kept talking to me for much of the flight."

"That's why I always book the seat next to me when I fly. I don't like to talk to anyone."

Strampello took Rossi by the arm. "Cathy is preparing lunch. Have you eaten yet?"

"No, sir. I snacked on peanuts on the plane."

Strampello chuckled. "Peanuts. It wasn't long ago that you were given a meal on flights. Now you're lucky to get peanuts!"

"They did serve breakfast, but I pretended to be asleep. I didn't want to talk to that lady."

"I hope you like fish," said Strampello. "I have to watch my cholesterol these days."

"Yes, sir, I eat seafood."

Strampello mixed Rossi a cocktail, and they walked outside to the pool area. Rossi sipped on his drink before addressing the elderly gentleman. "I'm grateful for your seeing me, Mr. Strampello."

"How can I help you?"

"When I first met you, you said you'd be able to find the man who killed my daughter. At the time, I didn't think I needed your help . . . I thought the police would have been able to do their job. But the police aren't any closer today in making an arrest as they were back in October. In fact, a policeman recently told me there were only two officers assigned to this case." Rossi moved closer to Strampello. "I'm asking for your help, Mr. Strampello. I'm very frustrated. If you can help me find this man, I would be forever grateful to you."

Strampello zeroed in on Rossi's eyes. "What do you know about me Bill?"

"My father said you were a friend of my grandfather . . . that the two of you were involved with organized crime."

"Your grandfather saved my life. When I was eighteen, I thought I was a tough guy. Me and a couple of my friends used to rob gas stations and drug stores to get some spending money. None of us had a job. Hell, we never even *wanted* a job.

"We heard there was a man downtown that was a bookie, and on Mondays, he took in large sums of money. My buddy Sammy and I decided to rob him this one particular day. I entered the house through an open window above the back porch while Sammy stood guard outside. When I came downstairs, I was surprised to find the bookie alone. He was sitting at the kitchen table, counting and stacking the money in piles of $100. When he saw me walk into the kitchen, he reached for his gun. I pointed my gun at him and told him to keep his hands on top of the table. He said the money was not his. He said it belonged to 'the outfit.' I told him he was wrong . . . that the money belonged to me. I demanded he put the money in the leather bag and give it to me.

"Later that night, Sammy and I got together to divvy up the money. While we were splitting everything up, two men carrying sawed-off shotguns burst into the room. One of the men walked toward me and slammed his rifle butt into my stomach. I doubled over in pain . . . then I got knocked to the ground. As I raised my head to face him, he placed his foot on my chest, cocked his shotgun, and placed the barrel of the rifle against my head. I begged him not to shoot. He held the barrel against my head for several minutes. He then asked what would possess me to steal from 'the outfit.' I told him I wouldn't have robbed the guy if I knew he was connected with the mob. The man removed the riffle barrel from my head and told me to get up. He then blindfolded us, led us out of the house, and shoved us into the backseat of a car.

"After a short ride, Sammy and I were taken into a building before someone removed our blindfolds. I then realized we were standing in front of the commission. I tried to be brave, but the perspiration dripping from my forehead betrayed me.

"The 'Don' said he had to make an example out of us . . . that people needed to know that if they steal from them, they will die! That's when your grandfather and his buddy, Bruno, spoke up for us. They told the 'Don' that Sammy and I didn't know we were stealing from them, and they pleaded for our lives. The 'Don' said he would honor your grandfather's request if he vouched for me and Sammy. Your grandfather agreed, so we were allowed to live.

"Your grandfather put his own life on the line for us that day. When he vouched for us, he understood if me or Sammy fucked up, then he would be held accountable for our actions. From that day on, your grandfather kept a close watch over us. He wanted to make sure we didn't fuck up!

"Your grandfather knew we weren't model citizens. He knew we preferred making money the easy way whether it was legal or illegal. Your grandfather started taking me and Sammy with him whenever he had some small jobs to do. Before long, we accompanied him wherever he went. We were like the three amigos. We were completely loyal to each other. And when your grandfather became more powerful within the organization, he always bumped me and Sammy to a position of more responsibility.

"The guys who were with the organization longer than us were jealous, but they knew better than to say anything. They knew they'd get wacked if they bitched. And we knew it too. So we did just about whatever we wanted to do without worrying about anything. We were shrewd young guys carving a place for ourselves in the group. That's how I got my nickname Slick."

"You two were really good friends," said Rossi.

"I loved your grandfather. I would have died for him!"

"How can you help me?" asked Rossi.

"First of all, I'll inform the other families that I'm searching for this guy. Second, we're not like the police. We don't reassign people to other duties if we fail to find our man within the next several months. We'll keep searching for him for as long as it takes."

"That's the most encouragement I've had in months."

"Bill, you must understand that even though my 'family' is in South Florida, I can touch people anywhere in the United States. We're kind of like one big fraternity with local chapters throughout the entire country. I can ask and receive help from any of my 'brothers' in any state since I'm the 'Don' of the South Florida family. But I must show respect to the other 'Dons' when I go out of town. For example, if I want to go to Las Vegas for a vacation, I'd contact the 'Don' of the Las Vegas family and tell him I'm coming. He would welcome me with open arms and make sure that I enjoyed myself. I'd be given all the respect from his associates that he himself commands. However, if I went to Las Vegas without telling the 'Don,' then my presence in town would be perceived as threatening. The 'Don' may think I was planning to muscle in on his territory, and then he'd put a contract out on me."

"I wouldn't want you to jeopardize yourself, Mr. Strampello."

"I'll be fine, Bill. I've been involved in this business too long not to know how things are done. Just go back home and relax. I'll take care of everything from now on."

"Can I call you periodically to see how things are going?"

"I don't want you to contact me at all. I'll contact *you* when I find him."

"Thanks, Mr. Strampello."

"We'll find him for you, Bill."

CHAPTER 50

Later that night, Andrew Watson arrived home from his business meeting in New York. Allison informed him of Andrea and Michael's arrival, and she began to relate the story Andrea told her about Bill earlier in the day.

"That's terrible," he said. "Did you tell Andrea to move back with us?"

"Yes, dear."

"What happened?"

"Andrea thinks he's having a nervous breakdown. She said he's becoming more aggressive and more hateful every day."

"Has he hurt them?"

"She said no. She said he just sits in a chair and mumbles to himself for hours at a time."

"Does she realize that Bill needs psychological counseling?"

"Andrea made that suggestion to him, but he wouldn't listen to her. He said there's nothing wrong with him. He said it's normal to feel the way he feels and to behave the way he's behaving."

"I want you to take Andrea and Michael clothes shopping tomorrow. They're never going back there!"

"You can't make her stay here, Andrew."

"I'll talk to her in the morning. I'll make her realize it's dangerous for them to move back home."

Andrea was surprised to find her father seated at the breakfast table when she entered the Florida room. She thought he would still be asleep since he arrived home late last night.

"Good morning, Father. I'm surprised to find you awake so early in the morning."

"I don't sleep much anymore. I think all the medication I take disturbs my sleep cycle."

"How have you been?"

"I'm fine, but I'm concerned about you."

"I guess you've spoken with Mother."

"Yes. She told me everything when I arrived last night. It's very disturbing."

"I don't know what to do, Father. Bill is such a great father and wonderful husband. But lately, he's been different. To tell you the truth, he frightens me."

"Bill *was* a wonderful husband. He may not be the same person you married."

"If he were to get some help . . ."

"That's the point. He needs help, but he has to seek it himself. You can't force him into counseling."

"I don't think Bill will seek out help on his own. He insists there's nothing wrong with him."

"He's dangerous, Andrea. He's going to snap, and you don't want to be there when it happens!"

"I feel so helpless, Father. There should be something I can do to help him."

"Stay away from him. Does he know where you've gone?"

"Yes. I left him a note."

"Give him some time to collect himself. He's a smart man. Perhaps in time he'll realize that his hatred and volatile nature may cause him to lose his family. Let's hope this encourages him to get counseling."

"I hope you're right, Father."

Rossi caught the last flight from Fort Lauderdale and arrived in Philadelphia at 11:35 pm. He stopped at the restroom near the baggage claim area to wash his hands and face. He didn't care that his five-o'clock shadow made him look gruff, nor did he care that his shirt had pulled out from his wrinkled trousers. He only wanted to go home and get some much needed sleep.

Other than feeling exhausted, Rossi returned home from his meeting with Strampello with a bounce in his step. For the first time in months, he believed justice will prevail, and he believed that he will finally get his satisfaction. Rossi kept telling himself to remain patient; his day will come!

The following day, Rossi attended church service for the first time since Courtney's death. He decided to follow Strampello's advice and get back into his normal daily routines.

Following mass, many of the parishioners told Rossi how great it was to see him in church again. Rossi responded by telling them that, even though he appreciated their support and understanding, he just needed time to come to terms with Courtney's death.

When asked how Andrea and Michael were doing, Rossi said they were great and that Andrea wanted to spend some time with her parents. Rossi also said Andrea's visit to New York could not have come at a better time. He said he got so far behind with his responsibilities at the hospital that he just wanted to bury himself in his work.

Rossi felt great when he returned to the clinic Monday morning, but he knew he'd feel much better when he got his hands on Walker. He realized he shouldn't get overly excited about the possibility of Strampello finding Walker soon; after all, the police haven't been able to locate him in nearly a year. He just needs to be patient and wait for Strampello to call. And when the call finally comes, he will go anywhere in the world and confront the man who killed his daughter.

But what would he do if Andrea had already returned home when Strampello calls? How could he leave on a minute's notice without raising suspicion? Rossi needed to devise a plan to keep Andrea with her parents and away from Derry.

Rossi telephoned the Watson residence later in the week with hopes of speaking to his wife.

"Watson residence, Maria speaking."

"Hello, Maria. This is Dr. Rossi. May I speak with my wife please?"

"One moment, Dr. Rossi."

After a few minutes, Andrea picked up the telephone. "Hello, Bill . . ."

"How are you, Andrea?"

"I'm okay. How are you?"

"I'm doing a little better. I read the letter you left me and—"

"Bill, I feel so terrible for leaving without saying goodbye. I didn't know what else to do."

"You were right to leave. I *was* bitter and hateful. I apologize for my unacceptable behavior." Rossi heard Andrea crying through the telephone receiver. "Not only were you saddened by Courtney's death, but you were also burdened with my outbursts. I apologize for everything."

"My parents want me to stay with them for a while longer."

"I agree. I'm beginning to feel better, but I still have several issues to resolve. I plan to consult with the hospital psychologist in the near future. Perhaps he can exorcise my inner demons!"

"Please make the appointment. I'm sure he'll help you."

"I'll call again soon to see how you and Michael are doing. Stay with your parents until I resolve my problems. I want everything to be as it was when we reunite."

"I love you, Bill."

"I love you too. Good night, Andrea."

After hanging up the telephone, a sinister smile formed on Rossi's face. *That should keep her put until I conclude my business with Mr. Walker.*

CHAPTER 51

After interrogating Armor for forty-five minutes, Sheriff Manning returned to the police station and replayed his recording of the question-and-answer session with the hope of finding inconsistencies with Armor's answers. He hammered Armor with questions pertaining to his reasons for leaving Los Angeles, and he drilled Armor about how could he not have accumulated any possessions throughout the years.

Armor despised Manning's relentless questioning, and he became concerned that Manning could present a problem for him. He tried to put the interrogation behind him, but he was unable to do so. Living on the streets, he encountered people like Manning all the time; people who continue to hound you until you breakdown or you leave town. They just keep coming around, asking benign-type questions with the hope of uncovering that missing piece of the puzzle. Armor found these people as annoying as a pebble in a shoe.

Jim Dumbrowski returned from lunch and asked Armor if anyone came by to see him. Armor said Sheriff Manning stopped by and questioned him as though he were a criminal on a witness stand. Armor stopped working and walked over to where Dumbrowski stood.

"Do you have any idea why Manning has a hard on for me?"
"Not really."
"It was strange . . . I never saw it coming."
"What did he want?"

"He wanted to know why I moved here from Los Angeles. And he said he's going to keep an eye on me. Can't a person move from one town to another without being harassed by the police? It's just not right."

"The only thing I can think of is you didn't have a single thing with you when you came here . . . not even a penny! He probably thinks you're running away from somewhere!"

"I'm not running away from anything. I just wish people would leave me alone."

"If you're not hiding out, then don't worry about anything. Manning will try to construct the pieces of *your* puzzle. If the pieces don't fit, then he'll move on to another project. But if you *are* running away from something, then you'll discover how relentless Manning can be."

Armor turned away from Dumbrowski and reached for a towel to dry the perspiration off his face. "I'll be back in a little while . . . I have to get something to eat."

What am I going to do? thought Armor. *Dumbrowski said the sheriff will busy himself with other matters if he doesn't find anything on me. But that's what worries me. Manning won't find anything on me because I don't exist. There is no Jack Armor. And as soon as Manning discovers that I'm using an alias, he'll jump on me like flies on shit! And he won't stop until he takes me down. Why did I ever take the Rossi girl away from the festival that night? Why didn't I leave Derry when the police asked me to leave? If I had left town when I was told to do so, then I wouldn't be worrying about anything. But I didn't leave, and now I got a sheriff, who thinks he's Sherlock Holmes, trying to take me down. I don't know what to do. If I leave town now, the sheriff will get suspicious and put out an all-points bulletin on me. If I stay, then it's only a matter of time until he finds out my true identity and arrests me for kidnapping. Manning's becoming a pain in the ass.*

CHAPTER 52

Five months after the meeting with Strampello, Rossi received the telephone call he had been waiting for. The person on the other end of the telephone asked, "Do you recognize my voice?"

"Yes," answered Rossi.

"I have the information you want. I need you to meet me here in Florida so I can explain everything to you. When can you come?"

"I'll take the first flight tomorrow morning."

"My associate will meet you at the airport. Look for him."

"Thank you, sir."

"I'll see you tomorrow, Bill."

Rossi felt euphoric after speaking with Strampello. There were times when he wondered whether Walker would ever be found, but Strampello proved to be a man of his word. He walked the walk and found Walker, something the police were unable to do!

Rossi found this flight to Fort Lauderdale more pleasurable than his previous flight because no one required any medical or psychological advice. He was able to recline his seat and focus on what he planned to do to Walker when the two of them finally meet.

Marcello met Rossi near TWA's baggage claim area and directed him to his vehicle in the short-term parking lot. Upon arriving at the Strampello residence, Rossi was informed that Mr. Strampello was waiting for him on the patio. Rossi walked through the French doors leading to the patio and found Strampello sitting at the table nearest the swimming pool.

"I hope you like Cuban food," said Strampello.

"I like all ethnic foods."

Although Rossi enjoyed the conversation he had with Mr. Strampello while dining on roasted chicken, rice, and black beans, he felt like a child on Christmas morning finding wrapped gifts and not being able to tear the paper off the boxes until his parents came downstairs. He couldn't wait until Strampello told him all about John Walker.

Cathy removed the dishes from the table following lunch and returned indoors. She knew Mr. Strampello had business to discuss with Rossi, and she was not permitted anywhere near Strampello when he conducts business.

Unable to contain himself any longer, Rossi said, "I'm surprised you were able to find him so soon."

"It wasn't easy . . . If it wasn't for a certain cop, we may not have found him at all."

"A police officer?"

"A sheriff named Manning. He had a hunch this guy, who called himself Jack Armor, was not who he said he was. Manning asked him all kinds of questions, but he wasn't satisfied with his answers. As Manning kept snooping around, he came across some information I distributed through our contacts in the Midwest. From this information, Manning realized that his guy, Jack Armor, was really John Walker."

"Where is he?" asked Rossi.

"Omaha, Nebraska."

"Let's go get him."

"Not so fast . . . We gotta make sure we don't leave any trails."

Rossi nodded in agreement.

"What are you going to tell your wife?" asked Strampello.

"Andrea's not a concern. She's staying with her parents until I send for her."

"What would you like us to do with him?" asked Strampello as he poured himself another cup of coffee.

Rossi leaned closer to Strampello and whispered into his ear. Strampello pushed his chair back and said, "That's pretty fuckin' nuts . . . but because you're a doctor, it just might work."

"What if Walker skips out of town and we can't find him?"

"No problem, Doc. We know where he is . . . We won't lose track of him. He's under *our* surveillance."

"Tell me what I should do."

"Register for a medical seminar in a state near Nebraska so that you have a reason for being in the Midwest. One of our associates will meet you at the seminar and drive you to Omaha. Another associate will pluck Walker off the street and take him to a secured location where you can do your thing."

"I'll register for a seminar as soon as I get back home."

"Call me when you finalize your plans. And don't worry about anything—everything's under control!"

Rossi couldn't wait to return home and sift through his medical journals in hopes of finding a seminar near Nebraska. Although it was late at night when he arrived home from Fort Lauderdale, Rossi had no intentions of going to sleep. He immediately made his way to his study and sorted through the journals which were neatly stacked in groups of ten on the shelf above his roll-top desk. He only had to scan through three journals before finding a seminar which suited his needs.

He found a seminar titled "Plastic Surgery for the General Surgeon." The seminar will be held at the Marriott Hotel and Conference Center in Oklahoma City, Oklahoma. Rossi registered for the seminar and paid by credit card so to have a record of the transaction should he need an alibi.

Rossi telephoned Strampello the following day and provided him with details pertaining to the seminar. Strampello absorbed the information as quickly as a Bounty paper towel absorbs spilled water.

"So you say the seminar begins on the weekend of November 5?"

"Yes, sir."

"I'll call Johnnie Scarfone. He's the boss of the Midwest area."

"What do I do now?"

"Nothing . . . I'll call you when everything's worked out."

"Should I—"

"Do nothing until I tell you. Just wait for my call."

"Yes, sir."

CHAPTER 53

Officer Druzak drove to the Rossi home on October 28, the anniversary of Courtney's death. He was anxious about approaching the house, fearing that this meeting with Dr. Rossi would be as ugly as their last encounter. Disregarding his own apprehensions, Druzak knocked on the door. He realized he had a job to perform.

"Officer Druzak, I'm surprised to see you!"

"Can I have a few minutes of your time, Dr. Rossi?"

"Come in."

Druzak wiped his shoes on the welcome mat before entering the house. "Is Mrs. Rossi home?" asked Druzak.

"No. She and Michael are at my in-laws."

"I trust they're doing well."

"What can I do for you, Officer Druzak?"

"It was a year ago today that Courtney was killed."

I'm surprised you remembered, thought Rossi. "That's awfully nice of you to remember, Officer Druzak."

"As you know, we still haven't found John Walker."

That's because you're an incompetent fool! "I'm sure you're doing the best you can."

"I appreciate your patience and understanding, Dr. Rossi."

Save it for someone who cares. "I'm confident you'll find him."

"We'll find him, Dr. Rossi. You can count on it!"

I'll give you a hundred to one odds that you don't. "I hope so."

Rossi called the Watson home shortly after Officer Druzak left the house. He had not spoken with his wife in over a week, and he wanted to be certain that Andrea would not be coming home unexpectedly. Officer Druzak's visit was an excellent excuse for calling Andrea.

The telephone rang several times before someone picked up the handset.

"Andrea, it's Bill."

"I was just thinking about you."

"How's it going?"

"Things are okay . . . but I would like for us to be back together again."

"We will. The psychologist says I'm making progress, but I'm not quite there yet."

"I'm proud of you for seeking counseling."

"Officer Druzak stopped by the house a little while ago."

"Did he have any new information?"

"No. He stopped by to say he's still searching for Walker and that he's confident that Walker will eventually be arrested."

"You weren't rude to him, were you?"

"Not at all."

"Perhaps this counseling has helped you more than you think!"

"You're probably right."

"When do you think we'll get back together?"

"I'd say in about a month . . . I still need to put a few more issues behind me."

"I miss you, Bill."

"I miss you too. I'll call you soon."

CHAPTER 54

Strampello opened the front door and motioned for Marcello to come into the house. "What can I do for you, boss?"

"Come into the study . . . and close the door behind you."

Marcello eased himself into one of the two high-backed chairs as Strampello walked toward the bar.

"Can I fix you a drink?" asked Strampello.

"How's about a rye and water?"

"Rye and water coming up."

Strampello handed the drink to Marcello. "We got a job to do. Call Lefty, Nicky, Louie, and Vinnie and tell them I want them here at noon tomorrow. This Walker guy is in Omaha, Nebraska. I want you to take the boys to Nebraska and get everything set up. Rossi will be in Oklahoma, November 5, for a medical meeting. I want you there so that he doesn't do something stupid."

"Did you call Johnnie Scarfone yet?"

"I'm calling him later tonight."

Marcello got up from his chair and walked toward the bar. "Boss, I hope you don't mind me asking, but what is this Rossi guy to you anyhow?"

"He's the grandson of my mentor, Dominic Rossi. When the organization opened up the books, Dominic arranged for me and Sammy to be made."

"I'll make sure everything goes right, boss. Don't worry about nothing."

"Get in touch with the boys. I'll see you here tomorrow."

Strampello waited for Marcello to leave the room before pouring himself another drink. He kept thinking about the conversation he had with Rossi the other day. He listened as Rossi explained in detail what he planned to do to Walker.

Strampello was uncomfortable with Rossi's plan, but he approved the plan provided he stays within certain parameters.

Later that night, Strampello telephoned Johnnie Scarfone.

"Johnnie, Tony Strampello from Florida. How are ya?"

"Fine, Tony. How's the weather?"

"Better than yours, I'm sure. Johnnie, I'd like to ask a favor of you."

"Anything, Tony."

"There's a friend of mine I want to help. Somebody raped and killed his daughter. I found out the guy who butchered the girl is hiding in Omaha. With your permission, I want to send a few of my boys to take care of him."

"What can I do to help?"

"I'm not sure yet. I'm still working out the final details."

"When's this going down?"

"Around November 5."

"That's next weekend!"

"I know there's not much time, but my friend has been waiting a year for justice."

"Whatever you need, you got it."

"Thanks, Johnnie. I knew I could count on you. If there's anything I can do for you someday—"

"Forget about it. Call me if you need some help."

"Thanks, Johnnie."

The following day, Strampello met with several of his associates at his home. They didn't know what was going down, but they knew they weren't summoned to discuss the weekly take from the gambling and prostitution operations. The last time these men were in each other's company was when Strampello sanctioned the hit on Jim "Boom-Boom" Bochichio.

Marcello closed the door and pulled down the blinds after Strampello entered the room. Strampello looked at the four men seated in front of him.

"Boys, we got a job to do," he said. "The grandson of a friend of mine needs our help. About a year ago, someone raped and killed his daughter. This man skipped town, but I found out where he's been hiding." Strampello walked toward the bar and mixed himself a scotch and water. "We got something special planned for this guy. Marcello will fill you in on all the details during the next few days. But we're not working on this by ourselves. We're hooking up with Johnnie Scarfone, and I don't want any problems with Scarfone's men. If anybody fucks up, he'll answer to me!"

Nicky and Louie looked at each other without uttering a single word.

"Does everyone understand me?" asked Strampello.

The four of them responded simultaneously, "Yes, boss."

"Good. Go home and pack. This job will probably last about a month, so bring enough clothes. Does anyone have any questions?"

The four men just sat there shaking their heads no.

"Be ready to leave in a few days."

"We'll be ready, boss," said Louie.

"Now get out of here."

Marcello and the other guys stood up and walked toward the door. Strampello grabbed Marcello by the arm as he walked by. "Stay here . . . I have a couple of things to discuss with you."

"Yes, sir."

After the boys left, Marcello closed the office door and mixed himself a rye and water.

"The mark is John Walker," said Strampello, "but he's using the alias Jack Armor. He's hiding in Omaha, Nebraska. I want you to go to Nebraska and tell Scarfone that Dr. Rossi registered for a medical seminar in Oklahoma City, Oklahoma, beginning November 5. Arrange for Rossi to be picked up in Oklahoma and then taken to Nebraska. Meanwhile, I want you to find a cabin or a house in a secluded wooded area where no one will see or hear anything. Then I want you to grab Walker and take him to the cabin. Rossi will be there waiting for him. I don't care who you give what jobs to. Just make sure you're at the cabin with Rossi in case something goes wrong."

Marcello stood up and walked over to Strampello. "Don't worry about nothing, boss. I'll take care of everything."

"I know you will."

CHAPTER 55

After meeting with Strampello, Louie and Nicky reflected on the time when they were young and thought they were tough guys who had everything figured out. They hung out at the Casa di Mia bar and restaurant. The Casa di Mia was a hangout for "wise guys" and want-to-be "wise guys." The everyday bar patrons, who amused themselves by playing pool and throwing darts, stayed in the front room of the establishment. The wise guys and their friends threw dice and played poker in the back room.

Louie and Nicky frequented the Casa di Mia nearly every afternoon and evening, but they rarely played cards. They were busy working. They sat at a table in the corner of the room for hours at a time, taking bets on sporting events, running numbers, dealing drugs, and hustling women. Their business was open seven days a week, and business was good.

Louie and Nicky were best of friends since their high school days at St. Raphael's Catholic School in South Philadelphia. They were inseparable. Their classmates nicknamed them "the Dago twins," even though they didn't look anything alike. Nicky, who stood six feet two inches tall, towered over his smaller buddy who measured five feet eight inches short. However, Louie's strength more than compensated for his shorter stature. Louie knew from growing up in Philadelphia that if you were shorter than most people, then you better be stronger than they. Otherwise, you were going to get a regular ass kicking.

Louie started lifting weights and taking protein supplements when he was fourteen years old. By the time he graduated from high school, he wore XL shirts. He didn't need to wear those oversized shirts because of a larger than normal waistline. He needed to wear those shirts in order to fasten the button around his nineteen-inch neck and to facilitate sliding his fourteen-inch biceps through the shirt sleeves.

The Dago twins were fascinated with gangster movies. All they ever wanted to do was to live the life of a gangster; and it didn't take them long to live their dream. They distributed sports betting sheets and ran a numbers racket. Louie generated additional monies by protecting the smaller and weaker people who were harassed by school bullies. Louie acquired a reputation as being a tough guy, and this suited him just fine.

One afternoon, a young man, who was dressed in black and wearing a gold necklace, approached the shorter boy.

"Are you Louie?" he asked.

"Who wants to know?"

"You ever hear of Tony Strampello?"

"The mob guy?"

"Yea. I'm with him."

"You're with Strampello?"

"We've been watching you."

"I'm not bothering nobody."

"Tony likes how you've been running your little business. How would you like to work for us?"

"I thought I was working for you guys already."

"Running numbers and sports sheets don't mean you're working for us."

"What did you have in mind?"

"Driving some of the guys around and doing errands for our friends."

"Is that it?"

"We might use you for collections since you look like you could go a few rounds with someone."

Louie always dreamed of associating himself with the mob.

"Yea. I'm interested."

"I'll arrange for you to meet Lefty. He'll go over everything with you."

"What's your name?" asked Louie.
"Vinnie."
"Well, Vinnie, I got a partner that I do things with."
"You mean Nicky?"
"How did you know?"
"I told you we've been watching you."
"Can I bring him with me when I meet Lefty?"
"No problem. You know where the Casa di Mia bar is?"
"Yea."
"I'll see you guys there tomorrow at noon."
"Thanks, Vinnie."

The hairs on Louie's arms stuck straight up when Vinnie walked away. Louie was thrilled to be asked to be a member of the organization, and he couldn't wait to tell Nicky. For Louie, being invited to join the mob was as exciting as a high school student from the Bowery receiving an acceptance letter from Harvard University.

When Louie stopped at the pizza shop later in the day, he pulled out a chair and sat down next to Nicky.

"Guess what happened to me today?"
"You got arrested," Nicky said sarcastically.
"I'm serious, man. Guess what happened?"
"I don't know. You asked Ashley out on a date?"
"I was asked if I wanted to work for the mob."
"What?"
"No lie. A guy named Vinnie asked me if I wanted to work for them."
"Doing what?"
"Doing things for them and their friends . . . and maybe muscling some people."
"What about our betting and numbers business?"
"I guess we can still do that, but Vinnie said what we've been doing didn't mean we were associated with them."
"Way to go, Louie."
"You were invited too."
"You straight with me?"

"Yea. Vinnie knew all about us, and he wants us to meet a friend of his named Lefty. We're supposed to meet him tomorrow at noon at the Casa di Mia."

"We made it, Louie."

"Yea, we made it."

Louie and Nicky darted across the street when they saw Vinnie standing near the Casa di Mia.

"Vinnie," said Louie. "I'd like to introduce you to Nicky . . . He's a friend of mine."

"He's *not* a friend of yours."

"Yes, he is . . . He's one of my best friends."

"Nicky is a buddy of yours, but not a *friend* of yours. You guys need to learn the lingo if you plan on associating with us."

"What do you mean?"

"If I say a guy is a 'friend of mine,' that means he's affiliated with our organization. If I say he's a 'friend of ours,' that means he's a made man."

"I thought you said me and Nicky were working for you guys."

"Not until Lefty says so. Do you guys have any questions?"

"Yea. What did ya mean when you said he's a made man?"

"Do you guys know how a college fraternity works?"

"Kind of," said Nicky.

"When somebody first joins a fraternity, he's called a pledge. After he gets voted in, he's called a brother. If our bosses vote somebody in, then he's a 'made man.' *Capisci?*"

"Yea, I got it."

"Let's go see Lefty."

The three men entered the bar and walked through a double door leading to a back room. There, Louie and Nicky saw a man giving orders to two tough-looking men wearing thick gold rope chains over their silk shirts. When the man saw Vinnie walk into the room, he dismissed the two thugs and motioned for Vinnie to bring the two neophytes over to him.

Louie was mesmerized by the sight of Lefty. Lefty was wearing a black pin-striped suit with a black silk shirt and a white tie. He looked exactly how Louie imagined a gangster to look. Louie also couldn't help from noticing that Lefty sported a gold Rolex watch around his left wrist and a wide gold bracelet on his right wrist.

Even though Lefty stood six feet two inches tall and weighed two hundred forty pounds, Louie couldn't take his eyes off the scar on Lefty's left cheek. Louie wondered whether Lefty earned the scar from a fight or whether the scar was a self-inflicted wound to make him look more like Al Capone.

"Lefty, I'd like you to meet Louie and Nicky."

"How you boys doing?"

"Fine, sir," they replied.

"Call me Lefty.

"We're good, Lefty," said Louie.

"Vinnie said you guys might want to do some work for me."

"Yes, sir," said Louie.

"The name is Lefty."

"Sorry."

"Do you guys know how to keep your mouths shut?"

Louie swiped a hand across his mouth to indicate that his mouth was zippered shut.

"We got rules we follow, and the number one rule is no one talks. Do you guys understand?"

"Yes, Lefty," they replied.

"Good. Listen to what Vinnie tells you. If you listen to what we tell you and you keep your mouth shut, you'll make more money than you'll ever imagine."

Louie and Nicky glanced at each other and smiled. "That's why we're here, boss," said Louie. "We like the action, and we like money."

"You guys can go now. Vinnie will get in touch with you."

"Thanks, Lefty. We won't disappoint you."

Louie and Nicky left the bar realizing they were given an opportunity to live their dream of becoming gangsters.

"We're in, Louie."

"Ain't it great!"

"Do you think Lefty's a big player?"

"Na. Probably somewhere in the middle of the pack."

"How far do you think he's from Strampello?"
"I don't know. Probably a couple of people."
"Do you think he ever talks to Strampello?"
"How many questions you going to ask me?"
"I'd like to meet Strampello."
"You will, don't worry."
"How do you know?"
"Because we're going to be big in this business someday."

The next day, Vinnie called Louie and said he wanted to talk with him.
"Meet me at the bowling alley on Front Street. I need you to make a drop at the Casa."
"What is it?"
"It's none of your business. Don't ever ask what something is again."
"I thought I was one of the guys?"
"You are one of us. If we want you to know something, we'll tell you. If not, don't ask."
"No problem, man. Who do you want me to take this to?"
"Mr. Big."
"Who?"
"Tony Strampello."
Louie couldn't believe what he heard. He was about to meet the boss of bosses.
"I didn't think I'd meet Mr. Strampello so soon."
"He said he wants to meet the new guys. Do you know what he looks like?
"Who doesn't?"
"All right then. Pick up Nicky and get over to the Casa."
"My pleasure, boss."

Louie drove to Nicky's home and blew the car horn.
"Keep your pants on!" shouted Nicky. "I'll be right out."
Nicky ran down the stairs from his apartment and stepped into Louie's car. "What's up, cuz?" said Nicky.
"We got a job to do."

"Vinnie get a hold of you?"

"You'll never guess what we got to do."

"Knock off someone?"

"Make a drop to Strampello."

"Get the fuck out!"

"I'm serious as a heart attack. Vinnie said Strampello wants to meet the new guys."

"What's in the bag?"

"I don't know. Vinnie said not to ask any questions."

Nicky and Louie rode down the road a few blocks without saying anything to each other. Then Nicky said, "Maybe they're testing us."

"I thought about that myself."

"They might be setting us up to see if we looked inside the bag. Hell, I bet Strampello's not even there. I bet it's a setup."

"I don't know. I'm just going to do what I'm told to do."

Louie and Nicky entered the Casa di Mia. At first glance, they didn't see anyone they recognized. But that didn't surprise them; they didn't expect to know anyone in the front area of the bar. They knew all the guys kept to themselves in the back room.

In the front room of the bar were two women and two men. The women, wearing pink Betty Boop jackets, debated which songs to select from the juke box. The men, sporting shoulder-length hair that needed washed badly, held a pool stick in one hand and a bottle of beer in the other. These middle-aged men wore black motorcycle vests with a Harley emblem on the back. Black chest hairs could be seen beneath their unbuttoned vests.

Nicky and Louie entered the back room and saw Strampello sitting at a table in the corner of the room. He was talking to Lefty.

Nicky tapped Louie on the shoulder and said, "That's Strampello over there with scar face."

"Yea, I know."

"Should we wait here or what?"

Louie looked at Nicky and said, "Let's go."

As Louie and Nicky approached the table, Strampello stopped talking and focused his attention on Louie. Lefty then leaned closer to Strampello and said, "These are our new guys, Louie and Nicky."

"Nice to meet you, sir," said Louie.

"Yea, nice to meet you, Mr. Strampello," said Nicky.

"Call me Tony."

"We got something for you."

Louie handed Tony the bag and waited for a response.

"Thanks, boys. You did real good," said Strampello.

Tony opened the bag and pulled out the "take" from the South Philadelphia district.

"Looks a little light," said Strampello. He turned toward Lefty and said, "Make sure nobody's skimming off the top."

"Yes, boss."

Strampello looked at Louie and Nicky and said, "If you guys mind your own business and keep your mouths shut, you'll go far."

He then stood and looked at Lefty. "Take me home."

At that precise moment, the sound of broken glass and yelling could be heard from the front section of the establishment. Strampello and the boys walked into the bar area to see what was happening. There, they saw one of the gruff-looking men holding a broken beer bottle alongside the face of the bartender.

Strampello yelled out, "Yo! Don't do nothing stupid. Put the bottle down."

"Mind your own business, pops."

"This is my business. I own this place."

Strampello, along with Lefty, Louie, and Nicky, walked toward the man. "What's the problem?" asked Strampello.

"He stole the money I had laying on the bar."

"I didn't steal anything," said the bartender.

"You lying piece of shit . . . I'm going to cut you up."

Strampello then said, "He never stole anything in his life. Maybe you made a mistake."

The gruff man turned toward Strampello and held the broken bottle underneath his neck. "Maybe I should cut you up!"

Without hesitation, Louie knocked the biker to the ground with a thundering right cross and said, "If you ever threaten or talk to Mr. Strampello like that again, I'll kill you." Louie then kicked the biker in the stomach. "Get the fuck out of here and take the sluts with you."

The two men and the Betty Boop girls took their remaining money from the bar and walked out the door. As they were leaving the bar, the biker who was punched turned around and said to Louie, "I'll be back."

"Not if you know what's good for you."

Strampello was impressed with how quickly Louie reacted to the altercation. "You did good, Louie."

"Thanks, Mr. Strampello."

"Call me Tony."

"Thanks, Tony."

"Louie, from now on I want you with me. I want you and Lefty with me wherever I go. Understand?"

"Yes Tony."

From that day on, Strampello regarded Louie as one of his most loyal and trustworthy lieutenants. He continually counseled Louie about the operation of the organization. And whenever the time was appropriate, Strampello promoted Louie to positions of higher importance within the organization.

Nicky also benefited by Louie's achievements. Each time Louie was promoted within the organization, he recommended that Nicky be bumped up also. Louie never forgot his twin.

Strampello trusted the Dago twins and knew they would not botch up any assignments. He didn't use the twins for all situations, only the sensitive ones. That's why Strampello insisted that Louie and Nicky be involved with the Rossi case.

"Sounds like Tony thinks this Rossi guy is somebody special," said Nicky.

"Yea."

"What do you think the connection is?"

"Don't know."

"Hope nothing goes wrong."

"Nothing better go wrong . . . for our sake."

CHAPTER 56

Marcello caught the first flight from Fort Lauderdale, Florida, to Omaha, Nebraska, the morning of October 30. Strampello never permitted any of his people to fly on a commercial aircraft when they were on the job. He feared the police may trace someone's whereabouts back to him. However, an exception had to be made for this assignment because there was insufficient time for Marcello to drive to Nebraska and make the necessary arrangements for the Walker situation. November 5 was only six days away.

Patsy Falvo, one of Johnnie Scarfone's boys, met Marcello at the airport. Patsy approached Marcello and introduced himself.

"I'm Patsy. I work for Scarfone."

"Thanks for picking me up."

"Johnnie's looking forward to seeing you."

As they walked down the concourse, Marcello said, "I got a lot of things to do in a short period of time."

"Don't worry about it. You'll get it done. We'll give you all the help you need."

"I appreciate that. My boss says you guys are all right."

Scarfone's house was a forty-five-minute ride from the airport. Turning onto the governor's driveway from Maple Road, Marcello noticed that there were men positioned at various locations throughout the premises. The Scarfone property looked as if it were a secured prison compound, with outside security lighting, surveillance cameras situated strategically throughout the property, and five Rottweiler dogs roaming the grounds. There was also barbed wire strung on top of the ten-foot high fencing outlining the perimeter of the property. Marcello chuckled to himself as he wondered whether these security measures were meant to keep intruders out or to keep them in once they penetrated the compound.

Patsy led Marcello to the patio at the rear of the home. When Marcello saw Scarfone, he walked over to him and kissed him on both cheeks.

"Thanks for all your help," said Marcello.

"My pleasure. How do you like your steak?"

"Bloody," said Marcello as he walked toward the barbeque pit.

"How's Tony doing?"

"He's good . . . Mr. Strampello sends his regards."

Scarfone flipped the steaks over before sprinkling them with Worcestershire sauce. "How can I help?" asked Scarfone.

"Mr. Strampello would like you to secure a house or a cabin where no one can hear and see anything. Our boys will do the rest."

Marcello waited for a response from Scarfone, but he said nothing. Scarfone was posturing Marcello.

Marcello again addressed Scarfone. "If you would grant Mr. Strampello this one request, he would be eternally grateful to you."

"When do you want the place?" asked Scarfone.

"November 5. We'll need it for about a month."

"No problem. Tell Tony I'll take care of it for him."

"Thanks, Mr. Scarfone."

Scarfone flipped the steaks that were searing on the grill before reaching for the gin and vermouth. "Do you want one or two olives in your martini?

CHAPTER 57

Dr. Rossi entered the lobby of the Downtown Marriott Hotel in Oklahoma City and made his way to the registration desk. Resting on an easel adjacent to the desk was a placard indicating that Dr. Thomas Starzel, the renowned transplant pioneer from Pittsburgh, Pennsylvania, would be the featured speaker for this year's medical conference.

The hotel lobby was bustling with men and women. Rossi believed many of the people in the lobby were physicians, like himself, who were here to attend the medical conference. However, unlike himself, Rossi knew the other registrants had actually planned on attending the seminars. Rossi had made other plans to amuse himself.

"May I help you?" asked the front desk clerk.

"Yes, I'd like to check in. My name is Dr. William Rossi."

The clerk typed in William Rossi and waited for the registration information to appear on the computer screen.

"You reside in Derry, Pennsylvania?" asked the hotel clerk.

"Yes, sir."

"I have you registered for a nonsmoking room with a king-size bed. Is that correct?"

"Yes."

"And you'll be checking out Sunday?"

"Is it possible to get a late check-out for Sunday?" asked Rossi.

"No problem, Doctor. Let me make that notation on the computer." As he typed in the request for a late checkout, the clerk discovered that a message for Dr. Rossi was attached to his preregistration. "There's a package here for you, Dr. Rossi." The clerk handed Rossi a small rectangular box, and Rossi placed it inside one of the pockets of his garment bag. He then asked the clerk where he should go to pick up his conference packet.

"Make a right at the gift shop and take the elevator to the mezzanine level."

Rossi replaced the credit card inside his wallet and made his way to the mezzanine level.

Rossi glanced at the seminar information as he rode the elevator to the eighth floor. Once inside his room, he opened the box which he received at the registration desk. Two objects were inside the box, a cellular telephone and a written note. The note, which was signed by Marcello, instructed him to dial a particular telephone number as soon as he unpacked his bag.

Minutes later, Rossi dialed the number using the cellular telephone. He immediately recognized the voice on the other end of the telephone. It was Marcello.

"Doc, is that you?" asked Marcello.

"Yes, it's me."

"Are you alone?"

"Yes."

"Listen very carefully," said Marcello. "We want you to be seen by as many people as possible at the hotel. Go to the lobby or to the bar and talk to other doctors. Make sure you introduce yourself so that you'll have an alibi."

"When can I leave for Omaha?" asked Rossi.

"Don't interrupt me again," barked Marcello. "If you can't follow instructions, we'll call this whole thing off. Understand?"

"I'm sorry," said Rossi in a softer tone of voice.

"All right. What's your room number?" asked Marcello.

Rossi glanced at the number listed on the telephone adjacent to the bed and said, "Room 8028."

"Make sure you put things in drawers and on countertops so that the maid thinks you're there," instructed Marcello.

"I will."

"One of my boys named Vinnie will come up to you at the bar and introduce himself as Dr. Ostrowski. Give him a key to your room. He'll be in and out of your room all weekend so that it looks like you're around."

"How will I recognize him?" asked Rossi.

"Don't worry about it. He'll know you."

"Do you have any questions?" asked Marcello.

"Yes. How do I get to Omaha?"

"At six thirty this evening, go out the front door and look for a dark blue Lincoln Continental. There'll be a limousine placard in the rear window. Get in the car and look at the driver's registration. It will be clipped to the passenger side sun visor. Make certain that the driver and the picture on the registration match. The driver's name is Nicky. He'll drive you to Omaha."

"I appreciate all your help," said Rossi.

"Forget about it. If you're a friend of Mr. Strampello, then you're a friend of mine."

CHAPTER 58

A chilly wind blew across the Western plains as the people of Omaha prepared themselves for the upcoming winter. The meteorologists predicted that the Midwest will have a relatively mild winter this year because of the effects of El Niño. However, the farmers and ranchers were not buying into their theories. The ranchers relied more on the *Farmer's Almanac* than anything else, and the almanac warned that the Midwest will experience a harsh and snowy winter this year. The ranchers, anticipating a bitter winter, packed their barns and silos with hay and corn so the horses and livestock would have an abundance of food for the winter months.

Jim Dumbrowski had mixed emotions with the coming of the winter season. He disliked this time of year because people had no need for his services, and this deprived him of the opportunity to make money. Yet he longed for the time off work to hunt, fish, and visit out-of-town friends and relatives.

However, winter had not yet arrived, and there were several things that Dumbrowski still needed to do before the first snowfall. Foremost on his to-do list was to inform Jack Armor that he would be laid off beginning next week. Dumbrowski enjoyed working alongside Armor, and he felt badly that he needed to let him go. He hoped Armor would stay in Omaha throughout the winter, but he realized he would probably leave town in search of work. He wouldn't have the money to sustain himself during this period of unemployment.

After placing his bagged lunch into the refrigerator, Armor walked toward Dumbrowski to find out what needed to be done this morning.

"Good morning, Jim."

"Hey, Jack."

"It's chilly this morning."

"It's getting that time of year."

"I hate the cold. Days like this make me wonder why I left LA."

"If you ever find out, be sure to tell Manning. He's dying to know."

"Hell with Manning. That guy pisses me off."

"He's really not a bad guy."

"Yea, he's a regular Yankee doodle dandy."

"He's a good guy once he gets to know you."

"I just wish he'd get off my case."

Armor reached for the coffee pot before strapping on his work apron. "What do you want me to do today?" asked Armor.

"How about fixing the wheel on DeMarco's cart?"

"No problem, boss."

Armor looked at the cart and discovered that there were several spokes missing from the right wheel. He removed the wheel and searched for a one-inch dial rod which was needed to repair the wheel.

Minutes later, Dumbrowski approached Armor and said, "Jack. We need to talk."

"What's up, boss?"

"I got to let you go."

"Did I do something to upset you?"

"Not at all . . . I've enjoyed having you here with me. It's just that things slow down this time of year, and I don't have any work for you."

Armor was disappointed to hear that he was going to lose his job. "No problem, boss. I understand."

"I wish I didn't have to let you go."

"I'm just appreciative that you gave me a job."

"What are you going to do?"

"I'm not sure. Maybe go back to LA."

"That'll confuse the hell out of Manning."

"Why would you say that?"

"Because his theory of you running away from something in Los Angeles will blow him away."

"I'd feel real bad about that."

"I'm sure you would."

Dumbrowski took out $50 from his wallet and offered it to Armor.

"What's this for?" asked Armor.

"Just a little something to help you get to LA."

"I'll be all right, Jim."

"Just take it. It'll make me feel better."

Armor shoved the money into his shirt pocket. "Thanks, Jim. Thanks for everything."

"I'll miss you, Jack."

"I know you will."

Armor opened the refrigerator door, removed his lunch, and waved goodbye to Dumbrowski as he left the stable.

CHAPTER 59

"What can I get you?" asked the bartender.

"Johnnie Walker Red with a splash of water," replied Rossi.

Dr. Rossi glanced at his watch and realized it was only 6:00 pm. He still had to wait a half hour before meeting Nicky. Rossi strolled around the lounge and looked for a familiar face from medical school or for a person he may have met at a previous conference. He didn't see anyone he knew. Rossi remembered that Marcello wanted him to mingle with other doctors so to establish an alibi in case he's implicated in the John Walker incident.

Rossi spotted a woman sitting by herself at a table near the piano player.

"Excuse me," he said. "Are you here for the medical seminar?"

"Yes, I am."

"May I buy you a drink?"

"I'm married."

"So am I. Would you like a drink?"

The woman hesitated for a moment and then said, "Whiskey sour please."

Rossi motioned for the waitress and ordered a whiskey sour for the woman and a scotch for himself. He then turned toward the woman and said, "My name is Bill Rossi."

"Nice to meet you, Bill. My name is Cindy."

"Where did you attend medical school?" asked Rossi.

"University of Pittsburgh. And you?"

"Temple University." Rossi groped for something intelligent to say, but his mind was as blank as a washed blackboard.

"Do you work in Pittsburgh?" asked Rossi.

"Yes. I'm affiliated with the University Health System."

"Pittsburgh is well respected in the health field. In fact, I believe Dr. Starzel is with the Pittsburgh group."

"Yes, he is . . . and I've had the opportunity to assist in one of his surgeries."

"That's great."

"Where do you practice?" asked Cindy.

"In a small community named Derry."

"You don't strike me as a small town guy."

"I'm really not. I had a surgical position at Mount Sinai Hospital in New York. But once my wife became pregnant with our daughter, we thought it best that we leave New York."

"How old is your daughter?"

"She would have been ten this year, but she passed away last October."

"I'm sorry to hear that," said Cindy.

"She died from complications from thalassemia."

Just then, the waitress returned with their drinks.

"Thalassemia is a terrible disease," said Cindy.

"Yes, it is."

Rossi took a sip from his drink and asked the woman, "What do you do for fun in Pittsburgh?"

"I follow Pitt football."

"No kidding. I would never have believed you to be a football junkie."

"My husband's the head coach."

"You're married to Tom Bailey?"

"Yes, I am."

"He's had a lot of success at Pitt. I still believe his 1981-1982 team was the best college football team ever."

"A lot of people feel the same way."

"That team was loaded with tremendous athletes: Dan Marino, Jumbo Covert, Mark May, Russ Grimm, Hugh Green, Ricky Jackson. What a team!"

"That certainly was an exciting year," said Mrs. Bailey.

The waitress interrupted Dr. Rossi and asked if there was anything else she could do for them. Rossi said they were fine. He then slipped her a $10 bill for the drinks and told her to keep the change.

"And Pitt played in the Sugar Bowl that year against Georgia," said Rossi.

"Yes. New Orleans was jumping that year."

"Perhaps you can answer this question for me?"

"What's that?"

"Why doesn't Pitt play Penn State any longer?"

"I don't know."

"You don't know, or you're not at liberty to say?"

"I really don't know. It's been said that Coach Sheffey holds some animosity against Pitt for a failed Eastern Football Conference."

"That's unfortunate," said Rossi. "Pitt and Penn State have battled each other for years."

"My husband thinks the series will start up again someday."

"I hope so."

Rossi glanced at his watch and realized it was 6:35 pm. "I'm sorry, Cindy, but I have to go. I promised my wife I would call her around six thirty."

"Thanks for the drink."

"See you later," said Rossi.

Rossi excused himself and proceeded to the exit sign. Before reaching the front door, he felt someone tap him on the shoulder. "Excuse me, but aren't you Dr. Rossi?"

"Yes, I am."

"You may not remember me, but I was a classmate of yours. My name is Stan Ostrowski."

"I remember you."

"I believe you have something for me," said Vinnie.

Rossi reached into his coat pocket, removed his room key, and handed it to Vinnie.

"Your limo is parked outside," said Vinnie.

"Thanks."

CHAPTER 60

Marcello and Louie were parked in the alley, waiting for Walker to appear from around the corner.

"You sure he comes this way?" asked Louie.

"That's what Scarfone said."

"Then where is he?"

"How the hell do I know?"

"Maybe he's not coming."

"Maybe you ought to shut the fuck up," said Marcello.

"Don't get bent out of shape. I didn't mean nothing."

Marcello glanced at his watch and realized it was seven twelve.

"If he's not here by seven thirty, we'll go to his house," said Marcello.

"I'm hungry," said Louie. "Do you mind if I go around the corner and grab a burger?"

"Go ahead, but hurry up."

"Do you want anything?"

"Bring me back a chocolate shake."

Louie got out of the car and ran up the alley. Shortly afterward, he returned to the car with a large bag of food. "What time you got?" asked Louie.

"Seven twenty-five."

Marcello glanced at the side mirror on his automobile and saw a man with a suitcase walking down the alley. "Stuff the burger down, big guy. I think our boy's coming."

"Tell him to wait until I finish eating."

"He's about forty feet away."

"Damn it."

As Walker neared the car, Marcello said, "Get ready."

Louie jumped out of the car and grabbed Walker by the arm. "Leaving town, John?"

"My name's Jack. You got the wrong guy."

"Jack, John. Whatever the fuck you call yourself. Get in the car."

Louie shoved Walker into the backseat and slid in beside him.

"Who are you guys?" asked Walker.

Louie and Marcello didn't say a word.

"What's this all about?" asked Walker.

Again, Louie and Marcello didn't respond.

"You're making a mistake."

Louie placed his gun against Walker's head and said, "You say another word, and I'll kill you."

Walker didn't say anything for the remainder of the time he was inside the car. Marcello drove an hour before reaching the dirt road which led to the cabin.

"We're almost there," Marcello told Walker. "Your new home is at the end of the road."

Walker, feeling anxious about all that had happened, hoped that Louie hadn't noticed the perspiration that was forming on his forehead and hands.

"Welcome to Chez, Walker," said Marcello. "We hope you enjoy your stay."

The A-frame cabin was nestled in the woods, miles away from any neighbors. On the wraparound porch sat two white wicker rocking chairs, positioned on both sides of the front door, and angled ever so slightly toward each other.

The area was void of chirping crickets or passing cars; it was eerily quiet. Walker believed if he were here for any other reason, he would probably enjoy the serenity. However, he had no idea why he was abducted. And more importantly, he had no idea what these people planned to do to him. But he sensed that whatever was planned, it would be unpleasant.

"Keep moving," said Louie. "We need to get you settled in before your host arrives."

Walker cautiously walked up the stone walkway as he scanned the area for a possible means of escape. Louie opened the front door and shoved Walker inside the cabin. Upon entering the room, Walker stood before a large stone fireplace which extended from ceiling to floor. Remnants of burnt logs were still in the fireplace. Two recliner chairs, situated on either side of the fireplace, outlined the north wall of the Great Room. An overstuffed couch and a round eating table with four chairs were also in the great room. But what concerned Walker the most was the door at the southeast corner of the room. He believed the door provided access to the basement, a portal to unholy things.

Marcello grabbed Walker's right arm. "Sit down," he commanded.

Louie walked toward Marcello and asked, "Should we tie him up?"

"Na. He's not going nowhere."

Marcello looked toward Walker and said, "Johnnie, I'd like to take you downstairs, but your host wants to personally escort you to your suite. He wants to see the expression on your face as you enter the room."

Walker was petrified; he didn't say anything.

Louie looked at his watch and whispered to Marcello. "Rossi won't be here for a while yet. How about a game of gin?"

"Nickel a point?" asked Marcello.

"Deal."

CHAPTER 61

Rossi walked out of the Marriott Hotel and saw the Lincoln Continental parked near the hotel entrance. As he approached the Lincoln, the chauffeur got out of the car and opened the rear passenger side door.

"Good evening, Dr. Rossi. My name is Nicky Salvatore."

Rossi slid into the backseat and immediately looked at the registration on the sun visor. The name and the picture of the person on the registration indicated the chauffer was who he said he was. Rossi then leaned forward and tapped the driver on the shoulder.

"Mr. Salvatore," said Rossi.

"Everybody calls me Nicky."

"Nicky . . . how long does it take to drive to Omaha?"

"About seven hours."

"So we won't arrive until one thirty?"

"Something like that."

Rossi slid back into a more relaxed position and picked up the *Playboy* magazine resting on the seat beside him. "I didn't realize Lincolns came equipped with *Playboy*," said Rossi.

"I had to amuse myself somehow," replied Nicky.

"You could have read *The Grapes of Wrath*."

"Right."

Rossi grinned, thinking this guy probably doesn't read anything other than smut magazines.

Nicky turned to face the backseat. "You been waiting a long time for this day!"

"It's been 373 days," said Rossi. "And I mentally rehearsed what I'll do to him each one of those days."

"What are you going to do to this guy?"

"What would you do to someone who raped and killed your daughter?" asked Rossi.

"I'd torture the motherfucker!"

Rossi chose the appropriate words before responding.

"That's inhumane," said Rossi. "I won't bring myself down to his level."

"Then what are you going to do?"

"I'm not sure . . . I'm supposed to be here for a medical seminar. Maybe I'll do something educational."

Nicky cocked his head in such a way to convey that he was confused by the doctor's statement.

"What's that supposed to mean?" asked Nicky.

Rossi didn't say a word. The sinister smile on his face said it all.

CHAPTER 62

The drive to the cabin was uneventful. However, with less than two miles to go, Nicky became confused as to which fork in the road to take. He mapped out the route to the cabin just the week before with one of Scarfone's men. They made the trial run to the cabin during the day, not at night; all the roads looked alike to Nicky at night.

Nicky realized he had chosen the wrong pathway when the road ended abruptly. Consequently, he and Rossi didn't reach the cabin until 2:00 am.

The headlights of the Lincoln shined as brightly as a Hollywood movie premier as Nicky navigated the car along the tree-lined driveway leading to the cabin. The light beams danced across the front windows of the cabin. Marcello saw the lights of the approaching car and shouted out to Louie.

"Turn off the lights! It might be the cops."

Louie turned off the lights as Marcello kept his eyes glued to the approaching car. Moments later, Marcello watched as a dark-colored Lincoln emerged out of the darkness. "It's them," he said.

Louie turned on the lights and walked toward Walker. "Johnnie, your host has arrived."

A creaking sound was heard as the front door swung open. Walker's heart thumped at twice its normal rate. The palms of his hands and his forehead were wet with perspiration. Walker was frightened. He sensed danger. He had no idea who was about to walk through the front door, but he had no doubts that this person wanted to harm him.

Louie and Marcello greeted Nicky as he walked into the room. Nicky looked at Walker and said, "I hope you haven't been waiting for us *too* long . . . We got here as quickly as possible."

Walker felt a surge of adrenaline flow throughout his body. He was afraid he would lose control of his bladder and urinate in his pants. Walker couldn't take his eyes off the front door, knowing the next person to pass through the threshold would be his so-called host.

Walker's jaw dropped as Dr. Rossi walked into the room.

"Hello, John," said Rossi. "Long time no see."

Walker didn't say a word. He was surprised to see Dr. Rossi walk through the doorway.

"Have my friends been cordial to you? Can I get you anything? Perhaps a beer or a cup of coffee?"

"What's this all about, Dr. Rossi?"

"You have to answer for Courtney's death."

"What are you talking about?"

"Don't deny what you did, John. Or should I call you Jack?"

Walker hesitated momentarily before answering. "There has to be a mistake, Dr. Rossi. I didn't kill your daughter."

Rossi bit his lower lip as he rolled his head in a circular fashion. "I guess she molested herself . . . I guess she cut her own throat."

"I didn't do anything like that, Dr. Rossi."

Rossi turned and slowly began to walk away from Walker. Without looking back Rossi asked, "If you didn't kill my daughter, then why did you change your name and run away to Nebraska?"

"I didn't kill your daughter," said Walker. "Really, I didn't."

"Then why did you run and hide?"

"I was afraid I'd be arrested for kidnapping."

"What?" asked Rossi.

"I was angry because I was forced to leave your precious little town. I kidnapped your daughter to scare everyone."

"And you didn't kill her?"

"No, I didn't."

"I guess you left her unharmed, left her where you knew we would find her."

"I swear that's what happened."

"You expect me to believe this?"

"That's the truth Dr. Rossi."

Rossi walked toward Walker and positioned himself directly in front of his guest. "I *don't* believe you. And if you keep denying that you killed my daughter, then I'll kill you right here and now."

Rossi stared at Walker and waited for a response. When Walker didn't say anything, Rossi inched closer. He now stood chin to chin with this man. "If you lie to me, I'll kill you right now. If you tell me the truth, I promise I'll spare your life."

A lump formed in Walker's throat as he regurgitated the burritos he ate for dinner.

"Tell me the truth," screamed Rossi.

Walker lowered his head and said, "I killed her."

Rossi maintained a poker face as Walker confessed to killing his daughter. He just stared at Walker with piercing eyes. Minutes later, Rossi lowered himself into one of the wicker chairs and said, "How could you have killed my little girl?"

Rossi stood up and walked toward Walker. "I've fantasized about killing you for an entire year. I've dreamt about doing unspeakable things to you. Now, that I've finally found you, I can't kill you . . . I promised I would let you live if you confessed to murdering my daughter."

Rossi paced back and forth as he searched his mind for the appropriate words to say. "I promised to let you live and live you will. But before I'm through with you, you'll beg me to kill you!"

Walker didn't say anything. He knew he was damned whether he admitted to killing Courtney or whether he denied doing so. He prayed that Sheriff Manning would walk into the cabin and break up this lynch mob. He wished he had never seen or heard of Dr. Rossi or the town of Derry.

"John, let's go downstairs. You and I are going to have some fun . . . At least I'll enjoy myself."

CHAPTER 63

Rossi opened the door that led to the basement, flipped up the light switch, and walked down the stairs. Reluctantly, with a little nudging from Louie, Walker followed Rossi. When Rossi reached the bottom of the stairs, he stepped to his right and methodically surveyed the basement.

"Is this how you wanted everything set up Dr. Rossi?" asked Louie.

"It's absolutely perfect."

Rossi walked around the basement and repositioned some of the equipment. Walker, on the other hand, quickly scanned the entire room when he reached the basement floor. Walker's greatest fears were now realized. He stood as motionless as a mime. He could not believe what he was seeing.

"Does any of this look familiar to you John?" asked Rossi.

Walker said nothing.

"I suppose not . . . You were close to death the last time you were near anything like this."

In the center of the basement stood a wooden picnic table draped with a white unfitted bedsheet. On either side of this makeshift surgical table were two pole lamps fitted with spotlights. The lights were angled in such a way that the beams of light converged at the top half of the table. A mobile cart, filled with syringes, zylocaine, sterile gauze, sutures, scalpels, and hemostats, was positioned adjacent to the surgical table. There were also two one liter bottles of 5 percent dextrose and saline solutions suspended from a portable carrier on the side of the bed opposite the cart.

"What are you going to do with me?" asked Walker.

"I'm going to make sure you'll never be able to do anything like that again."

Rossi walked toward the work area and situated himself along the right side of the table. He then turned toward Louie and said, "Help our patient onto the bed."

Louie grabbed Walker by the arm and led him to the sheet covered table. Louie then handed Walker a bed gown and told him to put it on.

"You guys are nuts!" shouted Walker.

Louie fired back, "Shut the fuck up and get on the table!"

Walker climbed onto the table and turned his head to the left. He watched Rossi as he removed a needle from a plastic sheath and placed the needle on the mobile cart. Rossi then took a second syringe from the cart, pushed the plunger to make certain there were no air bubbles trapped inside the carpule, and positioned himself next to Walker.

"Before I begin," said Rossi, "I want to inject you with penicillin. One cannot be too cautious these days. If you become infected, you may decide to sue me."

Walker turned his head away in disgust.

"John, are you allergic to penicillin?"

Walker didn't respond.

"Well, I'll assume you're not allergic to penicillin. If you go into anaphylactic shock, don't blame me."

Rossi took the syringe filled with penicillin and injected the contents into Walker's left arm. He then picked up the other syringe and said, "I'm going to insert this intravenous needle into the large vein on your left hand. You may feel a slight burning sensation."

Walker winced as Rossi inserted the needle.

"I'm sorry if that hurt," said Rossi. "I normally have one of my surgical nurses start the IV for me."

"What are you going to do to me?" asked Walker

A sinister smile again formed on Rossi's face.

"We'll talk again when you wake up John. Count backward from 5."

"You guys are crazy," said Walker with a slurred speech due to the effects of the anesthetic. "You're all . . ."

Those were the last words spoken by Walker before succumbing to the effects of the anesthetic.

Rossi placed tourniquets above Walker's wrists before reaching for the instrument which resembled a metal cutting tool. With great expertise, Rossi removed the fingers and thumbs on both hands. Although Dr. Rossi took precautions to minimize blood loss, a stream of blood flowed along the creases of the bedsheet onto a single puddle of blood. Louie thought the merging of the various lines of blood looked like rivers flowing downstream to a common tributary.

"Louie, can you assist me?" asked Rossi.

"What do you want me to do?"

"Get some gauze and apply pressure to these stumps."

"I don't know about this, Doc."

"I need your help to control the bleeding."

Louie reluctantly approached the triage site and grabbed a handful of gauze. He applied pressure to areas where moments ago were lined with fingers.

"Is this right?" asked Louie.

"You're doing great."

Rossi began to suture the amputation sites. After making certain that the bleeding was controlled, Rossi started an IV drip of dextrose and saline solutions to guard against dehydration. He also inserted a morphine drip to permit Walker to self-administer the narcotic as needed to control pain. Rossi then bandaged Walker's hands and checked his vital signs before removing his surgical gown and gloves.

"Thanks for your help," said Rossi.

"Anytime, Doc. But wouldn't it have been easier to just shoot him?"

"Sometimes easier isn't better. I have plans for Mr. Walker."

"And people think *we're* a barbaric bunch of guys."

Rossi glanced at his wristwatch and was surprised to discover that it was 6:15 am. "Let's get some sleep . . . It's been a long day."

"What do we do if Walker wakes up before we do?" asked Louie.

"If he wakes up before we do, we'll hear him on this battery-operated intercom. But I doubt he'll wake up because of the IV and the morphine drip."

"But what if we don't hear him because we're in a deep sleep?"

"So what? He's not going anywhere."

"You're right, Doc. Go to bed. I'll be up as soon as I clean up this mess."

Louie was abruptly awakened by Walker's moans at 10:30 am. He slowly dragged himself out of bed and staggered to his feet. *I don't know why we just didn't shoot the son of a bitch,* Louie thought to himself.

He walked down the hallway and rapped on Rossi's bedroom door. "Doc, I'm sorry to disturb you, but your patient's calling."

"What's happening?" responded Rossi in a bewildered-like manner.

"I heard him moaning."

Rossi got out of bed, washed his face, and made his way to the basement to check on Walker. "How's my patient doing this morning?" Rossi asked sarcastically.

"What have you done to me?"

"I noticed that gangrene was developing in your thumbs and fingers. I thought it was in your best interest to amputate them before the necrotic tissue spread to your wrists and arms."

"You what?"

"I had to control your infection."

"I don't know why you're doing this to me."

"You know why . . . Just think about it."

Walker slowly turned his head from one side to the other.

"Are you in a lot of pain, John?"

Walker nodded.

"Whenever the pain becomes too intense, use your elbow to push this button. Morphine will be released and the pain will go away. Go ahead, push the button."

Walker struggled at first but eventually managed to dispense the narcotic.

"Get some rest, John. You need to regain your strength to fight off the infection."

Rossi checked on Walker several times throughout the day, making certain that he was not bleeding more than expected. Walker faded in and out much of the day, remaining conscious only for the amount of time necessary to dispense another measured dose of morphine.

The next morning, Rossi went to the basement to evaluate Walker's medical status. He was surprised to find Walker awake and lucid.

"Good morning, John. How are you feeling today?"

Walker turned his head away from Rossi.

"Is your pain still intense?"

Again, Walker ignored Rossi's question.

"I know you're upset with me, but I need to know how much pain you're experiencing.

"Go fuck yourself."

"It sounds like you're feeling better . . . That's great because we need to wean you off the narcotics. I don't want you to become a drug addict."

Walker didn't find that last statement amusing.

"Are you hungry?" asked Rossi.

"No . . . How could anyone have an appetite after having his fingers and thumbs cut off?"

"I'm going to insert a feeding tube into your other hand. We need to maintain proper electrolyte and nutritional values for you.

Rossi inserted a second IV needle into Walker. "This should replenish your electrolytes."

"I hope you're not expecting a thank you from me."

Rossi smiled at Walker. "You don't have to thank me, Mr. Walker. I'll do everything humanly possible to keep you alive. And that's a promise!"

Knowing that his daughter's murderer was asleep in the basement, Rossi entertained thoughts of ending this charade by slamming Walker's head with a ten-pound sledge hammer. However, he did not succumb to this temptation. Instead, he decided to leave the cabin for a few hours to clear the cobwebs from his mind and to refocus on the task at hand. He wandered through the woods until he came upon a large oblong-shaped boulder. He decided this was as good a place as any to sit and relax.

Walking through the woods reminded Rossi of the many walks he took in Central Park while working as a surgical resident. He remembered how he longed to stroll through the park after a strenuous day at the hospital. Other hospital residents frequented bars or exercised at gyms as their choice of relaxation. Rossi preferred to go to the park. There was no better therapy for him than to take a nature walk and observe the creatures in their natural habitat.

While resting on the bolder, Rossi thought of Andrea. He reminisced about the day when he first met her. He recalled how beautiful she looked, sitting on the park bench reading a book, with the wind gently blowing through her hair. He remembered how it excited him to telephone her at the end of a hectic day and how the sound of her voice relieved all his tensions. How simple life was back then.

One memory after another raced through his mind. He reminisced about the weekend trip they took to Paris, the romantic dinner at Maxim's and the entertaining show at the Lido. He also mentally relived the excitement he experienced with the birth of his children.

But not all memories that entered Rossi's mind were pleasant. He remembered how his father-in-law, the mighty Andrew Watson, intimated him and made him feel inferior. He relived the moment when Dr. Gaffney confirmed that Courtney had a terminal genetic blood disorder. And he could not repress the morbid thoughts of his daughter's sexual assault and murder, regardless how hard he tried.

Rossi became filled with rage each time he thought about how frightened his little girl must have been moments before her death. Whenever he thought of the pain and suffering Courtney endured that night, his abdominal muscles became so tense that he would double over in pain.

Rossi was certain that Walker was the person responsible for these sordid memories, and he vowed to hold Walker accountable for them.

Rossi returned to the cabin at dusk. As he walked through the doorway, he was greeted by Louie. "I thought you got lost. I was ready to organize a search party for you."

Rossi smiled as he shut and locked the door behind him. "I was just taking a little stroll . . . I needed a few minutes alone."

"You hungry, Doc?" asked Louie.

"That depends . . . What's for dinner?"

"We have Stouffer's macaroni and cheese or Swedish meatballs. Which one do you want?"

"I'd prefer a three-pound Maine lobster," said Rossi.

"I want a blonde with big tits, but we no got."

Rossi walked toward the stove and said, "I guess I'll take the meatballs."

"Coming right up."

Rossi took off his jacket and hung it in the hallway closet.

"How's Walker doing?" asked Rossi.

"All right, I guess. He's been pretty quiet today."

"I'm going to check on him."

Rossi opened the basement door and walked down the stairs. He placed two fingers on Walker's left carotid artery, felt for his pulse, and discovered that the pulse rate was sixty-eight. Walker awakened during Rossi's cursory examination.

"How's my patient doing?" asked Rossi.

"Peachy."

"I want to clean the wound site and change the gauze."

Rossi carefully cut away the bloodied gauze and exposed the hands.

"Everything looks great, John. I'd say the surgery was successful."

Walker looked at his hands for the first time since having his fingers amputated. The muscles around Walker's mouth seemed to move up and down in response to the anger and tension that he felt.

"Hey, John . . . how about giving me a hand," Rossi said in a sarcastic manner.

"You're a sick fuck," said Walker.

"And you're a predator."

Rossi cleaned the wounds and again wrapped the hands with sterile gauze.

"I'll be back in a few days," said Rossi. "I have other patients to see back in Derry."

"You can't leave me alone like this."

"My associates Louie and Marcello will check up on you periodically. You'll be okay."

Walker turned his head away from Dr. Rossi.

"See you next weekend, John."

Marcello drove Rossi back to Oklahoma City. Later that evening, Rossi checked out of the hotel and made his way to the airport. There, he waited until it was time to board the late-night flight to Philadelphia.

Louie was instructed to remain at the cabin. He was charged with the responsibility of caring for Walker.

CHAPTER 64

Rossi was back to work early Monday morning. Even though he was unable to sleep on the airplane, he felt as rested and as invigorated as he had in months. The weekend activities Rossi shared with Walker had more of an effect on him than if he had ingested a vial of stimulants.

Rossi bumped into his friend Dr. Wilson at the hematology laboratory later that morning. He had not crossed paths with Wilson in several weeks, and the lab was the place he least expected to see him.

Wilson darted toward Rossi with an extended hand. "How have you been, Bill?"

"Never been better!"

"I can't remember when I saw you last. What have you been doing?"

"A little this and a little that."

"What?"

"I just returned from Oklahoma . . . I took a continuing-education course last weekend."

"Did you find the seminar enlightening?"

"Extremely," replied Rossi. "Dr. Starzel spoke on human organ transplants."

"How much did this seminar set you back?"

"Just $2,000."

"Pretty steep."

"Not really . . . the tuition includes three weekends of seminars."

"That's still a lot of money."

Rossi thought of Walker. "I believe I'm getting my money's worth."

"And you're going back to Oklahoma again this weekend?"

"The next *two* weekends."

"You seem to be at peace with yourself."

"To tell you the truth, I've mourned for Courtney for so long that I became depressed. Just getting away and associating with other physicians, even if only for a few days, has done a world of good for me."

"I've been a little bummed out myself lately," said Wilson. "Perhaps I should go with you next weekend."

Rossi was startled by Wilson's suggestion that he accompany him to Oklahoma City. "I don't know if you can still register for the seminar," said Rossi. The conference involves three consecutive weekends, and you already missed the first weekend."

"Settle down, big guy . . . I was only joking. I can't go anywhere right now. I have four ladies with buns in the oven who are ready to drop any day now."

Rossi was relieved to hear that Wilson was not serious about joining him in Oklahoma. "That's too bad . . . I think we would have had a great time together."

"Perhaps another time."

"I'll look forward to it."

The remainder of the week was uneventful for Rossi. Other than his daily rituals of working till late and eating a Swanson TV dinner while watching the evening news on CBS, his only other obligation for the week was to call Andrea.

Rossi called his wife Thursday night. Although she was pleased to hear from him, she wondered what motivated him to do so. Rossi confessed that he had missed her and that he couldn't stop thinking about her. The truth be told, he wanted to be certain that she had not planned on coming home this weekend. Rossi didn't want his plans for the upcoming weekend ruined. He anticipated another fun-filled weekend!

Rossi felt more relaxed this weekend than last. He knew exactly what to expect and what to do. He mentally prepared for this weekend with the same thoroughness as he displayed as a surgical resident.

Rossi knew the routine. He would register at the hotel and mingle with some physicians until it was time to meet Nicky. Immediately upon arriving at the cabin, he would examine Walker and reevaluate his medical condition. However, this would be a cursory evaluation; Rossi already knew what his findings would be without having to examine his patient.

When Rossi entered the cabin at 8:30 pm, he detected a pungent odor. The stench permeated throughout the entire two floors. Rossi became concerned that the source of the odor may have been coming from the basement. However, after a quick inspection of the cabin, he realized the odor emanated from the kitchen. Dishes, with hardened bits of food, were stacked high in the kitchen sink.

Rossi searched for Louie and found him asleep on the bed, with soiled clothes strewn across the bedroom floor.

"The place looks like a pig sty," said Rossi.

"*Excuse me* . . . I gave the maid the day off."

"And how's our boy doing?"

"I hardly knew he was here."

Rossi carried his valet into the bedroom and began to unpack his clothes. He placed a picture of Courtney on the left corner of his bedroom dresser to help him focus on the task at hand.

Louie knocked on Rossi's bedroom door. "You hungry, Doc?"

"Do you have any Swedish meatballs?"

"Nah. I got some Hungry Man Dinners. Can I fix you one?"

"I'll pass."

"Suit yourself."

After placing his valet under the bed, Rossi decided to check on Walker. "How's it going, John? Did you miss me?"

Walker didn't respond to the sarcasm.

"Are you in pain?"

Again, Walker was silent.

"Let's see how you're healing."

Rossi removed the bandages and examined Walker's hands. "Now I want you to wiggle your fingers."

Walker wanted to spit in Rossi's face, but he thought otherwise. Rossi sensed Walker's resentment and said, "Don't flick me off, John."

Rossi stepped to the rear of the gurney. "John, I apologize for being insensitive . . . that was very rude of me." Rossi then repositioned himself alongside Walker. "I'm concerned that your surgical sites look angry. I'm going to administer an antibiotic to help control the infection." Rossi connected an antibiotic drip to the IV tube. "This should help," he said.

Rossi removed his latex gloves and threw them into the waste receptacle. Before returning upstairs, Rossi again addressed Walker. "I think you'll be okay . . . I'll check on you in the morning. But I want you to promise me that you won't leave. Can I trust that you'll be here when I return in the morning?"

"Fuck you!" shouted Walker.

"I'll check on you in the morning. Hopefully, the antibiotic will take affect by then."

Rossi walked upstairs and saw Louie standing in front of the sink basin, washing the filth from the dishes which accumulated from last week's meals. "I didn't know you had it in you," said Rossi.

"What's that?"

"I didn't realize there's a domestic side to your rough and tough persona."

"There are a lot of things you don't know about me," said Louie.

"So the less I know about you, the better it is?"

"It's more like, the less you know about me, the *healthier* you'll be."

Rossi awoke early Saturday morning and jumped into the same clothes he wore the night before. He was eager to check on Walker. As he made his way from the bedroom to the basement, Rossi passed by the kitchen doorway. There, he noticed that Louie had whipped up a batch of hotcakes.

"How's about a short stack?" asked Louie.

"No, thanks . . . I'm not very hungry this morning."

"Are you going downstairs?"

"I need to check on our boy."

Rossi walked down the stairs and noticed that Walker was awake. "Hey, buddy. How's it going?"

Walker remained motionless; he refused to acknowledge that Rossi had spoken to him.

Rossi moved closer toward Walker and pulled back the bedsheet. "We have a problem, old boy."

Walker quickly turned his head to face Rossi. "What are you talking about?"

"I don't know how to say this, but it doesn't look like the antibiotic is working."

A frightened look appeared on Walker's face. "What do you have to do?"

"There's only one thing that can be done," said Rossi. "I need to operate."

"Please don't cut off my hands," pleaded Walker.

"I won't . . . I need to cut off your toes."

Walker couldn't believe what he heard. "Are you nuts?"

"They're infected, John . . . Don't you understand?"

"There's nothing wrong with my toes."

"Who's the doctor here, me or you? If I say your toes are infected, then they're infected."

"You're really fucked up."

Rossi prepped Walker for surgery. He doused the surgical site with an antiseptic, and he introduced an anesthetic into the IV line. He again asked Walker to count backward, beginning with 5.

As soon as Walker fell into an unconscious state, Rossi began to amputate his toes. Beginning with the "pinky" on the left food and ending with the "pinky" on the right foot, Rossi removed all ten toes.

Curiosity got the best of Louie, so he decided to go to the basement to observe what Rossi was doing. But he got to the basement too late; Rossi had already discarded his gloves into the wastebasket. However, he noticed that Walker's feet were wrapped with surgical gauze. "You didn't do what I think you did . . . did you, Doc?"

"His toes were infected."

"Sure they were. And I was Cinderella in another life."

Rossi chuckled.

"Remind me not to get on your bad side," said Louie.

Rossi adjusted the feeding tube and the IV line before heading upstairs. "Let's get out of here," said Rossi. "He'll sleep most of the day."

CHAPTER 65

Sheriff Manning drove to Dumbrowski's at daybreak. He wanted a face to face discussion with Armor. He walked inside the livery stable and looked for Armor, but he was nowhere to be found.

Manning then saw Dumbrowski standing near the horses. "What's going on, Jim?" asked Manning.

"Just putting things away for the winter."

"Where's Jack?"

"Had to let him go. Things been pretty slow the last couple of weeks."

Manning picked up a minisledge and looked at it as if he had never seen a sledge hammer before in his life. "Where did he go?"

"Not sure. I heard him say something about LA."

Manning placed the sledge back on the workbench.

"You were tough on him," said Dumbrowski.

"There's something about that boy that doesn't sit right with me."

"Like what?"

"Don't know. But I got a feeling there's some history with that boy."

Manning paced back and forth as Dumbrowski continued to put things away in their respective drawers.

"I liked the boy," said Dumbrowski. "I just think he had a bad childhood."

"Don't be surprised if we haven't heard the last of him."

"I hope you're wrong, George. I really hope you're wrong."

CHAPTER 66

After spending ten consecutive days and nights at the cabin, Louie felt as if he had done a stretch in "the big house." He didn't care where he went or what he did—he just needed to go somewhere, anywhere!

"What do you want to do?" asked Rossi.

"Want to see a movie?"

"Nah . . . Movies are so violent nowadays."

"I can understand how you feel . . . You've shown a real aversion for violence," Louie stated sarcastically.

Rossi was surprised that a thug like Louie would use a word such as aversion in his everyday speech. "Let's go to a shopping mall," said Rossi.

"I don't know, Doc. Strampello wouldn't like that. He'd say that someone may recognize us and connect us with Walker."

"I guess you're right."

After a few moments, Rossi suggested they get a bottle of wine and find a quiet place to party. They stopped at a gas station and asked the attendant if there was a liquor store nearby. The attendant, wearing a grey tee shirt underneath his grease-stained overalls, said there were two liquor stores about a mile away. One establishment, the Pigley Wigley supermarket, was located on Constitution Boulevard; the other facility was the Wal-Mart near the intersection of Broward and University. He suggested we go to the Pigley Wigley because its prices were better.

The Pigley Wigley had a liquor section as diverse and as complete as any liquor store that Louie or Rossi had ever visited.

Two complete aisles were set aside for alcoholic products, eliciting a comment from Louie that people in Nebraska probably had nothing better to do than get drunk.

The wines stood upright on aisle 2, toward the rear of the store. Rossi scanned the shelves before finding the wine he most preferred. He reached for the bottle of white Zinfandel and placed it inside his basket. Moments later, Louie called out from the end of the aisle, "I don't do white wines, Doc."

Rossi put the Zinfandel back on the shelf and picked up two bottles of merlot. Louie grabbed a king-size bag of Snyder's of Berlin Potato Chips, a container of sour cream dip, and an inexpensive cork screw before joining Rossi at the checkout line.

They drove approximately fifteen miles out of town before coming upon a vacant patch of land formerly known as the O.K. Campgrounds. This campground was anything but okay. The lawn areas were overgrown with straggly looking grass, the men's restroom door was hanging by a single hinge, and there were weeds growing within the cracks of the ceramic tiled swimming pool. The facility looked as if it had not been used in years. What better place to sit and drink than a deserted parcel of land, thought Louie.

Louie ripped open the bag of potato chips while Rossi struggled with the cork. "I hate cheap cork screws," said Rossi. "The corks never come out like they're supposed to." Just as Rossi voiced his displeasure with inexpensive cork screws, the cork fractured, leaving the larger portion of the cork embedded within the neck of the bottle.

Louie looked at Rossi and said, "Give me the bottle, Doc."

Rossi handed the bottle of wine to Louie. "I'll show you how to pop a cork." Louie grabbed the car key and jabbed at the cork until it slid inside the bottle. "Problem solved."

"Where's the wine glasses?" asked Rossi.

"I thought you brought the glasses," Louie answered sarcastically.

"What do we do now?"

"You got AIDS, Doc?"

"No. Why do you ask?"

Louie put the bottle in his mouth and took a big gulp. "Do you want a swig?"

"Why not?"

They drank wine and snacked on chips and sour cream until the sun fell from the sky. Louie placed his hand on Rossi's wrist and said, "I never hung out with any doctors before. You're different from what I imagined."

"What did you expect me to be like?"

"Some uptight asshole who thought he was better than everyone else."

"What do you think of me now?" asked Rossi as he hoisted the wine bottle to his lips.

"You're not uptight at all . . . You're just an asshole!"

Rossi burst into laughter, causing the wine to dribble down his chin and onto his shirt.

"Can I ask you a question?" asked Louie.

"Shoot."

"What made you want to become a doctor?"

Rossi hesitated momentarily. "I had a sister who died when she was very young. She had cystic fibrosis."

"Cystic what?"

"Cystic fibrosis . . . It's a disease that affects the lungs and makes it impossible to breathe."

"That's it?" asked Louie.

"I was touched by the care given to my sister. It made a lasting impression on me."

"You're a compassionate guy . . . How were you able to do what you did to Walker?"

Rossi again hesitated before answering the question. "Because of what he did to my daughter."

"I understand," said Louie.

"And I hate him for making me do this to him."

Louie took another drink from the bottle. "You didn't have to chop the guy up, Doc . . . You could have called the police and had him arrested."

"I would never have had him arrested."

"Why not?"

"I'd be worried that he'd get off on some technicality."

"How would that happen?"

"He'd hire a good attorney, like Lucky Bowers, who would work his magic and make it appear like Walker was a choirboy. Or perhaps some incompetent policeman would compromise the evidence, resulting in a ruling that the evidence is now inadmissible in court."

"You got a point, Doc."

"I'm making sure that justice *will* be served," said Rossi.

Rossi took one more swig from the bottle before passing it to Louie. "Let's get back to the cabin . . . I need to check on my patient."

Rossi approached Walker and found him conscious and alert. He reached for Walker's wrist to check his pulse.

"Why did you do this to me?"

Rossi was not concerned with answering Walker's question; he was more interested in monitoring his vital signs. "Your pulse rate is seventy-six. It's slightly elevated, but considering all that you've been through, it's not too bad."

Rossi removed the bandages covering Walker's feet and noticed that the tissues were healing nicely. There were no signs of inflammation. "Everything looks good, John. Don't worry about this yellowish-looking tissue outlining the incisions. That's granulation tissue. It's normal healing tissue."

Walker attempted to lift himself off the table, but he was unable to do so. He looked at Rossi with disgust. "I can't believe you mutilated me."

"You haven't seen anything yet," responded Rossi.

"You're making a mistake, Dr. Rossi. I didn't kill your daughter."

"I suppose it was just a coincidence that the only serious crime committed in Derry since the beginning of time occurred when you were in town."

"All I can say is I didn't kill her."

Rossi turned away from Walker and faced the makeshift surgical table. "Yes you did!" shouted Rossi.

"Someday you'll find the person who killed your daughter. Then you'll have to live with yourself for the rest of your life for doing this to me."

Rossi didn't respond to anything Walker said. He just continued to organize the instruments in an orderly fashion.

"I wish I died the day you operated on me," said Walker.

Rossi turned toward Walker and said, "Me too."

"Just kill me now if it will make you feel better."

"Killing you would be too humane . . . I never want you to forget me or forget what you did to Courtney."

Realizing he could not reason with Rossi, Walker made one final plea for clemency. "If you're not planning to kill me, then let me go. There's not much else you can do to me."

"You'd be surprised what I can still do to you."

"What are you going to do . . . castrate me?" Walker asked sarcastically.

"I'm offended that you think I'm capable of doing something like that. I would *never* castrate you . . . I wouldn't want to deprive you of your masculinity. But don't you worry, my friend . . . I still have one or two more things that I'm saving just for you."

"There's nothing more you can do to make me feel any worse than I feel now."

"Everything will be over soon. By this time next week, you'll be feeling peachy.

"Like I said before, go fuck yourself. I don't care what you do to me. You're not a doctor. You're not even a human being. You're a monster who never deserved your daughter."

"I'll tell you what, John. I was going to conclude my business with you next weekend. But since you seem to harbor some resentment toward me, I'll do you a favor and complete my treatment of you right now."

Rossi slipped into his surgical gown one last time. He then leaned over Mr. Walker and said, "When you wake up this time, your life, as you know it, will be over. You won't be able to speak, you won't be able to hear, and you won't be able to see. The last thing you will see is me before drifting off into an unconscious state. Once you recover from the surgery, you will be taken to town and left on a sidewalk. You will live the remainder of your life knowing who did this to you, but you won't be able to tell anyone. You'll be unable to speak because you won't have a tongue, you'll be unable to write because you won't have any fingers or toes, you'll be unable to see because you'll be blind, and you'll be unable to hear because your auditory nerves will be damaged. It will be our secret who mutilated you."

Rossi thought Walker would beg him to reconsider, but he did not.

"Would you like to say anything before you fall asleep?"

"I hope you find the person who killed your daughter, Dr. Rossi."

"Pleasant dreams, John."

Louie wondered why Rossi was taking so long to come upstairs, so he climbed down to basement to investigate. He was surprised to find Rossi dressed in surgical scrubs. "What are you doing, Doc?"

"Phase 3."

"I thought you were doing phase 3 next weekend?"

"He pissed me off . . . so I thought what the fuck."

"Look what happens when I leave you alone for a few minutes!"

Rossi looked at Louie and winked at him with his left eye. "Would you like to help?"

"You go ahead. You can have all the fun."

"You can pop one of his eyes out if you'd like."

"If I do anything, I'd wack the poor fuck to put him out of his misery."

Louie watched as Rossi placed the final suture at the base of Walker's severed tongue.

"I believe everything went well," said Rossi.

"What's the game plan now?"

"There's really no need for my returning here next weekend. Why don't you and Nicky dump him on some street corner three weeks from now?"

"Will do."

"Thanks, man. I really appreciate it."

What will you do next weekend, Doc?"

"I may actually attend the medical conference. After all, I paid for it."

"Maybe you can tell the other doctors what you've been doing these past couple of weeks."

Rossi smiled at Louie and said, "I'll think about it."

Louie began cleaning up the mess. "Let me know whenever you're ready to leave, Doc."

"Let me help you clean up."

"I'll take care of it . . . I have nothing to do all week long."

"I appreciate everything you guys have done for me."

"No problem. Like I said, if you're a friend of Strampello's, then you're a friend of ours."

CHAPTER 67

When the airplane reached twenty-five thousand feet, Rossi leaned his head against the window and closed his eyes. He was overcome by a feeling of tranquility, a sensation he had not experienced in over a year. Although Walker paid a price for what he did to his daughter, he didn't pay the ultimate price; he was still alive. However, Rossi was content with all that occurred during the past several weeks, and this feeling of satisfaction provided him closure for Courtney's death.

As Rossi reflected on the many events that transpired during the past year, he was most appreciative of the support and assistance he received from Tony Strampello. He envisioned Strampello's arms to be like tentacles on a giant octopus, extending out to people in every geographic region of the United States. Strampello accomplished what the Derry and the Pennsylvania Police Departments were unable to do. He found John Walker.

Rossi had previously told Louie that he planned to attend the medical seminar in Oklahoma next weekend. But he was now reconsidering his decision. He believed it would be best if he were not anywhere near that part of the country when Walker was found. He realized the better option would be to surround himself with people from home in case he needed an alibi.

"Excuse me, sir," interrupted the flight attendant. "May I get you a drink?"

Why not have a drink, Rossi thought. *You have much to celebrate.* "I'd like a gin and tonic, please."

Rossi took a sip from his drink before closing his eyes once again. He enjoyed the serenity of the moment. Tony Strampello made it possible for him to feel this way again. *Here's to you, Tony,* thought Rossi as he gulped down a mouthful of gin.

Thoughts of failure and insensitivity resonated throughout his conscience mind during the flight to Philadelphia.

How difficult things must have been for Andrea this past year, thought Rossi. *Not only did she grieve over Courtney's death without any emotional support from me, but she was also burdened by my insensitivities. Andrea had always been supportive of me during my residency and during my first years of medical practice, but I was not there for her in her time of need.*

I failed her terribly. If I had not been obsessed with finding Walker, I would have been there for my family . . . I would have been their "Rock of Gibraltar." However, due to the inadequacies of the police departments, I had no choice but to seek other means of assistance. Thank God for people like Tony Strampello.

Here's to you, Tony, as Rossi took another gulp of his gin and tonic.

Rossi decided it was time to put his professional career back on track. He now realized that the bitterness and hatred he felt this past year had adversely affected his ability to practice medicine. To be a good practitioner, you must not only have a thorough knowledge of medicine, but you must also be sensitive to the concerns and fears of your patients. Rossi knew he had not connected emotionally with any of his patients this past year.

Rossi also realized he was still very much in love with Andrea and decided that his first priority upon returning home was to resolve all issues with his wife. He needed to become reunited with both Andrea and Michael.

Regardless of the time of day, Rossi decided he would drive to the Watson residence and bring Andrea and Michael back home with him. It was imperative that he reestablish his family life as soon as possible. Rossi prayed that Andrea would feel the same way.

"We'll be landing in a few minutes, sir," advised the flight attendant. "I need to have your glass."

"One moment, please," said Rossi. He swirled his glass, causing the last bit of liquid to splash onto the ice cubes. He then hoisted the glass into the air in a ceremonious way and toasted his wife before handing the glass to the flight attendant.

CHAPTER 68

The airplane landed at 7:34 pm at the Philadelphia International Airport, and Rossi maneuvered his way along the concourse with the same swiftness as O. J. Simpson in his Avis rent-a-car commercial. Once outside the terminal, Rossi jumped into his Lexus and drove to his home before continuing his drive to the Watson residence.

Upon arriving at his home, Rossi pressed the message button on his telephone answering machine and discovered that eight messages had been recorded. The first message was from Dr. Wilson. Wilson said there was an opening for Saturday's eight thirty tee time and asked Dr. Rossi to call him as soon as possible. Rossi deleted the message. One by one, Dr. Rossi played the other messages; none of which required an immediate response.

It was ten thirty before Rossi reached the Watson home. He approached the gated entrance and pressed the intercom button.

Rossi was asked to identify himself. He immediately recognized the woman's voice. "Maria, this is Dr. Rossi."

"Good evening, Dr. Rossi."

"Are my wife and son here?"

"Yes, sir," said Maria. "They're playing cards with Mrs. Watson in the library."

"Can you open the gate please?"

"Right away, Dr. Rossi."

Rossi passed through the gate and steered his Lexus to the front entrance. He then followed the slate pathway leading to the entryway and waited for Maria to open the door. However, it was not Maria who opened the front door. It was Mr. Watson.

"What are you doing here?" asked Andrew Watson.

"I came to take my wife and son home."

"Andrea said you haven't been yourself lately."

"I've never felt better, sir."

"I think Andrea and Michael should stay here with us."

"No disrespect, sir, but Andrea and Michael belong at home with me."

"I won't allow you to take them."

"Bill, what are you doing here?" asked Andrea.

"I came to take you and Michael home."

"Go upstairs, Andrea!" barked Andrew Watson. "I'll take care of this."

"Andrea, don't go . . . I need to talk to you," begged Rossi.

"Go upstairs, Andrea," commanded Mr. Watson.

Andrea turned and began to retreat to the upper level.

"Andrea, please don't leave. I love you."

Andrea ran down the stairs and threw her arms around her husband. "I've missed you so much."

"I'm ready to patch things up with you and Michael."

"What did the psychologist say?"

"He said I've resolved all of my issues . . . that I finally came to grips with Courtney's death."

"If you go with him, I'll disown you," threatened Andrew Watson.

"You wouldn't say that if you love me," said Andrea.

"It's *because* I love you that I said it. You can't trust him . . . He may still be emotionally unstable?" "Nonsense!" barked Rossi. He then looked at his wife and said, "Go upstairs and get Michael."

"I think you should leave," demanded Watson.

"Not without my wife and son."

Andrea stood frozen at the base of the staircase, indecisive about whether to leave with her husband or stay in New York with her parents.

"Go upstairs, Andrea," said Mr. Watson. "We'll talk later."

"Father."

"We'll discuss this tomorrow."

Andrea looked at her husband with tears in her eyes. "Give me a little more time to think things out," she pleaded before running up the stairs.

"I love your daughter," Rossi said to his father-in-law. "I would never harm her."

Watson didn't say anything.

Rossi lay in bed for twenty minutes after the alarm clock sounded. Although he had six uninterrupted hours of sleep, his body told him it required more sleep.

He couldn't remember what day it was. He remembered flying home from Oklahoma on Sunday, but he couldn't remember if today was Monday or Tuesday. The last several days were a blur, with one day overlapping the other.

Rossi was disappointed that Andrea chose to remain with her parents rather than return home with him. *Why would she do so? Was it because Andrew Watson always got what he demanded? Or did Andrea fear that her father would cut her off from the family fortune? What other explanation could there be for Andrea's betrayal of him.*

Rossi always believed that Mr. Watson did not approve of his daughter's decision to marry him. Rossi always believed Watson felt Andrea married beneath herself. Watson wanted his daughter to marry a corporate executive or a politician. It was irrelevant that he was a physician. What mattered most to Andrew Watson was that Rossi was of Italian descent and that his parents were uneducated laborers.

Rossi didn't care if Watson liked him or not. All he cared about were his wife and son. Despite Andrea's refusal to come home last night, he still loved her, and he believed that she also loved him. He knew it was only a matter of time before Andrea realized that her place was with her husband.

Rossi again glanced at the clock, hoping that he had incorrectly set the alarm. No such luck. The red neon numerals on the face of the clock radio indicated that it was seven fifty-five. Rossi forced himself to jump into the shower. He needed to be at the hospital by 9:00 am.

Throughout the day, Rossi thanked his fellow colleagues and subordinate personnel for tolerating his erratic behavior during the past year. He acknowledged there must have been moments when they found it difficult to work with him. Rossi said he appreciated their patience, and he vowed to never be aggressive or argumentative again.

Other than the emergency appendectomy Rossi performed on Dr. Tony Scales, the radiologist at Derry Memorial Hospital, his first day back on the job was uneventful. And since Andrea was still at her parents' home, there was no need for Rossi to rush home to an empty house. He chose to remain at the hospital for several hours longer and attack the patient charts that were piled high on his desk.

Drs. Wilson and Casey were walking down the hallway leading to the doctors' office corridor when they noticed a beam of light emanating from Rossi's private office. They decided to drop in on Rossi and share with him a bizarre story they just read in the national news section of the *Philadelphia Inquirer* newspaper.

Rossi was surprised to find that his friends were still at the hospital. "What in the world are you guys doing here?" asked Rossi.

"Wait till you hear this," said Casey as he pulled out the article from his shirt pocket. "The mutilated body of a white Caucasian, in his midtwenties, was found last night on a secondary street in Omaha, Nebraska. The victim, identified by police as Jack Armor, was an apparent drifter from Los Angeles, California. The victim was alive, but without his fingers, toes, and tongue. He was also blinded and made incapable of hearing. The police are not speculating as to who committed this unimaginable brutal act of violence."

Casey put down the clipping and said, "Can you believe this? You got to be one sick puppy to do something like that."

"Unbelievable," interjected Wilson.

Rossi wanted to justify this heinous act of violence. "He must have really upset someone."

"Regardless how much someone pisses you off, you don't carve him up like a Thanksgiving turkey," said Wilson.

"I'm not defending what was done . . . I'm just saying you don't know all the facts," said Rossi.

"I agree with you, Jim," said Casey. "The guy is a real psycho."

Rossi went home as soon as Wilson and Casey left his office. He wanted to log on to the Internet and read anything and everything pertaining to the mutilation of Jack Armor, a.k.a. John Walker.

He typed the keyword "Omaha Gazette" into the appropriate box on the computer and waited for the home page of the newspaper to pop up on the monitor. He clicked into the "top stories" icon and found the article he wanted to read.

"A man, identified by Sheriff Manning as Jack Armor, was found sitting on the corner of Maple Lane and Beaver Street. He was incapable of seeing, speaking, and hearing; and all of his fingers and toes had been amputated. Manning said the victim was a drifter from Los Angeles, California, and he had been employed by longtime resident Jim Dumbrowski. Dr. Anthony Scalercio, the chief medical examiner from Omaha Presbyterian Hospital, stated that the victim's inability to hear, speak, and see was a result of intentional injury to sensory organs. Sheriff Manning said the motive for this mutilation was unknown, and there were no suspects at this particular time. A $10,000 reward has been offered by the Omaha Crime Stoppers Organization for information leading to the arrest and conviction of the person or persons responsible for this act of violence."

Rossi clicked out of the Internet and sat at his desk for a few moments. For the first time in a long time, he felt completely at peace with himself. He felt like the demon that haunted and tormented him for the better part of a year had finally been exorcized from his body. Rossi believed he could now move forward with his life.

His next task at hand was to convince Andrea and Michael to return home. The following day, Rossi, believing Mr. Watson had already left home to prepare for his daily round table meeting with his corporate executives, telephoned his wife at 9:00 am.

"Watson residence, Maria speaking . . . How may I help you?"

"Maria, this is Dr. Rossi. May I speak with my wife?"

"One moment, Dr. Rossi."

Maria walked to the family room where Andrea and Allison Watson were repositioning the furniture.

"There is a telephone call for you, Mrs. Rossi. It's Dr. Rossi. Shall I tell him you're busy?"

Andrea paused for a moment before responding. "No, Maria, I'll speak with him."

"Very well, Mrs. Rossi."

Andrea walked out of the family room and picked up the telephone receiver in the kitchen.

"Bill . . . is everything okay?"

"Everything's great."

"Can I do something for you?"

"I'd like for you and Michael to come back home."

"Bill, we've talked about this before."

"No. You and your father talked about it. We've never discussed it."

"What's the difference?"

"The difference is that you belong here with me. You're my wife. We belong together."

"You frightened me that day I left you . . . You were like a madman."

"I apologize for that, Andrea. I should not have said those things to you. I *was* emotionally unstable."

"Why should I come back?"

"Because I've changed. The counseling sessions made me realize how wrong I was to think and behave the way I did."

"How can I be certain that you resolved your issues?"

"Come home and find out for yourself. I don't know how else to prove it to you."

Andrea mauled over the words that her husband had just spoken.

"We had something great at one time," said Rossi. "Give me another chance. Do it for us. Do it for Michael."

After a few moments Andrea said, "All right, Bill. We owe it to Michael for us to be a family."

"Then you'll come home?" asked Rossi.

"Yes. I'll be home in a couple of weeks. But if you behave like you did that day, I'll leave and never come back."

"Fair enough . . . But why won't you come home now?"
"Don't pressure me, Bill. I'll be home soon."
"I love you," said Rossi.
"I'll be home soon . . . Goodbye, Bill."

Although Walker's death brought closure to Rossi, the same could not be said for Andrea. She did not know that Courtney's assailant was found partially dismembered. And there was no way he could *ever* tell her what he did to Walker. If Andrea were to discover that he had anything to do with Walker's dismemberment, she would leave him immediately and file for divorce.

Weeks turned into months, and Andrea and Michael had not yet returned home. Rossi remembered the last words Andrea said to him were not to pressure her. And he respected her request. He did not call again. However, it was now two months since they last spoke. He needed to know what her intentions were, and not by telephone; he would find out in person.

Rossi arrived at the Watson residence at 11:00 am. As he approached the electronically controlled gate, Rossi pressed the intercom button. He expected to hear Maria's voice on the intercom. But to his surprise, it was the voice of Andrew Watson.

"Who's there?" asked Watson in a gruff voice.

"Bill Rossi."

"What do you want?"

"You know what I want. Quit playing games."

"Andrea's not here."

"When will she be back?"

"I don't know . . . but I'll tell her you were here."

"If you don't mind, I'd like to wait for her."

"I do mind. I'll tell Andrea you were here."

"I'm not leaving without her and Michael."

"If you don't leave, I'll call the police."

Rossi pressed the accelerator pedal to the floor on his Lexus and broke through the gate. In no time, he was banging on the front door.

"I told you to leave," Mr. Watson said sternly.

Rossi shoved past Watson without saying a word. Once inside the house, Rossi shouted for his wife. "Andrea, are you here?"

"I'm calling the police," said Watson.

"Andrea, please answer me."

"Bill, why are you shouting?" asked Andrea.

"Your father refused to allow me to see you. He's on the telephone right now calling the police."

"What's going on?" asked Andrea.

"The last time we spoke, you said you'd be home soon. That was two months ago."

"I apologize, Bill. I didn't mean to be away so long."

"Can we go home now?"

"I can't. Not just yet."

"Then when?"

"I'll be home within a week. I promise."

Watson walked into the foyer and stood face to face with Rossi. "The police are on the way."

"Call the police and cancel your request," Andrea demanded of her father.

"I will not," Watson said defiantly.

"You will if you ever want to see me and Michael again."

Watson kept quiet. He refused to continue the verbal volley with his daughter.

"I'm leaving," said Rossi.

Rossi turned toward Watson and said, "I'm sorry for upsetting you, Andrew, but Andrea and Michael belong home with me."

At that very moment, the doorbell sounded.

"That must be the police," said Watson.

"Father, tell them to leave!"

Mr. Watson opened the front door and saw two uniformed policemen poised with their right hands on their revolvers.

"Someone called and reported that an intruder was on the premises," said one of the policemen.

"Yes, sir. I'm the one who called. But I was mistaken."

"What do you mean you were mistaken?"

"My son-in-law came here unexpectedly, and I didn't recognize him. I thought he was an intruder."

"What about the broken front gate?" asked the other policeman.

"I did that myself. I thought the car was in reverse, but actually it was in drive."

"You need to be more careful," said the first policeman.

"Yes, I know," said Watson.

"Are you sure everything's okay?" asked the second policeman.

"Positive."

"Then we'll be leaving," said the second policeman.

"Sorry for the inconvenience."

"No problem. We were in the neighborhood anyhow."

"Thanks again."

Watson closed the door after the policemen drove down the driveway.

"Thanks, Dad," said Andrea.

"Yes, thank you, Andrew," said Rossi.

"I didn't do it for you Bill. I did it for Andrea."

"Whatever."

"Goodbye, Andrea."

"I'll see you next week, Bill."

Rossi left the Watson home with mixed emotions. He was pleased that Andrea and Michael planned to come home next week, yet he felt animosity toward Andrew Watson. Regardless of how he felt about Mr. Watson, Rossi knew he would not lose any sleep because of him.

CHAPTER 69

Sheriff Manning interviewed everyone who may have had any information whatsoever pertaining to the mutilation of Jack Armor. Manning never liked Armor, but he pitied the son of a bitch for what he had become. No one should have to live out his life as a vegetable, especially someone who was capable of rational thinking.

Initially, Manning tried to gather some information from Armor himself, but the poor schmuck was unable to provide any assistance. He was as useless as a pair of shoes on a duck.

Manning stopped by Dumbrowski's home to see if he had any information which may assist him with the Armor investigation. He walked up the stairs leading to the wraparound porch and peeked into one of the ceiling-to-floor windows. He didn't see anyone inside the house. He rapped three more times on the door. When no one came to the door, Manning thought Dumbrowski may have already left for his winter trip.

Manning then walked around to the back of the house and found Dumbrowski draining the water from the outside pipes. Draining the exterior water lines was a ritual Dumbrowski performed every year so to protect his home from damage caused by burst water pipes.

"Getting ready to go?" asked Manning.

"I'm leaving in a couple of hours."

"I was afraid I missed you."

"Did you find out anything about Jack?"

"Not really. That's why I'm here. I was hoping you might know something which would shed some light into the investigation."

"Like what?"

"Did Armor ever express any concern for his safety or talk about being mixed up with any shady characters?"

"I don't think so. He never talked much about other people."

"He said he was from LA, right?"

"That's what he told me."

"I don't buy it," said Manning. "He must be running away from something."

"What makes you say that?"

"Something stinks. I don't think he's who he says he is. I think he's using an alias."

"You said there were no matches from the fingerprints you lifted off his beer bottle."

"That doesn't mean he's not wanted for something. It just means there are no outstanding warrants for his arrest."

"He seemed like a nice guy to me," said Dumbrowski. "I enjoyed him."

"I don't know what it was, but there was something about him that didn't sit right with me."

"I always said you're a great cop, George. You're one of those guys who have that intuition, that sixth sense, which differentiates great cops from good cops."

"I don't know, Jim. If I was a great cop, then Armor would look more like me and you and not like an aborted fetus."

CHAPTER 70

When Rossi returned home, he made a bee's line to the telephone answering machine to check if Andrea had called. He was happy to see that there was an unheard message on the recorder.

Rossi pressed the play lever, hoping to hear that Andrea and Michael would be returning home, but it was not Andrea who had left the message. It was Officer Druzak. "I need to speak with you," said Druzak. "It's extremely important. Call me as soon as you get home."

Rossi wondered why Druzak wanted to speak with him. Did he have information which implicated him to the Walker mutilation? He didn't think so. Rossi believed that he and Louie had covered their tracks quite well. But what else could be of such importance? Rossi felt beads of perspiration build on his forehead. He needed to compose himself before calling Druzak. Shortly afterward, Rossi picked up the telephone receiver and punched in the numbers that would connect him to Druzak.

"This is Officer Druzak."

"Officer Druzak, this is Dr. Rossi."

"Dr. Rossi. I have some important information for you."

"What is it?" asked Rossi.

"I'd rather tell you in person. I'm only five minutes from your home. May I come over?"

"Of course."

"I'll be right there."

Rossi tried to calm himself while waiting for Officer Druzak to arrive. *There is no way on earth he could connect me with John Walker,* he thought. *I bet Druzak's going to tell me they still have no idea where Walker is, and they'll remain on the case until he is found.*

Druzak parked his black and white outside the Rossi home and made his way up the porch steps. Just as he was about to press the doorbell button, Rossi opened the front door.

"Come in, Officer Druzak."

"Thanks, Dr. Rossi."

Rossi led Druzak into the living room. "Can I get you a cup of coffee?" asked Rossi.

"No, thanks, Doc. I only have a few minutes."

"What can I do for you?"

"I have some good news for you," said Druzak. "A man has been arrested for the murder of your daughter. He's being extradited to Philadelphia as we speak."

"Are you sure you have the right person?" asked Rossi.

"He stopped at a police station near Pittsburgh and confessed to the murder. He said he felt guilty for killing the little girl, and he couldn't live with himself any longer."

"Was it anyone from Derry?" asked Rossi.

"No. It was a homeless man, but it wasn't John Walker. This guy's name is Ralph Curry."

"Did he say why he killed Courtney?"

"He said he'd been living in the woods near the park when he saw Walker with Courtney the night of the harvest festival. But Walker didn't harm her. He let her go, and he then ran toward the train tracks. Curry, realizing that Courtney was all alone, assaulted her. When she wouldn't stop screaming, he slapped her, and she fell to the ground, hitting her head against a rock.

"Curry first thought Courtney was dead. However, minutes later, when she began to move, he panicked and cut her throat. He then stowed away on a train heading West. He had been living in Pittsburgh ever since."

Rossi sat in his chair facing Officer Druzak without uttering a single word.

"I thought you'd be pleased to learn that we finally caught this guy," said Druzak.

"I'm sorry. I am pleased with the arrest. I'm just shocked that it wasn't Walker."

"Tell you the truth, Doc, I'm glad it wasn't Walker. I kind of liked the guy."

Druzak stood up and walked toward the door. "I have to leave. I wanted to tell you the news myself."

"Thanks for coming over," said Rossi, and he escorted Druzak outside.

"Take care of yourself, Doc. I'll keep you informed about how the Curry case is shaping up."

Rossi walked back inside his home and locked the door.

What have I done to this man? I took an innocent person and turned him into a cubical mass of carbon and water. How could I have done such a thing? Am I incapable of differentiating right from wrong?

Andrea was right when she said I needed psychological counseling. Why didn't I listen to her? She suggested I seek counseling before it's too late. I ignored her advice, and now it was too late, too late for me and too late for John Walker.

Rossi paced back and forth inside his home.

I must answer for what I did to him . . . I must take responsibility for my actions. I have no choice other than to turn myself into the police. I pray that Andrea and Michael will forgive me for what I have done.

I must tell Strampello what I did. Considering everything that Tony has done for me, I owe him the courtesy of explaining my intentions to him personally. I'm sure he'll understand.

Rossi walked into the master bedroom and reached for the telephone that sat on the nightstand nearest his side of the bed. He didn't have to search for Strampello's telephone number. He had memorized the number many months earlier.

Marcello answered the telephone on the third ring. "Hello," said Marcello.

"This is Dr. Rossi. "Is Mr. Strampello at home?"

"Who is it?"

"Dr. Rossi."

"Hey, Doc. This is Marcello. I didn't expect to hear from you."

"There has been a terrible mistake. I must speak with Tony."

"Wait a minute. I'll get him for you."

Marcello motioned to Strampello to pick up the telephone.

"How've you been, Bill?"

"Tony, there's been a terrible mistake."

"What's the matter?"

"I destroyed an innocent person . . . Walker had nothing to do with Courtney's death."

"Are you sure?" asked Strampello.

"Yes. A policeman just left my home and told me that someone confessed to killing Courtney."

"What made you think that Walker killed your daughter?"

"Because he was seen several times hiding in the park prior to my daughter's death."

"And he had nothing to do with this?"

"He kidnapped Courtney from the festival and dragged her into the woods, but he didn't harm her. He let her go."

"That's too bad. But things happen sometimes."

"I can't live with myself, Tony. I'm turning myself over to the police."

"Don't be irrational! Think about what you're doing. It's not only you that's involved with this mishap. You can bring a whole lot of trouble to our organization."

"I don't have a choice," said Rossi. "I can't live with myself."

"Bill, listen to me. I want you to take a couple of days and think about this. This Walker guy . . . he's not completely innocent. If he didn't kidnap your daughter, then she wouldn't have been in the woods for that man to molest and kill." Rossi didn't respond. He was considering what Strampello had said. "Take a couple of days and think about this," said Strampello. "If after a few days you still want to turn yourself into the police, then you'll have my blessing to do so. I just want you to be certain you won't regret your decision."

"All right, Tony. I'll think about it. But I doubt if I'll change my mind."

"That's all I'm asking you to do. Take a couple of days to think about everything."

Immediately after hanging up the handset, Strampello placed a telephone call to Joseph Mirada, the head of the Philadelphia crime family.
"Joey?"
"Who's this?"
"Tony Strampello from Lauderdale."
"How have you been, Tony?"
"Not bad for an old-timer."
"What can I do for you?"
"Is the line clean?" asked Strampello.
"You don't have to worry about nothing."
"I got a little problem. I hope you can help me."
"Anything, Tony. What can I do for you?"
"There's a guy in Derry, not far from you, who's talking about going to the police. It could be bad for us."
"What's his name?"
"Dr. Bill Rossi."
"You don't have to say anything else . . . I'll talk to him for you."
"Thanks, Joey. I knew I could count on you."
"Forget about it."

Joey Mirada felt as strong and looked nearly as good as he did when he was in his twenties. He thought of himself as a relatively young man. However, at fifty-five years of age, he was on the back side of life's bell curve.

Joey stood five feet eleven inches tall and weighed two hundred eighteen pounds. People said he looked like an older Richard Gere.

He still believed himself to be the same lean, mean fighting machine he was when he first made his bones in organized crime. Joey fought anybody anytime. The other members of the Philadelphia organization called him "punchy." However, the number of fights Joey instigated eventually took a toll on his looks. Too often, people used his face as a punching bag.

Joey sent Mark Randazzo, one of his most trusted lieutenants, to take care of the Rossi situation. Joey knew Randazzo would handle the situation with expediency and without any fallout on the family. Randazzo understood the sanctity of the family superseded everything else.

Randazzo gathered the items he needed to deal with Rossi, and he started on his way to Derry by 4:00 pm. He preferred to take care of business during the day. He was always concerned about indoor lighting casting shadows to the outside. He didn't want to be seen. He wanted to be as inconspicuous as possible. The sanctity of the family must be preserved at all cost.

CHAPTER 71

Andrea informed her father that it was time that she and Michael returned home. Andrew Watson objected to her decision to leave, but Andrea told him it was important that they be a family for Michael's sake.

Andrea started down the stairs with suitcase in hand, but her father immediately reached for the luggage.

"I wish you'd reconsider, honey."

"Father, I can't. I need to be with Bill."

"Michael, hurry up," said Andrea. "We need to go."

Michael struggled with his suitcase as he descended the stairs.

"Allow me to help you, Master Michael," said Maria.

"I can do it . . . It's not heavy."

Watson waited outside as Andrea said her goodbyes.

"You understand I need to go home, don't you, Mother?"

"Yes, Andrea."

"Father's not happy with me."

"He's just concerned for your safety. He'll be fine."

"Thanks for everything, Mother. I love you."

"I love you too, Andrea."

"Michael, give your grandmother a kiss," said Andrea.

Michael put down his suitcase and gave his grandmother a big hug. However, he didn't kiss her; he was too embarrassed to do so.

"Give your grandmother a kiss," demanded Andrea.

Reluctantly, Michael kissed her on the cheek.

"Call if you need anything," said her father.

"I will, Father. But don't worry about anything. Everything will be all right."

"We love you, Andrea!" shouted Allison as Andrea drove away.

CHAPTER 72

Randazzo arrived at the Rossi home before 5:00 pm. He rang the doorbell, but no one was there. He returned to his car and waited for Rossi to return home.

Fifteen minutes later, Randazzo saw a man enter the house. He again rang the doorbell. Moments later, the door swung open.

"Dr. Rossi?"

"Yes, I'm Dr. Rossi."

"My name is Mark Randazzo. I'm a friend of Tony Strampello."

Rossi stared at Randazzo, wondering why Strampello would send someone to his home.

"May I come in?" asked Randazzo.

Rossi stepped aside and allowed Randazzo to enter his home before locking the door.

"Please excuse me, but all I can offer you is a cup of coffee. My wife has been away, and I haven't had the time to go to the grocery store."

"No problem, Doc . . . Coffee sounds great."

"How do you like it?"

"Black."

Rossi stepped into the kitchen with Randazzo following close behind. He grabbed a mug from the cupboard and poured Randazzo a cup of coffee.

"What brings you here?" asked Rossi.

"Will I have the opportunity to meet the missus?"

"I'm afraid not. She's visiting her parents in New York."

"That's too bad."

"How is Tony?"

"Tony is concerned that you're being too tough on yourself about this John Walker thing. He sent me here to help you work through your dilemma. He wants to make certain that you're thinking with your head and not with your heart."

"I don't know if anyone can help me. I took the law into my own hands, and I fucked everything up!"

"Mistakes happen. You can't blame yourself for the mix-up."

"I can't live with myself knowing what I did to him. I just hope Tony understands."

"Tony understands more than you think."

Rossi turned away from Randazzo momentarily to pour himself another cup of coffee. With his back facing Randazzo, Rossi said, "Tell Tony I'm turning myself over to the police."

When Rossi turned to face Randazzo, he noticed that Randazzo was screwing a silencer onto his Beretta.

"What are you doing?" asked Rossi.

"We can't allow you to go to the police."

"I won't implicate Tony . . . I'll tell the police I acted alone."

"He can't take the chance."

"If you kill me, there will be an investigation . . . then Tony *will* become involved."

"You're going to leave a suicide note," said Randazzo.

"I won't do it. Then the police will know that I was murdered."

"Let me explain something to you, Doc. You're going to die today whether you write a suicide note or not. If you write the note, then you'll be the only one who dies. If you don't write the note, then your wife and son will also be killed. The choice is yours."

Rossi pondered Randazzo's statement for a few seconds before answering, "I don't have a choice."

"Now you're using your head."

Randazzo dictated to Rossi exactly how he wanted the note to read. Afterward, he removed the clip from the Beretta, leaving only a single bullet in the chamber. Randazzo then pulled out another gun from his jacket and aimed it at Rossi while handing him the Beretta. Randazzo then told Rossi, "Pull out your hanky and wipe off my fingerprints."

Rossi did as he was told.

"Now place the revolver next to your temple and pull the trigger. Remember, you're doing this for your family."

With little hesitation, Rossi pulled the trigger and fell to the floor. Bits of human tissue splattered onto the walls as blood poured from the entrance wound. Randazzo then wiped off his fingerprints from the coffee mug and everything else he touched before walking out of the house. The sanctity of the family superseded everything else.

CHAPTER 73

Andrea and Michael reached the Derry exit of the Pennsylvania Turnpike at 6:15 pm. Less than ten minutes later, they were driving up Main Street.

They had not missed a beat since leaving Derry. Everything looked the same as when they left four months earlier. Andrea thought living in Derry was like a soap opera; regardless of how long it's been since you watched the last episode, you were able to pick up the story line within a few minutes.

Andrea and Michael each had their own reasons for wanting to return to Derry. Michael was excited to return home because he missed his friends. He enjoyed his stay with his grandparents, but there was not much there for a young boy to do. Andrea longed to return to Derry to renew her relationship with her husband. And she realized that it was important that she, Bill, and Michael be a family once again.

They continued their trek up Main Street, passing the high school on the left and the hospital on the right. They were now only two blocks from their home.

As Andrea turned right at the corner of Main and Elm streets, she noticed that her husband's car was parked in front of their home.

"It looks like Daddy's home," said Andrea.

"Can I go over to Jimmy's?" asked Michael.

"After you say hello to your father."

"But, Mom."

"After you say hello to your father," Andrea said sternly.

Michael ran up the steps leading to the house and rang the doorbell. When no one came to the door, he pounded his fist against the door.

"Looks like Dad's not here."

Andrea thought it strange that her husband had not yet opened the door. "Michael . . . go to the back of the house. Maybe Daddy's working in the garage."

Michael jumped over the railing and ran to the back of the house as Andrea struggled with her suitcase. She then dragged the suitcase to the front door before unzipping her purse and removing her house key.

Andrea unlocked the door and called out to her husband. But there was no response. She then walked into the living room and saw her husband lying on the floor, his body outlined in blood. Andrea let out a scream that could be heard a block away.

Upon hearing his mother's scream, Michael ran into the house. "Mom . . . where are you? What's wrong?"

"Don't come in here, Michael. Go over to Jimmy's and stay there until I come and get you."

Michael ran out of the house, wondering why his mother had screamed.

Andrea carefully approached her husband. As she knelt down, Andrea saw a note lying next to her husband's body. She began to read the note.

> *Dear Andrea,*
>
> *If you're reading this note, then I must be dead. I'm sorry for the grief I caused both you and Michael. I can't go on living any longer. I did a terrible thing. I found John Walker, the person whom I believed killed Courtney. He was living in Omaha, Nebraska. I kidnapped and tortured him. I amputated his fingers, toes, tongue, eyes, and ears before leaving him on a street in town. After mutilating this poor man, I discovered that he didn't kill our daughter after all. It was another homeless man who murdered Courtney. He confessed because he felt guilty for doing what he did. You and Michael are better off without me. I'm sorry for everything I did. I love you.*
>
> *Bill*

Andrea sat in the rose-colored high-back chair and collected her thoughts. She then took a bedsheet from the hallway closet and draped it over her husband's body before telephoning the police.

"Derry Police, Officer Druzak speaking."

"Officer Druzak, this is Andrea Rossi."

"Hello, Mrs. Rossi. When did you get back in town?"

"Officer Druzak. My husband is dead. He shot himself."

"What?"

"Please come to my home."

"I'll be right there."

Druzak grabbed the car keys sitting on the desk and ran out the door. He was at the Rossi home within five minutes. He knocked on the door before walking into the home.

"Where are you, Mrs. Rossi?"

"In the living room."

Druzak walked into the living room and noticed that there was a sheet draped over a body. He approached the body and removed the sheet to verify that it was Dr. Rossi. He saw Rossi lying in a pool of blood, a pistol resting near the body. Druzak took a handkerchief from his back pocket and carefully removed the pistol without contaminating the crime scene. He then looked at Mrs. Rossi.

"Do you have any idea why Dr. Rossi shot himself?"

Andrea extended her right arm and handed Officer Druzak the note. After reading the note, Druzak looked at Mrs. Rossi and said, "I told your husband that a homeless man named Ralph Curry confessed to murdering your daughter. But Dr. Rossi never mentioned that he found John Walker. I feel badly about what happened."

"It's not your fault, Officer Druzak. You were only doing your job."

"I'm glad you understand, Mrs. Rossi."

Andrea suddenly remembered that she told her son to go next door. "I forgot about Michael," said Andrea.

"What did you say?"

"My son, Michael. I told him to go to Jimmy Henson's house. He doesn't know his father is dead."

"Why don't you and Michael stay in a hotel room tonight? I have a lot of work to do here, and I need to make some telephone calls and find out what happened to Walker. I'll make sure that the house is cleaned before you return home tomorrow."

"Thanks, Officer Druzak. I don't think I could have stayed here much longer."

The first thing the following morning, Officer Druzak placed a telephone call to the police department in Omaha, Nebraska. The officer on duty answered the telephone.

"Sgt. Sam Napoli speaking."

"Sergeant Napoli . . . this is Officer Druzak from the Derry Police Department in Pennsylvania."

"What can I do for you?" asked Napoli.

"I'm working on a suicide case which may have some ties to your area."

"How's that?"

"The victim, Dr. William Rossi, left a note indicating he killed himself because of what he did to a person in Omaha. He wrote that he mutilated someone by the name of John Walker. Apparently, he cut off his fingers, toes, tongue, and did other things to this guy."

"We have someone who fits that description. But his name is Jack Armor, not John Walker."

"Is he missing fingers and toes, and a tongue?" asked Druzak.

"Yea . . . And he's also blind and deaf."

"It has to be the same person. Who's in charge of the investigation?"

"Sheriff Manning."

"Is Manning there?"

"Yea. Hold on. He's in the other room.

Napoli put the telephone down and yelled for Manning.

"Yo, Sheriff! Pick up on line 3."

"This is Sheriff Manning."

"Sheriff Manning, this is Officer Druzak from the Derry Police Department. I believe I have some information for you on an unsolved crime."

"And what might that be?" asked Manning.

"A body mutilation on a Jack Armor."

"How did you come up with this information?"

"The person who mutilated Armor was a doctor in my town. He recently killed himself and left a note describing in detail what he did to John Walker, a.k.a. Jack Armor."

"So that's his real name. John Walker."

"I'm afraid so."

"I knew there was something about this guy that didn't sit right with me. I figured he had a past that he was trying to shake."

"I guess he couldn't shake it off fast enough," said Druzak.

"You'd feel sorry for him if you could see this poor SOB."

"I don't think there's a need for me to come to Nebraska. The note confirms what you've told me about Walker, or whatever his name is. I'll write down on my report that the note is authentic and that the cause of death is due to a self-inflicted gun wound to the head."

"If I can be of any other assistance to you, don't hesitate to call," said Manning.

Druzak thanked Manning for all his help before hanging up the telephone.

CHAPTER 74

Andrea received the official police report from Officer Druzak, which stated that the cause of death was a self-inflicted gunshot wound to the head. She arranged for her husband to be laid out at the same funeral home as Courtney. She then moved back to New York with Michael to be near her parents. There were too many unpleasant memories for her to remain in Derry.

As Andrea packed the family belongings in preparation for her move back to New York, she came upon a handwritten note among her husband's personal papers. The note contained the name and telephone number of a man she didn't recognize. She never heard her husband mention the name Tony Strampello.

Andrea thought Tony Strampello may have some information as to her husband's mental state during the months preceding his death. She thought about calling Strampello but decided against it. Perhaps she would call him another day.

JOHN J. SCALERCIO is a dentist who spent most of his life in Pittsburgh, Pennsylvania before moving to South Florida in 2007. He began writing Before It's Too Late while still living in Pennsylvania. The story was born from notes he scribbled on a single piece of paper as he waited at Delta Airline's Crown Club at Dulles International Airport for his friend, Eric Knisley, to arrive on a flight from Ft. Lauderdale, Florida. When his friend arrived, he quickly gathered his notes and tucked them away in his briefcase, believing that he lacked the talent to format his words and thoughts in such a way that he could create a story anyone would enjoy reading. He stashed his notes in a time capsule with a note to himself, "warning, do not open unless completely restless and bored."

Both restlessness and boredom presented themselves simultaneously one cold, Saturday morning in January, 2002. The inclement weather, having forced him to remain indoors, prompted him to revisit his notes. As a result, Scalercio sat down in front of his computer screen and began typing on the keyboard. Words that he had stored in memory for the better part of a decade began to appear on the screen. He typed for most of the day until his wife arrived home. She looked at the computer screen and asked her husband what he was writing. He said that he had decided to transfer the thoughts he had stored in his mind into words. He shared what he had written with her and she told him that it held her attention.

Ironically, the following day, his mother-in-law came to the house and handed him an instructional book on writing. The book was being used at the time as one of the premier guides for beginning writers and was a standard textbook in writing classes and universities throughout the country. As Scalercio began reading the book, he quickly became discouraged and even more convinced that he was not ever going to be a writer. The author of the "how to book" criticized many of today's published and unpublished writers, stating that these "so called authors" lacked the skill and ability to write. The more he read, the less motivated he became. Nevertheless, he continued to plow through the book. He found that its author criticized accomplished writers, such as Stephen

King and John Grisham. The writer stated that they were both great storytellers, but not good writers. This inspired Scalercio, as his goal in writing was not to become the next Mark Twain, or Ernest Hemingway. All he wanted was to be a good storyteller.

Having regained his inspiration, now confident that being a good storyteller was a worthy undertaking, he visited the local Barnes and Nobel bookstore and purchased several books pertaining to "how to write dialogue," "how to create suspense," and "how to publish your novel." He also sought out a local writers club in order to obtain feedback on things he needed to do to improve his writing skills. He completed his novel the following summer and mailed nearly one hundred query letters to publishers and editors, most of whom did not respond. A few publishers and agents were courteous enough to acknowledge his manuscript and advised him that although the story seemed interesting, they were not accepting any work from unpublished writers. Scalercio again shelved his story for several more years because he did not want to go the self-publishing route.

Despite his apathy toward the project, Scalercio was blessed with an amazing support system of family and friends, all of whom kept encouraging him to complete what he started years before. He once again sat down in front of his computer screen and began making the changes he believed would improve the story. He then decided to self-publish his book because he finally believed that he did, in fact, have a story that was worthy of his efforts.

Many of the names which appear in his book are those belonging to his friends. However the story as it is associated with those names is entirely fictional and has no bearing on those individuals' real lives.

Scalercio and his wife still live in South Florida and have three grown children.

Made in the USA
Columbia, SC
18 April 2021